HANGING On To

Hope

PRIME OF LOVE: Book Two

LORI LEGER

**Sometimes you need to lose
all hope in order to find
true strength . . .**

Copyright © 2015 Cajunflair Publishing
(Lori Leger)

ISBN-10: 1940305365
ISBN-13: 978-1-940305-36-3
(Paperback - Createspace)

Copy Editor: Karen Sue Burns

Dedication

To the sufferers and survivors of childhood diseases such as Leukemia, God Bless you all. To the parents and loved ones who've lost their children to this horrific disease, may you find peace . . . and always, always . . . hang on to hope.

"Hanging On To Hope is for milestone women everywhere. It goes down like a full-bodied wine and a glass overflowing with faith to remind us the second time round can be better than the first."

~ Natasza Waters ~
Bestselling author of A Warrior's Challenge series and
Her Perfection Imperfection.

Musical Soundtrack

"I Should Have Been a Cowboy" – Toby Keith

"Angel Eyes" – Jeff Healey Band

"One on One" – Hall and Oates

"Hello" – Lionel Ritchie

"You Save Me" – Kenny Chesney

"I Want To Know What Love Is" – Foreigner

"Bring it On Home to Me" – Little Big Town

"Drift Off to Dream" – Travis Tritt

"Drive" – The Cars

"He Plays Piano in the Dark" – Brenda Russell

"Wicked Games" – Chris Isaak

"Breathe" – Faith Hill

"All I Wanna Do is Make Love to You" – Heart

"You Shouldn't Kiss Me Like This" – Toby Keith

"Thinking Out Loud" – Ed Sheeran

Map of South Louisiana
Real and *Fictional* towns in book

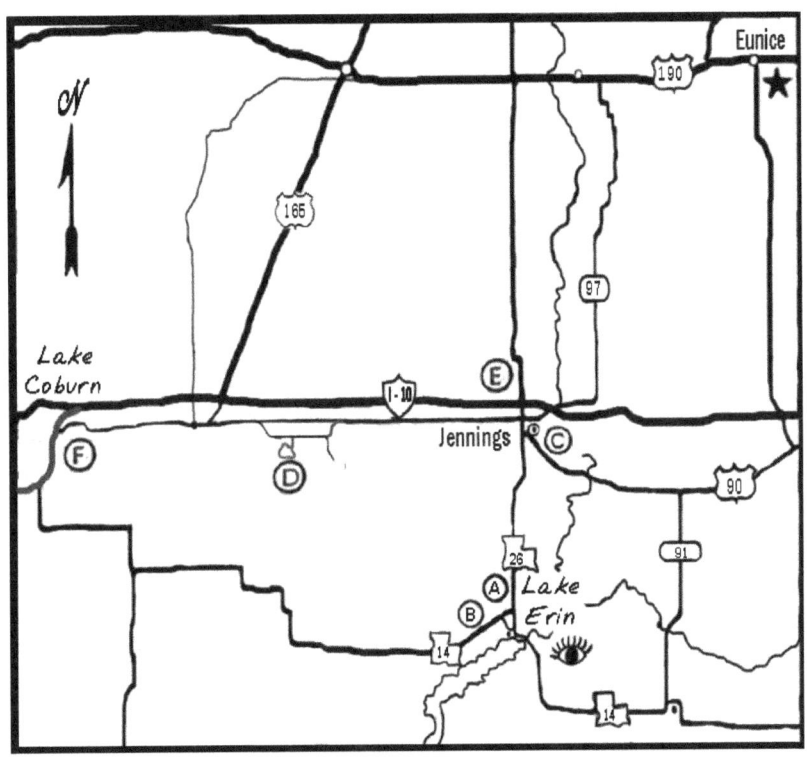

LEGEND:
Ⓐ *John Michael & Cyn's home*
Ⓑ *John David's (J.D.) home*
Ⓒ *Allie's home*
Ⓓ *Andrew's Pond (Clay's RV)*
Ⓔ *Jane Andrew's home*
Ⓕ *Margie's home*
👁 *1st Sighting (Clay & Allie)*

★ *Double Date* (Queen Cinema 3)

Prologue

December 1st

"Daddy?"

Clay opened his eyes and blinked twice, attempting to focus in the room's muted lighting. He moved forward in the chair positioned next to his daughter's bed. The eerie quiet had his heart pounding with dread until he saw the steady pulse and glow of Hope's heart monitor machine.

Still trying to decide whether she'd spoken or if he'd dreamed it, he heard the soft rustle of her sheets. He rose and crouched over the hospital bed set up in her room at home, lifted her thin, cool hand in his own. "Hope? What is it?"

"You have to, Daddy."

He reached out with one hand to toggle on the lamp, careful to avoid the silk sunflower arrangement on her bedside table. He turned to her, wearing a smile. "I have to what, baby-girl? Love you until the end of time?" It was their game; the "guess the answer" game they had played since she was five years old.

A solitary tear slipped from her right eye, created its own trail onto her temple. He thumbed it away before it hit her hairline.

"Let me go, Daddy."

I know.

He wasn't an idiot. He witnessed the punishment doled out by this disease. Still, he couldn't speak the words he knew she needed to hear and he needed to say. Once again, he chose the coward's path.

"I can't, Hope. It's not time yet."

Her eyes focused on something, or someone, that wasn't there, and she reached for it. A second before she started to fade away, her gaze landed on him again. "Let me go, Daddy . . ."

Clay Andrews woke instantly, his heart aching with the old familiar sense of loss. He lifted his head from the pillow of his king-size bed. He searched the premises, prepared to see some ghostly apparition floating around his bedroom.

Nothing.

He dropped back against the pillow, his peripheral vision registering the glow of his bedroom's digital clock. He didn't bother to check it. He knew damn well 3:03 would be glaring at him in luminous blue digits. Clay made a half-hearted attempt to go back to sleep, giving it a full ten minutes before he threw off the covers. He swung his legs over his bed and stood. He had no doubts the impending two-year-anniversary of his daughter's death had something to do with the rash of recent dreams of her last moments.

He shuffled to the kitchen to start the coffee brewing before hitting the john. Any day beginning at 3:00 a.m. was bound to leave him wrung out by the end of it.

By the time he exited his tiny bathroom, the smell of fresh coffee had permeated the entire area of his RV home on wheels. Some may question his style of living, but he was a single man who worked out of state more often than not. It suited his needs.

Mug in hand, he seated himself at the table to go through a week's worth of mail. He sorted the credible mail from the junk mail, wondering, as he always did, how many trees they could save if someone would put an end to the non-stop parade of sales circulars. He put a single bill aside and settled back to read the previous week's paper. Sifting through the pages, his gaze settled on a picture attached to his first cousin's wedding announcement.

Mrs. Bessie Robicheaux and Mr. J.D. Ferguson would like to announce the joining in marriage of their children, Dr. Cynthia Ellender and John Michael Ferguson. The wedding will take place 2:00 p.m. Saturday, December 1st at Our Lady of the Lake Catholic Church in Lake Erin, LA. Pastor Thompson of First Baptist Church and Father Guidry of Our Lady of the Lake Catholic Church will both officiate to bless the union.

The first, as in today? Hell, he'd nearly missed it, and he'd only seen his closest cousin a couple of times since Hope's funeral. It would be nice to catch up with Johnny and meet his new wife. He scratched his chin, asking himself if he was up to it. Did he want to spend the afternoon at a wedding reception with a room full of people, most of them strangers?

He stared at the photo of the couple seated on a wooden bench, their faces both stretched in Cheshire cat grins. His cousin's fiancée was a looker for damn sure, maybe even a few years younger than Johnny. "Way to go, Cuz. I wish you the best."

Clay set the paper aside. He approached the glass doors of the living area's built-in cabinetry and retrieved the official invitation he'd received weeks ago. He'd forgotten about the damn thing until now. After a moment's consideration, he decided to skip the joyous occasion.

A whisper-soft "Daddy" tickled his ear, prompting an automatic shoulder scrunch. The hair at the back of his neck stood up and his skin prickled. Whether real or not, a viable message from his daughter or a figment of his own imagination, this had happened before and often enough for him to take heed. If he could guess, he'd say Hope didn't want him sitting home on a Saturday afternoon if she could help it.

He nodded. "Okay, baby girl, you drive a hard bargain. I'll go. Way to look out for your old man."

Chapter One

The bride's granddaughter, adorable as the tiny flower girl, progressed toward the front of the church. Allie Sarver held her breath, no doubt along with others, fully expecting a slip, trip, and fall at any second. The toddler's chubby left hand clutched the handle of a wicker basket, while her right chunked handfuls of deep red rose petals on the floor in no particular direction.

Zoe made it halfway down the aisle before taking her first tumble. She recovered on her own, but at the three-quarter mark, she spied her mother, the matron of honor, waiting up ahead. She released an excited screech. "Mama!" Distracted from the task, she dropped the basket and ran the rest of the way to meet her, accompanied by laughter from the wedding attendees.

Allie stepped from her aisle seat to retrieve the basket, clearing the way for the bride. She returned to her seat in time to see Cynthia, accompanied by a son on each arm, start her short journey up the aisle. Cynthia tore her gaze from John Michael, her prospective groom, just long enough to toss Allie a quick wink. Allie forced herself to smile at her sister who was older by seven years. As crappy as she felt, today wasn't the day to rain on anyone's parade, particularly a bride's.

As expected, Cynthia made a beautiful bride.

Allie contemplated her sister's appearance, groaning inwardly at the physical differences between her own body and that of her always-put-together sister. Cynthia's champagne colored suit had needed little alteration to fit her like a glove. Her short hair highlighted and cut in a sassy style that complimented the shape of her face. For as long as Allie could remember, her big sis had exuded perfection—as a teenager, a young wife, and later, a young mother. Cynthia had always been the perfect height, shape, cup size in a bra, and possessed a brain to produce an exceptional A-average, all through school. Perfect, in every way. Her decision to become a doctor, a pediatrician to be exact, taken in stride with the rest of her flawless persona.

Allie's gaze landed on her brother, seated with his family in the pew in front of her. Even Kyle, the middle child, had gotten his dose of perfect in his own way. He'd always been good-looking and athletic, but with enough smarts to get a bachelor's degree in Mechanical Engineering while attending a Louisiana university on a sport's scholarship. He'd married the captain of the cheerleading squad and they'd pumped out two more impeccably beautiful children—one boy, one girl, neither of whom produced the slightest little ripple in their perfect family's lifestyle.

Then along came ordinary Allie to add a permanent wrinkle in the Ham and Bess Robicheaux "no-ironing necessary" group of children. Allie had long decided that her mother must have run out of the flawless DNA and had doled out mass quantities of whatever-the-hell was left to her third child.

Not that she felt unloved by her family. As the youngest child, she'd always enjoyed her share of spoilage from her older siblings, as well as her parents. But why couldn't she have inherited at least a small share of that perfection . . . something to pass on to her own offspring?

Allie's gaze shifted to peruse her own daughters, one dressed like a Bohemian bag lady with bright blue hair, the other embracing her emo phase in head to toe black.

Never one to judge any book by its cover, Allie could forgive her daughters' exterior trappings, if only they'd apply themselves to their school work, or a constructive hobby of some kind, or *something* that gave their lives meaning.

Her family, friends, and co-workers all insisted it was just a phase and they'd grow out of it. Would they? Cecily was already seventeen and still didn't have much to say, except that she couldn't wait to leave home. Allie suspected both her daughters were simply trying to distance themselves emotionally from their mother now, until they could physically move as far from her as possible. Why spend time with mom, the rule maker, when their rule-breaker dad offered incentives like later curfews and bigger allowances?

And that hurt like hell, because she loved her daughters. They'd been close once upon a time.

She reached out to push a stray lock of straight, pitch-black-dyed hair from Kayla's face. The fourteen-year-old shied away from her touch before glaring at her. Kayla whispered something in her sister's ear. As one, she and Cecily turned their critical eyes upon their mother, dispatching identical expressions of amused disgust.

Allie turned away from the familiar looks. She'd seen that same look from their father often enough during the last fifteen years of their marriage. It was the look that reminded her every, single day how lacking she was—as a wife, as a woman, and now obviously, as a mother.

It killed her seeing it from the two daughters for whom she'd give up her own life. She wiped a tear from the corner of her left eye, cringed inwardly at the snickers that passed between the two girls at their mother's display of soft-heartedness.

She released a sigh, determined not to give in to her feelings of dejection. Maybe one of these days, she'd accomplish something fabulous to change her daughter's low opinion of her.

The community center teemed with people, all there to share in the couple's joy. He turned at the sound of his name and came face to face with the groom.

"Clay! I'm glad you could make it here, man. It's been awhile."

Clay gave the cousin he'd always considered his closest, a one-armed hug and clasped his hand. "It's damned good to see you, Johnny. I wouldn't have missed this." No use telling him he nearly had.

"It's nice to meet someplace other than a funeral home, isn't it?"

"No kidding, man."

John shook his head. "Why is it as we get older, we tend to visit less unless there's a death in the family?" He stiffened as a look of chagrin came over his face. "I'm sorry, Clay. I'm a dumbass."

He waved off his cousin's concern. "Don't worry about it, and you only spoke the truth. We get too busy with our own lives." He gave his cousin a nod. "Sometimes it's work or taking care of the sick in our families, but sometimes it's just a matter of not wanting to move our asses off the recliner after working all day."

The bride took that opportunity to step up and loop her arm through her new husband's. "Did I hear the word recliner, John Michael? I could sure use one about now because my feet are killing me."

Johnny leaned in to give his wife a kiss on the mouth. "Take your heels off, babe. The hard part's over."

Her eyes widened. "You think so? The reception just started."

"Yeah, but it's party time." He placed one arm around her waist. "I want you to meet my cousin, Clay Andrews. His mom is my dad's older sister."

Cynthia nodded immediately. "You're Aunt Jane's son? That explains those Ferguson blue eyes you share with my husband."

Clay extended his hand. "It's a pleasure to meet you, Cynthia. On Uncle J.D.'s last visit with Mom he had nothing but wonderful things to say about you."

She accepted his hand and placed her opposite over her own heart. "I'm thrilled to meet you, Clay, and that's good to hear. I adore my father-in-law. I've known him forever."

Clay cocked his head, confused. "But, I thought you just moved here from Oklahoma?"

"My parents are from here, and this was my home. I left after high school to visit with my grandparents, met a man there, and never came home. After my husband died, I moved back home to be close to my mother."

Johnny pulled her close to place a kiss on her temple. "And once I saw Cyn again, I couldn't stop thinking about her."

"Cyn?" Clay frowned as a particular memory came to him. "Wait a minute, this is Cyn? *The* Cyn? From Junior High?"

Johnny gave him a sheepish nod. "The one and only."

Cynthia gave her husband a curious look. "Why does he know about me?"

Clay's guffaw of laughter resonated around them. "Because for two years of our lives, every time I saw this dude, it was 'Cyn said this' and 'Cyn did that'. Lady, this guy was crazy in love with you, or whatever it is a kid feels in junior high." He elbowed his cousin's ribs. "She doesn't know?"

Cynthia intercepted the look of warning Johnny sent him. "Know what?"

John cleared his throat and adjusted his collar. "You were my first dream, of the nocturnal emission sort, sweetie."

"Oh." Her expression turned curious. "Only the first?"

"A few more than that." Johnny lifted one brow and grinned at his wife. "I may as well admit that you were kind of my pin-up girl after that. You know; my inspiration. . ."

Cynthia raised a palm to stop Johnny. "Okay, okay. That's enough talk about wet dreams and teen-age boys' masturbation sessions."

Clay choked on his sip of beer.

She laughed and slapped him on the back. "I'm a doctor, Clay. There's not much I don't know about the workings of the human body, teenage males included."

He took a deep breath and stared at his newest cousin-in-law. "I didn't expect you to be so frank, but it's refreshing."

She laughed at his answer. "I'm still reeling from the fact that John Michael talked about me so much that you remember me. All he could manage was one quick kiss behind a stack of hay bales when we were thirteen."

Johnny draped his arm over her shoulders. "But it was a good kiss, wasn't it?"

"It was. I just would have liked a few more."

Clay shook his head at Johnny. "You may have been three years older than me, but I was wiser for my years. I kept on you to call her, remember?"

Johnny snorted. "Older yes, the jury's still out on wiser. I have to admit that you did stay on me to call her."

Clay smiled as Johnny reached out to touch Cyn's face. "You two look great together." He furrowed his brow as a particular memory came to him. "You know, now that I think about it, he pointed you out to me once, a long time ago. I was at the feed store with him and Uncle J.D. and you came in with your dad and a little girl."

"That had to be Al. My little sister was my shadow back then. She's here, somewhere." Cynthia twisted and craned her neck. "There she is."

She pointed to a pretty woman Clay had noticed in church. The one who'd picked up the flower girl's basket during the ceremony. "There's definitely a family resemblance between the two of you. She doesn't look like an 'Al' to me, though."

Cynthia's grin was contagious. "It's short for Allie. Have you met?"

He was quick to shake his head. "No, but are those her daughters with her?"

Cyn's face sobered. "Yes, her daughters are . . ."

"I witnessed a little scene in church between the three of them. They seemed—disrespectful—towards their mother."

"Her girls used to be so sweet, but now they're taking cues from their father." Cynthia's expression turned stony. "My ex-brother-in-law's a pig and a walking cliché."

"At least he's an ex."

"Yes, he found someone younger, controllable, shapeable . . . someone more suited to *his* needs." She dabbed at her mouth with her pinky. "I'll have to thank the bastard next time I see him."

"That is one beautiful woman."

Cynthia stared in the direction of her sister, her eyes clouded with sadness. "She is, but thanks to Bruce, she doesn't see herself that way."

Clay turned his perusal toward the younger sister again. "Bruce, the Bastard?"

"That's right. Allie is one of the most beautiful, generous, caring, loveable people I know. She owns a successful hair salon and has all the reason in the world to be proud of her accomplishments, but twenty years with that idiot turned her into a bundle of insecurities. She won't even think about dating again."

From Clay's perspective, there wasn't a damn thing wrong with what he saw in the younger sister. Allie was an inch or so shorter than Cynthia, with a few extra pounds that only made her more appealing to his personal tastes. Her fingers fluttered about nervously, ending in a self-conscious tug at the hem of her blouse.

Her body language fired off signals that she wasn't comfortable in large crowds, which he could relate to. More than that, she didn't appear to be completely comfortable with herself.

He considered the possibility of getting to know her. Remembering the latest dream, he pushed aside that thought. After all, he was still eyeball-deep in his own daily struggles. What the hell could he possibly bring to a relationship, at this point?

Allie eyed the delectable looking wedding cake, wished she could bury her face in it for once without worrying about the consequences. She tugged at the back of her blouse and smoothed the front over her stomach. She passed on a glass of champagne, opted instead for a bottle of water.

"Every little bit helps," she grumbled, and spun away from the table before she changed her mind. She plowed right into a man, plastering his plate of food onto the front of his dress shirt. Her hand flew to her mouth, covering her horrified gasp. "I'm so sorry!"

To his credit, he recovered in seconds. "It's fine, Miss—a couple of sandwiches, and some nuts and crackers."

"Are you sure? Let me help you with that." She grabbed a handful of napkins and tried to brush the crumbs from his shirt.

He placed one large hand over hers. "No harm done. It's my own fault. I was just—"

"Oh. My. Gawd! What did you do now, Mother?"

Allie didn't have to see her daughters to know they'd be wearing identical horrified expressions. Great—another humorous "mom" story they could run and tell to their father and his dipstick of a girlfriend. Even before her husband had left her for another woman, he and her daughters often enjoyed a stimulating game of "let's gang up on mom".

"It was my fault," the man said. "I ran into her."

"You don't have to do that," Allie whispered, giving the front of his shirt one last swipe with her hand. The abs she felt through the shirt were firm, nothing like Bruce's jelly-soft belly. The thought provoked a slow rise of heat to her face.

"I was coming to talk to your mother. She stopped and I didn't." He faced Allie and nodded. "I saw you in church earlier and wanted to introduce myself to you."

"You did?"

"I'm Clay Andrews, Johnny's cousin. And you are . . ."

"Allie Sarver and I'm the bride's sister. It's lovely to meet you." Allie's gaze followed her daughters as they walked away, snickering behind their hands. "I doubt they bought that story of yours. I can't seem to do a darn thing right in their eyes, lately." She deposited the napkins on a table. "Thanks for that, though. They're already ashamed to be seen with me."

"I don't know why. You're not the one with blue hair or trying to pass yourself off as the black widow."

"I know, right? But they've labeled me the most uncool mother on earth." Allie finally stopped to study the man's face and had to take a breath. She hadn't realized until that moment how out of her league he was, with the same build and good looks as his cousin, John Michael. His hair color was closer to dark blond than black, but his eyes . . . "Your mother must be a sibling to Mr. J.D. I can tell by those 'Ferguson blue' eyes. That's what Cynthia calls them."

"Guilty as charged. My mom is J.D.'s oldest sister."

"Well, it was certainly nice to meet you. Excuse me, please."

"Wait, I was wondering if you'd like to dance—"

She held up both hands. "Look, Mr. Andrews, you've fulfilled your good deed and social obligation by being courteous to the chubby klutz who dumped a plate of food on you. It's not necessary to keep up the pretense that you're interested in anything more." She left him then, quick stepping it to the women's restroom to get away from those piercing, blue eyes.

Clay watched her retreat, no other way to describe it. That poor woman couldn't get away fast enough. Her accusation had shocked him into silence—something that didn't happen often. She truly had no idea how lovely she was. It made him more determined than ever to wait for her to exit. He wanted to talk more. Wanted to let her know how wrong she was.

He grabbed a glass of champagne, then a second, and stood back to wait. As pretty as "Al" was from a distance, it turned out that up close, she was downright gorgeous. Her auburn hair curled around a heart-shaped face, and she had the slightest hint of a dimpled chin, with inquisitive green eyes, plump lips, and creamy, fair skin. All that beauty wrapped up in a bodacious body of soft, voluptuous curves. Her blouse, cut somewhat low, had given him a modest peek at quality cleavage. Of course, he'd always been a leg man, and the only leg he'd seen below her floor length skirt was two trim ankles in a pair of heels.

But it was her genuine nature that intrigued him. He'd seen no sign of false fawning or flirtatiousness, nothing but straight talk from the woman. She exhibited intelligence—the kind of girl who could give as good as she got in an argument, no doubt.

Barring the obvious self-esteem issues, she appeared to be everything he liked in a woman. Though he wasn't interested in a relationship, he could always use a friend. She emerged from the women's' room and stopped in her tracks when she saw him, her eyes wide with curiosity.

He approached, holding out one glass of champagne. "You look like you could use this."

For a second it seemed as though she'd take it, but then she crossed her arms. "No, thank you."

He cocked his head. "Are you sure? I'm more of a beer man, myself, but it's not bad for bubbly."

Again, she appeared to consider it, and then shook her head. "I'd better not."

"Driving?"

"Dieting."

He frowned. "Why?"

"I think that's obvious."

He sipped from one glass and considered her answer. "Not to me."

She sighed and placed both hands on her rear end. "I've been playing hide and seek with the same thirty pounds for fifteen years, that's why. The last time I checked, they found me out again."

He shook his head, impressed enough with her straightforward attitude to want to hear more. "Lady, if you lost thirty pounds there'd be nothing left to you."

She answered with a snort and another tug at her blouse. "If you knew me at all, you'd know I don't fall for lines like that."

"And if you knew me at all, you'd realize I don't use lines. I don't date, so I have no need of them."

She let her head fall back and sighed. "Look . . . Clay, is it? I don't want you to waste your time. I'm not interested in the drink or anything else for that matter."

"All right, then." He finished off one glass of champagne and sipped from the second. "There's no sense in wasting good champagne."

She nodded. "I agree. Have fun with that." She turned away and headed for the opposite side of the room.

"You sure you wouldn't want to have coffee with me sometime?" he called out to her.

She paused long enough to throw a curious look in his direction. "I don't. But thank you for asking."

Clay tracked Allie's path to the far side of the room before he turned and headed in the opposite direction. He set the empty glass of champagne on a table, deciding he deserved something a little more substantial after that fiasco.

He approached the large, open container of iced down beer and grabbed a cold one before approaching Johnny and his Uncle J.D.

J.D. extended his hand. "There's my favorite nephew!"

He shook his uncle's hand. "Hey Uncle J.D., how are you?"

"I'm right as rain. Life is good. How's it going on your end?"

Clay twisted the cap off his beer bottle and took a long pull from it. "I was fine, but I'm getting over it." He grinned at Johnny. "I just asked your new sister-in-law for coffee and she buried me, man."

"She's still stinging from her ex—"

"Bruce, the Bastard, I remember."

"What'd you say to her?" J.D. asked.

"I complimented her and offered her a glass of champagne."

"Maybe you need to brush up on your complimenting skills." J.D. elbowed his son. "Say, Johnny, you still got that list I gave you?"

"Pop, no."

"Well, *you* don't need it anymore, and *I've* got it all right here." He tapped his forehead with his forefinger. "So, why not pass it on to someone who can use it?"

John Michael wiped his forehead. "Jesus . . ."

Clay leaned in close to Johnny and lowered his voice. "He gave you a list of compliments?"

Johnny's warning came out through clenched teeth. "It was a list of lines, Clay. Trust me; you don't want any part of it."

"Well, hell, Son!" J.D. interjected. "I can't believe you'd be so selfish as to hold out on your cousin that way."

"You'd do better on your own, Clay."

J.D. stepped back to look from his son to his nephew. "Appears to me if he could do better on his own, he wouldn't be standing here with his finger up his butt, talking to us."

Clay smothered a laugh and rocked back on the heels of his just-polished western boots. "Man's got a point, cuz."

"Yeah, but I'm counting on you to prove him wrong." He frowned at his grinning father. "The old fart's annoying as shit when he's right."

The air rang with J.D.'s laughter. "You young pups always think you've got something over people who've been around long enough to know better. With age comes wisdom, boys." He turned away, chuckling under his breath.

"Not to mention dementia, incontinence, and the inability to filter your thoughts before you speak," Johnny called out to his father.

J.D. shook his head again but kept walking straight to the bride's mother. He stopped and spoke something into her ear. She nodded and let him lead her out to the dance floor for a waltz.

"Would you look at that?" Clay had no choice other than to admire the man.

"I know. A couple of months after Mom passed away, Pop and Cyn's mom, Ms. Bess, started spending a lot of time together. They'd all been friends for over fifty years." He gave Clay an elbow-nudge in the side. "It's a good thing."

Uncle J.D. took the opportunity to drive his point home as he and his dance partner passed Clay and Johnny on the first loop around the floor. "At least I'm smart enough to be out here. You two gonna dance with each other?"

Clay sipped from his beer. "He's right, you know."

"I know, dammit." Johnny turned to face Clay. "So what'd you say to offend Allie?"

"I offered her a glass of champagne. She turned it down, used dieting as an excuse. I don't know why she'd want to do that."

"From what Cyn tells me, her dick of a husband always ragged her about her weight. He screwed around on her and accused her of letting herself go."

Clay scanned the crowd for another glimpse of the lady in question. "Assholes like that never love anyone more than they love themselves." He leaned toward his cousin. "She's even more beautiful up close and personal."

Johnny grinned at his cousin. "Tired of being alone?"

Clay intercepted the knowing look from his cousin. If anyone knew what it was like to be without someone, it would be Johnny. It'd taken his cousin fourteen years to "move on" after his first wife died from a reaction to anesthesia during an emergency surgery. "I'm thinking it's been long enough."

"You ever hear from your ex?"

"Marge called from Paris around a year and a half ago. It was about six months after we buried Hope. Wanted to talk reconciliation . . . from Paris, freaking France . . . can you imagine?"

Johnny's brow creased in a frown. "Did you consider it?"

Clay shook his head. "She didn't just walk out on me. She walked out on our child too, a child fighting the biggest battle of her life at the time."

"Not an easy thing to swallow, I'd imagine."

He shook his head. "Try impossible."

Chapter Two

Monday, December 10th

Clay tapped on the door of his mother's two-story farmhouse before entering. "Anybody home?" He scanned the living area of the home where his parents had raised him and three other siblings, all brothers. Within seconds, his mother's five-foot-six inch silhouette filled the doorway into the kitchen.

"I'm in here, Son."

He lifted his nose to the air, inhaled the aroma of roasted poultry and fresh yeast bread. "Do I detect baked hen, Ma?"

"You have a keen sense of smell, my boy. Come on in here. I'm about to take the rolls out of the oven. Did you have a good week at work?"

"Everything went according to plan." He breathed in again. "Mm . . . yeast rolls. Did I pick a good day to drop by or what?" He wrapped his arms around his mother and gave her a big hug.

"I'm expecting company, but you know there's plenty. My brother and his lady friend should be here for lunch any minute." She pulled two pans of piping hot rolls from the oven and set them on the same cooling rack he'd seen her use since he was old enough to remember.

"Ms. Bess and Uncle J.D.?"

"Yes, I know you were working for Marilee's funeral, but it sounds like you've met her already."

"I have, at Johnny's wedding last weekend. She is the sweetest thing, next to you I mean." He leaned over to kiss his mother's forehead.

Arms crossed, she laughed as she straightened to her full height. "Are you sucking up to take home freshly baked rolls?"

"I'm hoping it works."

"You know I can smell bullshit from a mile away. But, I'd planned to put some of these aside for you anyway, so you're good."

"God bless you, Ma. I can't stay for the meal, though. I've got my annual wellness physical in an hour. I wanted to come by to check on you first." He reached for a roll, tossed it from one hand to another until he finally had to drop it back onto the tray. "Hot!"

"You don't say." She turned her back on him and shook her head. "Patience is the companion of wisdom, Son."

"I know, but the aroma of fresh baked bread has a habit of over-riding common sense or patience." He grabbed a plate from the cabinet and placed the roll on it to cool. "I wish you could have attended Johnny's wedding. You missed a good time."

"I do too. My arthritis from that cold front kicked my behind for a couple of days."

He grabbed the container of butter and a knife. "I saw family I hadn't seen in years."

"Well . . ." She paused a moment before continuing. "You were busy for a while."

"Yeah." The silence grew thick as mother and son stood there contemplating the white elephant in the room. Clay took a deep breath. "Two years this Saturday, Ma."

"I know, Son. I miss our girl so much."

He tapped his chest. "Sometimes I think I've lost a part of my heart, like it's missing. There are days I'm not sure if I'll ever be whole again."

"I've felt like that. Twice . . . once even before your father."

He stared, open-mouthed at his mother. "What?"

"I lost my fiancé, Tommy Killeen, during the Korean War. It was 1951, and I was only seventeen. I thought I would die." She smiled at her son. "Two and a half years later I married your dad." She placed her hand on his face. "Life goes on, Son. Always."

Clay took a step back to stare at his mother. "I can't believe I'm just hearing about this. Did Dad know?"

She smiled. "Evan was with Tommy when he got shot. They were pals over there. Tommy ended up in a MASH unit. He couldn't use his hand to write, so he dictated a letter to Evan and begged him to get it to me. Just after Evan walked away from the medical tent, the North Koreans bombed it. Your father mailed me the letter, along with some pictures he had of Tommy. I mailed him back, thanking him. That's what you did back then before cell phones and computers. We stayed in contact and when Evan got discharged, he came to see me." She shrugged. "Sometimes I wonder if Tommy knew and set it all up just to get his best friend and his girl together."

"Stranger things have happened, Ma."

She shook herself from her memories and used two potholders to pull a large roaster from her second wall oven. "Anyway, I woke up feeling fine this morning. That's why I called J.D. and invited them for lunch. I never thought I'd be getting a new sister-in-law at my age, but I'm thinking that's in the works."

"Johnny and Cyn think their parents won't make it official. If it happens, Johnny's new mother-in-law will be his step-mom. That will make his wife his stepsister. Even though it's not blood, Cyn says she doesn't know if her mom's psyche could handle it."

"Well, I sure hope they don't let that stop them. That's just ridiculous. Besides, what would they do? Live in sin for the rest of their lives?"

Clay laughed at his mother's reasoning. "You're a trip, Ma, you know that? What would it matter if they lived together and didn't get married? It's not like they'd consummate the relationship. I mean, they're too old for that."

"J.D.'s only seventy-seven. When your father was that age, he and I still—"

"Whoa!" Clay jumped out of his chair. "Holy crap, look at the time. I'd better get myself to the doctor's office."

In his defense, the last time this discussion came up it had taken several shots from a bottle of bourbon to clear his mind of that particular image. "Your offer to take some of these rolls with me still good, Ma?"

His mother clucked her tongue as she snatched a plastic container from her cabinet. "Aren't you a little long in the tooth to believe you were an immaculate conception?"

"Not as long as it works for me, and it still does, yes-sir-ree!"

"Just so you know, Clay, it was me and your dad that put money under your pillow in exchange for those teeth you lost as a kid."

Clay's mouth dropped open. "You're a cruel woman, Eliza Jane Andrews, crushing a man's belief in the tooth fairy like that."

Within two minutes he was back in his truck, the aroma of fresh bread filling the space as he fought against the mental image of his parents doing what kids today called "bumping uglies."

He started his truck and waved as his mom cackled from her covered porch. He'd always known his mother had a wicked sense of humor, but sometimes he wondered if she wasn't harboring a sadistic streak, as well.

With a clean bill of health, and another annual physical out of the way, Clay entered his home later that afternoon. He checked his voicemail and found a somewhat upbeat message from his mom, rampant with hidden inferences.

"Hey, Son. The visit with your uncle went well. That Bessie Robicheaux is a keeper for sure. I think you should follow J.D.'s lead and find yourself someone, Clay. Maybe there's someone you've recently met that you could ask out to dinner and a movie? Or maybe even dancing. . ." She followed up with a throaty chuckle and a final, *"We didn't raise you as a quitter, son. If at first you don't succeed . . ."* The call ended with a final beep.

"Keep on suckin' til ya do suck seed," he murmured, channeling Curly Howard and ended with a snort and shake of his head. He didn't have to wonder about the message. No doubt, his uncle had revealed how Ms. Sarver turned his coffee invitation into an abrupt and icy no, despite her paltry "thanks for asking". Hell, he had tried, but the lady wasn't receptive to the idea of meeting anyone new.

Clay grabbed his laptop before dropping into his recliner to check his business emails. He found the report he'd been waiting for regarding the next gas well location. The report gave him what he needed to proceed with this particular job. He opened the file and made some notes, and tried to make some headway. Several attempts later, he saved what little he'd accomplished and shut down the program, his concentration turned to shit.

He opened his favorite browser and typed in Allie Sarver, Jennings, LA. Several listings appeared, but only one mentioned a salon. He clicked on it and a picture popped up of her, along with several other people at a ribbon cutting ceremony. The caption under the picture explained.

Allie Sarver, owner/operator of Allie's Cut Above, opens the doors of her new salon located at 525 Magnolia Avenue in Jennings. Ms. Sarver had been operating from a room attached to her home for the past fifteen years. With the opening of her downtown location, she begins this new endeavor with an already impressive list of clientele.

Clay studied the building's front façade and sign. He knew that place. It was right next door to the diner he frequented when he was in Jennings for business. No wonder she looked familiar.

With one last glance at the photo, he typed in Bruce Sarver and hit the search icon, curious to know about the fool's business dealings. Several listings had him choking on his sip of coffee.

He was a car salesman? Cyn's accusation of her ex-brother-in-law being a walking cliché made more sense than ever. He zoomed in on the headshot of the man, wondering how somebody with that nose and receding hairline could have convinced his ex-wife she was the one lacking in the looks department. The man's ego far exceeded his looks, though not his waistline.

Clay closed the browser, re-opened the digital map of the area near the next location. He took a few notes, listing rivers, lakes, or ponds in the area as possible water sources at the south Texas location. Two of the landowners already had several wells set up in the area. His mind clouded with images of a woman instead, one with soft, round curves, and the barest hint of mouth-watering cleavage.

Well, shit. He closed his laptop, and attempted to clear his mind, but an image of inquisitive green eyes had him thinking about a second attempt to ask her on a date. He'd told himself when she shut him down the first time, he wouldn't call her. Now, if he and "Al" just happened to show up at the same place at the same time, Clay figured he would have no choice but take that as a sign to try again.

Chapter Three

Thursday, December 13th

"What'll it be today, Allie?"

She perused the daily menu written on the board and tapped her chin. "I'll have the grilled chicken salad today. No cheese or croutons, a cup of the vegetable soup, and a glass of water with lemon, please Jill."

"Sure thing, hon. Is that for here or to go?"

"That'll be for here, unless the lady's dead set on not having lunch with me."

The somewhat familiar masculine voice had her spinning around to see her new brother-in-law's cousin, Clay Andrews. "Oh, hello. I didn't realize anyone had walked in after me." The first sight of those blue eyes when he removed his sunglasses had her sucking in her breath. How could she have forgotten how handsome he was?

"I try to make it here a few times each month. It beats any fast food restaurant around when all I have time for is soup and a sandwich."

"Allie?"

Jill's question took her by surprise. "Huh? Oh . . ." She threw a quick glance back at Clay.

The man sent her an adorably sexy lopsided grin. "I don't bite, you know."

She faced Jill again. "Um, I guess I'll be dining in today."

"Good, then add her tab to mine, please. I'll have the hot ham and cheese. I'll also have a cup of whatever soup you have today and water, please."

"Sure thing, Mr. Andrews. That'll be $14.95."

He slipped his sunglasses into his coat pocket, pulled a twenty out of his wallet. "Keep the change, Jill."

"Thank you. You two take a seat anywhere and I'll bring your meal to you in a few minutes."

Without asking, he led her to a table in the corner, one hand placed at her lower back. "Is this okay?"

"It's fine." She took the chair he pulled out for her, for once thankful her back was up against the wall. At least the table hid her big butt. Once he sat across from her, she found herself wishing the place had bigger tables. Why had she said yes to this?

He rested his arms on the table. "So, I had business in Jennings today. What brings you here?"

His gaze landed on her shoulder and she checked the sunflower pin she'd worn to secure her scarf, making sure it was stilled clasped. "My salon is next door. I come here most days I don't have time to fix my own lunch."

He pointed toward her business. "Allie's Cut Above? That's you?"

"That's me." She forced herself to smile and stop fidgeting. If she didn't find a way to relax she'd bounce right off of this chair.

He sipped from the plastic cup of water Jill placed in front of him. "Are you sole proprietor?"

"Yes, I am."

"Are haircuts your only service?"

"I cut and style hair, give perms, dye jobs, add highlights, lowlights, minimal waxing, manicures, make-up application, and spray on tans."

"So, you're a full-service salon?"

"Semi." She went on to explain. "We don't do pedicures or any kind of massage services, no full-body waxing. There are only two of us and it's time consuming."

"Full body waxing—people do that?"

"Oh sure they do. Men do that all the time."

"No."

"Yes."

"Not real men."

"Yes, Clay, real men—real, hairy men."

He shivered. "I saw a scene in a movie once where a guy got his chest waxed. It looked excruciating."

"That's what they say. I did one man's back and chest twice. The first time he drove himself. The second time, he got one of his friends to bring him. He said it took at least half a fifth of Johnny Walker Red to get the courage to keep the appointment."

"Damn!"

"Yeah, that was my first experience at seeing a grown man cry. He claimed the nipple area was particularly rough."

"You mean the alcohol didn't dull the pain?"

"I suspect it only made him more emotional. I stopped offering the service after that—couldn't stomach it anymore." She smiled at Clay's burst of laughter. "That and tanning beds. . . I quit offering that service when I developed a couple of spots I had to have surgically removed. Now I see a dermatologist every six months. Spray on tans don't last as long, but they're much safer."

His facial expression changed. "Were the spots cancerous?"

"Yes, but not the kind that metastasizes and we found them early enough. The experience scared me enough to get rid of those beds. Now I try to talk all my customers out of using them anywhere else."

"It says something about your character that you place customer safety above profit."

She rested her arms on the table. "You can't imagine the guilt after I had that scare."

"I'm sure everyone had to sign a release form to use them?"

"Of course, and I had warnings posted everywhere. That wouldn't stop me from hating myself if it happened to anyone else. I had to shut down the bed." Something about his expression had her curious. "Have you lost someone to cancer, Clay?"

He lowered his head, tapped his thumb and forefinger on the table, his mouth drawn in a tight line.

"I'm sorry. That's too personal. Sometimes I don't think before I speak."

"No, no . . . it's fine. And yes, I have lost someone." He sat back in his chair, stretched one long leg before him, the pointed tip of his boot straight up in the air.

Allie wasn't usually one to pry, but something made her want to know more. "A parent?"

He released a long, low sigh and lifted his gaze to meet hers. "My daughter developed leukemia when she was ten years old. She passed away two years ago when she was fourteen."

Allie's hand covered her mouth as soon as he mentioned the word *daughter*. Dear God. How does one bury a child?

"I-I'm so sorry, Clay. I don't know what to say."

"That's enough. Thank you."

"I can't do anything for you except listen if you need to talk."

He stared at her, wide-eyed. "Do you mean that?"

"I wouldn't have offered if I didn't."

"Part of me still wants to go home and curl up into a ball." He reached for the bottle of Louisiana Hot Sauce on the table and turned it between his two hands.

"I can't even imagine that kind of loss."

He wiped his face with one hand, slid his foot back under the table. "It ain't pleasant, I can tell you that much."

"I'm so sorry." Inadequate words, but she didn't have anything else for him.

Jill approached, carrying their plates. "Here you go. Let me know if there's anything else I can get for you guys."

"Thank you. This looks good," Clay said.

"I'm good, Jill. Thanks."

Clay stirred his soup with the spoon then stopped. "Allie, would you consider keeping me company tomorrow evening? I could take you to supper, or a movie, or both."

She opened her mouth to say no. Closed it. Opened it again. "Are you sure you want to after the way I treated you at the reception?"

He lifted one shoulder. "Everybody has situations that make them uncomfortable."

"I'm not comfortable in crowds when I don't know a lot of people," she said.

"I figured as much." He studied her, his brow furrowed. "I don't want you to feel sorry for me. And please don't think this is some kind of ploy to get you to come out with me."

"I don't. Besides, you didn't bring up the subject of cancer. I did."

"You know, last year I had to leave the state to keep from hibernating in my bed around the anniversary date. This year, I squeaked by with less effort."

She nodded. "Any improvement is good."

"I think so." He took another deep breath. "So, what would you like to do tomorrow night?"

"Have I accepted your invitation?"

"You have, but were too busy talking to notice."

She grinned, and stabbed some baby spinach and a bite-size piece of grilled chicken. "Let me think about it. Why don't you give me your phone number and I'll call you once I've considered my options." She pulled her phone from her purse, entered the number he called out to her.

He picked up his own phone. "What's your number?"

"When I call you, you'll have it."

He quirked one brow. "You mean *if* you call me? Like, after you've checked up on me?"

She sent him a sweet smile. "A girl's got to take precautions these days."

He pointed at her with his soupspoon. "You're a smart lady. Besides, I'm not worried."

"You sound confident."

"I've always tried to stay as far from trouble as I could. Sometimes it found me anyway, but it wasn't anything I could have avoided."

"Yeah, I've always found that family trouble is the most difficult to escape." She gave her salad a violent stab.

"Yep," he said. "Especially when you're married to it."

Clay clutched his coat tighter before reaching for his ringing phone. His heart gave an unaccustomed flip at the unfamiliar number. "Did you get your all clear, Ms. Sarver?"

A short pause preceded a response. "This is an automated message. Do you have ten minutes to take a survey?"

He smiled. "That was a noble effort, Allie, but I'm not buying."

Allie's chortle carried through to him. "You're no fun. How'd you know it was me?"

"I had a hunch." Her laughter was just what he needed to warm his heart on this blustery, barely above freezing day. "Have you decided what you want to do tomorrow evening?"

"I have. Since my girls will be with their father and his 'dipstick' this weekend, I wondered if you'd like to come over for supper. I never get the chance to cook anymore. I survive on bland baked chicken and salads. My girls are never satisfied with anything I prepare. They'll eat sandwiches before they eat my cooking."

"You've been on your feet all week, Allie. The last thing I'd expect you to do is go home and cook a meal."

"Cooking is fun for me. I love it, especially when I'm cooking for people who appreciate it. Besides, my two o'clock cancelled for tomorrow afternoon, so I'll get to close up the shop early. On my way home today I stopped off at the grocery store and bought the ingredients for two different meals."

He held his breath and prayed for the gumbo he'd been craving all week long. "Lady, I'd have to be crazy to pass up a home-cooked meal. I don't care what it is."

"Well, I make a fabulous chili with old fashioned cornbread."

"I like chili."

"Or seafood gumbo, unless you're allergic to shrimp, crabmeat, or oysters."

His breath released in a rush of air. "Nope. No allergies. Would it be too presumptuous to hope for potato salad to go along with that?"

"That was my next question. Seafood gumbo and potato salad it is."

"You have made me a happy man. Can I bring anything? Do you prefer a particular wine?"

"I'll be drinking water, but if you want wine you're welcome to bring a bottle."

"Fair enough," he said, determined to make sure she enjoyed herself tomorrow night.

Friday, December 14th
Date night

Clay arrived at Allie's place at 6:00 p.m. per her instructions. She had a lovely home situated in a nice subdivision on the eastern outskirts of Jennings. He surveyed the cozy living area, thinking it suited her, and froze when he saw the framed painting of a sunflower in full bloom. He couldn't help but think of Hope when he saw sunflowers. She adored them. He peered closer at the painting, seeing Allie's initials in the lower right hand corner, he called out to her. "You're an artist?"

Her laughter carried from the kitchen. "Hardly . . . that's a product of one of those painting parties. You know, you pay forty-bucks and show up with your own bottle of wine. After a couple of hours, you leave with a slight buzz and an amateurish work of art."

"Oh yeah, I've seen a lot of fleur de lis paintings as results of those parties."

"I know, but sunflowers make me smile, and at the time, I really needed something to make me smile."

Something stirred in his heart at her admission. He joined her in her kitchen, not surprised in the least to see a spattering of sunflower accents throughout the space. Not enough to overwhelm like in Hope's room. This space held just enough so that the bright yellow and orange accents popped on the darker terra cotta colored walls. His smile turned into a chuckle. "You must smile a lot in here."

She looked up from her stove and grinned. "I do. It's my favorite room in the house." She lifted the lid on the pot, allowing the aroma of rich, seasoned, seafood gumbo to waft through the air.

The smell stopped him in his tracks. "God that smells delicious."

She smiled at him. "I hope you're hungry. The rice, condiments, and everything else is already on the table, but I thought we could just serve the gumbo from here." She filled a bowl half full with the savory concoction, and handed it to him. "Go ahead and seat yourself." She poured the same into a smaller bowl for herself.

They spent their time discussing various likes, and dislikes, and just enough politics and religion to know they shared the same views.

At the end of a very pleasant hour, Clay relaxed against his chair back, and placed two hands on his full belly. "I can honestly say I've never enjoyed a meal as much as I've enjoyed this one. That was perfection and so is the company. Thank you, Allie. I appreciate all the trouble you went through to have me here."

"You are very welcome."

"Your love of cooking for people comes through in the food you prepare."

She raised one finger. "I enjoy cooking for people who appreciate it. There's a difference. If I spend four hours prepping and cooking a meal, only to have someone tell me what I should have done better . . . not so much."

"Did your ex do that?"

She lowered her water goblet to the table. "Always."

"Not this particular meal. It was perfection." He couldn't imagine anyone finding fault with the meal he'd just enjoyed.

"He complained about this meal too many times to count. The thing is I prepared it the same way each time. He'd always find something different to criticize."

"You've got to be kidding me."

She lifted her chin and frowned as she rattled off a list. "The roux is too dark. The roux is too light. Too many onions, not enough onions, too seasoned, not seasoned enough." She pointed to a small, wooden box pushed against the tiled back of her countertop. "I have this particular recipe, along with a few others, down to precise measurements. I left nothing to chance, just to prove something to myself."

He studied her for a moment. The tightness around her mouth, the immediate tensing of her shoulders . . . all signs of the inconsiderate treatment she'd suffered at the hands of that selfish son of a bitch. Her husband had thanked her efforts with criticism, betrayal, and finally abandonment.

"I Googled him, you know. It didn't surprise me at all to discover he's a car salesman. His reviews are dismal."

She gave a feminine sniff of disapproval. "He loves it, too. I can't tell you how many days he came home bragging about how he'd made a profit from someone who didn't know enough to realize they'd been reamed." Allie shook her head. "I don't think he has a conscience. I used to ask him how he slept at night. He always gave me the same answer."

"What was that?"

"Like a newborn baby."

"You mean he peed his pants and woke up every three hours for a bottle?" Allie's low chuckle turned into a round of hysterical belly laughter that brought a smile to his face.

"Here you go," he said, handing her a napkin to dab the tears from her eyes. "I'm glad someone finds me so amusing."

"I do." She gasped, trying to catch her breath. "Oh, my gosh. I can't remember the last time I laughed this hard."

"I can't remember the last time I enjoyed myself this much. Period."

His confession cut off her laughter, had her studying his face. Whatever she saw there seemed to satisfy her. She smiled and nodded. "I'm glad I could help, Clay."

"What do you think about gathering around firepits in the wintertime?"

Her eyes sparkled with excitement. "Love it. Most people I know hate the wintertime, but I love it."

"Do you trust me enough to come out to my place?"

"Where is your place?"

"It's about ten minutes west of here. You can come with me and I'll drive you back later."

She glanced at the clock on the wall. "How about if I follow you there in my car and drive home later? Shanna's off tomorrow and I have to style a bride, three bridesmaids, and a miniature bride for an afternoon wedding."

"Deal."

Allie accepted the unaccustomed offer of help to put her kitchen in order. She handed over storage containers of all leftovers to Clay.

He took the containers and grinned. "I'm bypassing all the insincere 'you don't have to do that's,' and jumping straight to 'Lady, I could kiss your ass for this!'" He gave her a one-armed hug. "I appreciate your generosity, and I know this will be even better tomorrow. Thank you."

"You're welcome. I'm going to change into something warmer. Then I'll expect you to deliver that roaring fire."

Within ten minutes of leaving her place, Allie turned off from a parish road onto something that resembled more of a trail than an established driveway. She parked behind his truck, next to a large RV. During her call to John Michael earlier, her brother-in-law explained that Clay had turned the house over to his ex-wife after the death of their daughter and purchased this camper as his permanent home.

She could understand him wanting no part of a place with bad memories of his daughter's long illness.

When she stepped out of her car, he approached, shrugging into his coat. "You want to wait inside while I get the fire started? It's not as cramped as it looks."

Allie couldn't deny being curious about his place. "Cramped? This place is huge for one person. What size?"

"Inside length is just under thirty-eight foot, with two slide-out sections on each side. I hadn't planned on anything this big, but I got such a great deal I had to take it. It turned out to be one of my better decisions."

She made her way around to view the backside of the camper, nodding in appreciation at his set-up. It may be a portable home, but he'd gone to the trouble of pouring a slab with room enough for two campers, and built a sturdy wood-structured roof large enough to encompass the slab. The process had added a twelve by forty foot covered patio area and carport, with overhead protection from the elements.

He walked around the back to meet her. "What's the verdict? I figured since it doubles as my home *and* home away from home, I'd just as soon build it to last."

"You've got a nice set-up, Clay. John Michael said you worked out of state a lot and didn't feel it necessary to maintain a house."

"That's right. What's the use of all that square footage when I'm home less than half the time? Maintenance of a house and yard is such a huge time suck. The RV meets all my needs, for now, anyway, and the majority of my pay goes into savings and a retirement fund. Come on, I'll give you the grand tour."

He opened the door for her so she could walk inside first. Something else her ex had never done for her. He always barged ahead, expecting her to trail behind him like a dog. It shamed her to admit she'd always done just that.

Upon entering, she sucked in her breath at the unexpected beauty of the interior. The pleasing, muted colors of the tiled floors, the walls accented with rich wood cabinetry and trim. The living area housed high quality leather furniture in a light taupe color, including a full sofa and a loveseat, placed at ninety-degree angles to each other. She pivoted to examine the kitchen area, with beautiful granite counter tops, full-size, glass-surfaced range, stainless steel fridge, and microwave. The sink was located on one-half of the center island, while the other half doubled as storage area and an extra work surface. It truly did have all the comforts of home.

"My parents had a camper when I was a kid. It did *not* look like this." She swiveled to meet his amused gaze. "This is fabulous."

"We had an old Winnebago for a while; a real home on wheels," he said. "I think dad accepted the title as payment for a carpentry job he'd done for somebody."

"Ours was one of those pop-up type campers. We were on top of each other in that thing." She shook her head at the luxuriousness of his living area. "Hell, I could live here." Her gaze landed on a spot under the huge wall-mounted flat-screen TV. "Electric fireplace?"

He pulled a remote from a container on the island, pushed a button, and a 3-D flame appeared behind the glass. "It's more of an electric heater than a fireplace, but it'll take the nip out of the air." He pointed to one end of the trailer. "The bedroom and bath are back there and the bunk house is on the opposite end."

She checked out the bedroom, impressive with its king-size bed and built-in storage units. The bath boasted a large, walk-in shower, a regular size toilet, and a sink, set in the same granite counter top used in the kitchen.

Allie emerged into the living area shaking her head in amazement. "You said something about a bunkhouse?"

He grinned and pointed to the left. "The grandkids love it."

She paused. "I didn't realize you had grandchildren. I guess I should have expected it though. You mentioned that Hope was your youngest child, you didn't say anything about her being your only child."

"She was the youngest of three. My son, Brian, is twenty-three. He's raising his three-year-old son, Sean by himself. My daughter, Terri, is twenty-two and she and her husband have a daughter, a one-year-old munchkin named Everly."

"I'm looking forward to being a grandmother."

"Grandkids are the absolute best. Mine got me through some rough times after Hope passed away." He opened a door and showed her a room with a bank of built-in cabinets on one end, and a TV in the center. Both sidewalls held hinged platform beds, all of them holding mattresses. A bench in the middle held a set of free weights. "Sean and Everly love sleeping in here."

"Do you ever have all of the family here at once?"

"Oh, sure, they all come a few times during the year. My sofa opens up into a queen-size bed also, so this place sleeps eight people. They come mostly during the spring and summer months though, so they can swim and fish—let the kiddos run around." He jerked his head to one side. "Come on outside and I'll show you."

She stepped out of the cozy warmth of the RV into the chill of the December night. Clay walked over to a switch on one patio post that powered a light at the end of a good-size boat dock. "This is fabulous, Clay!" She pointed to a large blackened pit next to the dock and along the bank of the pond. "Is this the fire pit?"

"It is. Do you still want me to fire it up for you?"

"You promised me a fire, Mr. Andrews. It's too late to back out of your offer."

"I wouldn't dare." Clay walked away for a few minutes and returned with an armload of roasting logs, some kindling, and a lighter. Within five minutes, the kindling blazed. Soon, the manufactured logs had caught to make a roaring blaze.

"That was quick." She sat in the fold out chair he placed for her next to the pit.

"Yeah, they're an easy and renewable source. There's no sense starting up a big log. It'll just get going good by the time you have to leave."

"I love this!" She stuck her hands out to warm them next to the fire.

"I have to admit, I'm surprised you like this outdoorsy stuff."

She stared at him, wondering if he was serious. "Why?"

"I don't know. You being a hair stylist and all, I figured you'd be more high maintenance."

"Pfft! I don't know where you got that idea." She relaxed in the chair and dropped her head back to gaze up at the sky. "Oh, look at all these stars. You have the best of both worlds here, don't you? You have a luxury camper and the great outdoors in one spot. When one gets to be too much for you, just step outside or inside into another world."

His laughter echoed over the glass-like surface of the water. "On a small-time scale, I guess. I know a guy who bought land on a lake up in Colorado years ago. His cabin puts most permanent homes to shame, and his camper . . . sheesh . . . you haven't seen luxury until you've stepped inside that thing. We're talking kitchens with full-size stainless steel appliances, windows all around to take in the gorgeous views, everything top-notch."

Allie couldn't help but think about what she could do with the money it took to buy something like that. "If he's got a fancy cabin on a lake, why the heck would he need a camper?"

He pulled up a chair alongside her and sat. "I guess it's kind of like your ex, Allie. I mean you cooked about the best meal I've ever had tonight, but from what you tell me, he wouldn't have been satisfied with that, would he?"

She tapped the arm of the chair with her fingers. She had to agree with him. "He would have complained about the seasoning."

"It was perfection."

"Or told me I should have cooked chicken instead."

"It was perfection."

"It was good, wasn't it?"

Clay buried his hands in his pocket. "It. Was. Perfection. But, for some people, even perfection isn't good enough." He shook his head and returned to host mode. "Would you like something to drink? I've got a couple of light beers in the cooler."

"No, thanks, it's too cold for beer."

He jumped from his chair. "Stay here. I've got just the thing for you."

Allie walked onto the boat dock and stared out over the water, relaxing to the sound of tiny waves lapping at the shoreline, and the pleasing tinkle of a wind chime hanging in the patio area. She strained in an effort to gauge the size of the pond. Had he stocked it? She used to enjoy fishing with her family and wondered what it would be like to spend a lazy afternoon out here casting a line.

When the camper door opened and shut again, she met him at the fire pit. "I smell chocolate."

He handed her a cup of hot cocoa. "I even had miniature marshmallows to put on top."

She took a sip and licked the sticky sweetness from her top lip. "Mmm . . . delicious! Thank you."

"I have the regular marshmallows too, if you want to roast some over the fire."

"I doubt I'll have room after the cocoa." She jutted her chin toward the pond. "Is it stocked?"

He adjusted a log on the fire pit. "I keep it stocked with bass and bream for fun. Do you like to fish?"

"I do, I just haven't been in years."

"I'll make sure to call you when it warms up."

"I'd like that." A lot, she suspected. "Did you buy this place after . . ." She managed to stop herself from saying "after your daughter died".

"We've had the land for about sixteen years. I invested in a huge family-sized tent after I bought the place. The kids and I would come out here every so often. It'd give their mom some time to herself. My work had always kept me away from home a lot, so I figured I owed her."

She studied his handsome profile, wondered what it would have been like to be married to someone who possessed that level of consideration for his spouse. "You already know what I do for a living. What is it you do that keeps you gone so much?"

"I'm self-employed as a completions consultant in the oilfield."

"As in completing oil and gas wells? My ex-father-in-law was a tool pusher, so I know some about the drilling end of that business."

"My work is different. I've been in the oilfield all my adult life but never on a drilling rig. I got a bachelor's degree in Petroleum Engineering, but my impeccable timing had me graduating just in time for the mid 1980's oil glut. My dad talked me into staying in school and getting my Master's degree. That helped me to get my foot in the door of the industry at the end of the decade. I started in Production and worked all across the U.S. and all over the world. Ten years later, I decided to start working for myself. I'm still at it."

Allie shivered and pulled her coat closer. "I watched a program on how fracking was done a few weeks back. I found it interesting how the process pulls out every drop of oil and gas from those shale deposits."

"Yeah, it's a lot more effective to drill horizontally than vertically."

"But, it also mentioned the possibility of waste water pumped into those injection wells triggering earthquakes and contaminating water tables in the areas." She held up one finger. "I also realize the process creates jobs in depressed areas around the country."

"And it lessens our dependence on the Middle-East for fuel." He leaned closer to the pit and adjusted the logs to get the fire burning again. "I wish our government would stop talking about alternative fuels and renewable energy and start doing something about it. Sure, wind farms are popping up all over the country, and a few electric cars. I know dozens of people using solar panels to supplement electricity. Where are solar powered cars, and cost efficient hydrogen powered cars, as well as the fueling stations?"

"Somebody will have to get the auto and transportation industry on board with alternative fuels before anything will truly change."

"You're right. Trust me, the automobile industry knows far too much about it to be relying on fossil fuels. The thing is, the industry needs fossil fuels to produce solar panels and rechargeable batteries for those electric cars, and most of the electricity used to power those cells still comes from coal, another fossil fuel."

"I never thought about that."

"Most people haven't. Hell, I've never been afraid of learning. I'm not too old to get a degree in some other field . . . wind turbine and solar energy, hydrogen energy—"

"Turning all this excess humidity down here into energy," she said.

"Sure. We'd have enough to run the world if we could just find a way to harness and convert it."

Allie inched her chair closer to the roaring fire for warmth. "That's a great attitude. I was a B-C student in high school. I didn't have the brain power for college then, much less now at forty-six years old."

He whipped around in his chair to face her. "You are not forty-six years old."

"I'm afraid so."

"I thought you were late thirties, at the most."

She rolled her eyes. "Oh please. I already fed you. It's not necessary to flatter me with lies."

He laughed and shook his head. "What do you have against compliments, lady?"

She spoke before she had a chance to think about her answer. "Nothing, if they're sincere."

The sad fact was that compliments were rare, non-existent even, for the bulk of her marriage.

"I swear to you, I thought you were thirty-six when I first saw you in church. Thirty-eight . . . tops. The close encounter at the reception didn't change my opinion. You don't look your age."

"Well . . ." She paused to face him, thankful for the darkness concealing the blush creeping up her neck. "Thank you."

His head bobbed. "You see how easy that was? And you're welcome."

"You're about my age, right?" She eyed him curiously.

"I'll be fifty December thirty-first." Before she could ask, he answered. "A few minutes after 11:00 p.m. and I know what you're going to say. Why couldn't I have waited one stinking hour to be the first baby of the year?" He raised his hands. "I have no idea."

"I missed being born on Halloween by this much." She held up her thumb and forefinger, indicating a tiny gap. "12:02 in the morning, November first."

"Ah, you were almost a "Boo Baby"." He smiled. "Hope was a Halloween baby. Her parties were always a blast."

"Kids in costumes, right?"

"Yeah . . . and we'd leave from there and go trick-or-treating."

He seemed lost in the memories of parties for the moment.

"I'm sorry, Clay."

He gave her a silent nod before wiping his face with one hand.

"In the diner you mentioned something about it being more difficult on the anniversary date. Did it just pass?"

He turned to her then, his mouth tightened in a grim line. "It's tonight, or 3:03 a.m. tomorrow morning, to be precise."

"Oh. Oo-oooh . . ."

"Yeah. I can't tell you how many times I've woken up to see that time on my clock."

She looked into the flames of the blazing fire-pit, the full implication finally dawning on her. "Okay. I get it now."

"What's that?"

She stood, handed him the half-empty cup of cocoa. "I should go, Clay. I just remembered I have to do the bride's make-up tomorrow, too. Thanks for tonight, though. It was a pleasant change."

"Allie? What—"

"Hey, call me when springtime rolls around if you still want some company fishing."

"Um. Okay."

He said something else, but by then she was halfway to her car. She couldn't hear anything over the pounding in her chest, anyway.

Allie got to her car, cursed under her breath at the long driveway. She wasn't that great at backing-up in broad daylight. Dead of night, pitch-black, rural areas with no lights added a completely new level of difficulty to the process. She started her car and threw it into reverse. Her determination to get the hell out of there overriding all fear of driving into God knows what. She left her car door open, the interior's illumination helping her enough to see the trail she needed to follow. Somehow, she managed, made it back to the paved roadway without sinking a tire in a drainage ditch.

She shifted into drive, forced herself not to floor the accelerator. Don't let on that you're upset. Don't let them see you cry. Never let them know when they've hurt you. Years of conditioning took over as she drove home.

Of course. They had been the only two people in that diner yesterday. He hadn't reached out to *her*, specifically. He'd simply reached out to the only other person around. How had she not seen it? No way would a man with his looks be interested in her.

Chapter Four

Clay sat for a full ten minutes, staring into the fire, and wondering what he'd done to offend Allie. Once it hit him, he swore under his breath. She couldn't possibly think . . .

He pulled his phone from his pocket, and found her name in his contact list. He brushed it with his thumb, decided against it, and slipped the phone back into his pocket. After repeating the process twice more, he covered the fire pit to smother it and headed to his truck.

Ten miles, driven well over seventy miles per hour, found him ringing her front doorbell eight minutes later. He knocked when she didn't answer, pulled out his phone to call her when she didn't answer that. After several rings, her automated voicemail greeting asked him to leave a message.

"I'm outside your front door, Allie. I'm not leaving until I speak face to face with you. So, if you want to get rid of me, you'll have to come to the door."

He waited a full two minutes before knocking again, deciding it was far more personal than a doorbell.

She pulled the door open, her face tight with frustration. "None of this is necessary, you know."

There it was. Further proof of how insignificant she believed herself to be. "It is necessary. Your feelings matter."

She crossed her arms and sighed. "It's not a big deal."

"It is to me."

"Look, I get it, you know? You were dreading the anniversary and didn't want to face the night alone. I was the only one in the diner yesterday. I'm not clueless. It's okay. Go home."

He put his hand out to stop her from closing the door. "You *are* clueless if you think my entering that diner a minute after you did was any kind of coincidence."

She opened the door enough to peek around the edge. "What did you say?"

"You heard me." He took a step into the opening, situating himself between the half-opened door and the jamb. "I Googled you and found a Jennings newspaper article about your shop's grand opening. I thought you looked familiar. I eat in that diner often and must have seen you there. Our chance meeting only happened because it was the first time you left your salon for lunch this week."

Her eyes narrowed. "I brought my lunch Tuesday and Wednesday."

"I know. I parked outside your shop both days, waiting for you to leave for lunch."

He gave himself an imaginary fist pump at her reaction: an intake of breath, and slight widening of her beautiful green eyes.

She swallowed. "You're not serious."

"I am."

"Why would you do that? All I did was empty a plate of food onto your shirt at a wedding reception."

"I really was on my way to speak to you at the reception when you turned and ran into me. Didn't you wonder why I was right on your heels when you turned?"

"Why didn't you tell me this at the diner yesterday?"

"Admit I'd stalked you for three days? Hell, I wouldn't be telling you now if I could see any other way to convince you."

She crossed her arms. "Convince me of what?"

"That I'm interested in you, dammit!" The look that passed over her face elicited a frustrated groan from him. "Is that so inconceivable?"

"To me, it is."

"That just pisses me off." Before he could clarify his position, her answer proved his point even further.

"Big surprise. I'm accustomed to having a man pissed off at me."

"I'm not pissed off at you, but I wouldn't mind planting my fist in "Bruce, the Bastard's" face right now."

The look in her eyes grew hard and dangerous. "Where'd you hear that?"

"That's what—" He stopped.

"That's what Cynthia calls him. Did my big sister guilt you into asking me on a date? Am I just some charity case with an asshole for an ex-husband? Somebody you should pity?"

He shifted from one booted foot to another, annoyed as shit at the spin she'd put on this conversation. He wasn't used to having his motives questioned. Christ-a-mighty, it'd been decades since he'd dated anyone new. Had the process changed so drastically in recent years?

He took a deep, calming breath, attempted to keep his tone even as he defended his actions. "I noticed you in church, even before I met your sister. And I'm pissed at Bruce for treating you so badly over the years that you have no idea how beautiful, how *attractive* you are."

Disgusted with the situation, Clay stepped back from her door. He turned to walk away but stopped to throw back one last comment. "Fair warning; I still may punch the SOB if I ever have the opportunity."

He drove home to lick his wounds in the peacefulness of his spot next to the pond. Thank God, she didn't call. He didn't know what to say to her if she did. Rather than dwell on it, he drank a beer and went to bed early.

"Daddy?"

His eyes opened and he blinked twice to focus in the room's muted lighting. The eerie quiet had his heart pounding with dread until he saw the steady pulse and glow of Hope's heart monitor machine.

Still trying to decide whether she'd spoken or if he'd dreamed it, her sheets rustled. He crouched over the hospital bed set up in her room at home, lifted her thin, cool hand in his own. "Hope? What is it?"

"You have to, Daddy."

He reached out with one hand to flip on the lamp and his fingertips brushed the silk sunflower arrangement on her bedside table. Clay turned to the daughter he adored and smiled. "I have to what, baby girl? Love you until the end of time?"

A solitary tear slipped from her right eye, trailed down onto her temple. He thumbed it away before it hit her hairline.

"Let me go, Daddy."

He'd seen it then. The pale face besieged by exhaustion, the toll her will to live had taken on her frail body. There would be no miracle cure, no last minute effort to rally the troops and march forward into another battle. She was done.

He realized, finally, that Margie's accusations before she'd left had been sickeningly accurate. Their daughter had been clinging to this painful, miserable existence—for him. She'd prolonged her agony, her suffering— and how she had suffered—to accommodate him and his inability to live without her.

He held his breath until his lungs burned with the effort to breathe, with the need to speak the words that had always kept her with him.

I can't . . . it's not time.

Neither could he say the two words she'd take as permission to sever her delicate tie with this world.

I know.

He chose the coward's path.

"Do I?" He'd hoped she wouldn't hear the whispered words, or wouldn't answer if she did. Her soft sigh indicated otherwise, and he tensed, dreading her answer.

"Yes."

He closed his eyes, lowered his head to rest it upon the fragile hand he held in his own. His hot tears dripped onto her skin.

"I'm sorry, Daddy."

He lifted his gaze, unable to hold back the sob that had been building. Like a giant wave, it crashed onto him, destroying the levee he'd constructed as his last line of defense, flooding him with sadness, and washing away every trace of the hope he'd clung to for so long. He reached up to caress her cheek and kissed her forehead. "You have nothing to be sorry for, sweetie. You've been so strong."

Her eyes stood out even larger against the pale skin of her thin face. Eyes similar to, but not quite the same shade of brown as his dad's, the grandfather she'd followed around like a puppy. The words came to him then, as though the man had reached across the boundaries of heaven and earth and spoken them himself.

"Pops will be so glad to see you, baby girl."

She smiled then, an actual smile—not one she forced for his benefit. She'd adored her "Pops".

"We'll fish."

He returned her smile, wiped the steady flow of tears from his face with the back of one hand. "Mind your limits."

"No limits."

He nodded, recalling his father's infamous line in regards to his favorite activity: *All I need in heaven is my old rod and reel, a sunny spot full of hungry bass, and no limits.*

"Do you know how much I love you, sweet girl?"

"I know, Daddy . . . I love you . . . so much." The answer came out in a gasp, as though she sucked oxygen from the last dregs of a reserve tank.

It shattered him. He dropped his head onto her frail body and uttered a broken, desperate prayer for his brave child. "Oh, God . . . God, please help us both. Help me to let her go, and help my baby girl to leave all this suffering behind her. Take her in your arms. Forgive my selfishness for wanting to keep her with me." He released a low sob and struggled to catch his own breath. After several moments of agony, he felt her arms go around him and he relaxed.

"Daddy?"

"Yes, Hope?" Somehow, he got the courage to corral his emotions at the exact moment she needed him the most. He lifted his gaze to hers, completely taken back at the look of wondrous anticipation on her face, and realized . . . this was it. He would always be grateful to have the memory of that moment. To have that eye contact with his youngest child as she quietly, peacefully slipped away from him. Her gaze softened and he had to wonder. What did she see? He knew what he hoped she was seeing. Acres of sunflowers in full bloom . . . her Pops waiting with open arms . . . and Evie, the black Miniature Schnauzer that shared a mutual adoration with her. He could only hope. As though his thoughts suddenly converted into flesh and blood before her, Hope's eyes widened, her lips parted with the barest hint of a smile. Seconds later, she passed from this world into the next—a world with no pain, no suffering, and nothing to hold her back.

The pulsing light of the heart monitor slowed, gave intermittent flashes, until it finally stopped completely. He crouched there, with his child's thin hand still clutched in his. He stroked his thumb back and forth over her cool, soft skin, remembered the feel of her arms around his shoulders. He stared at the hand he held, had never released, and realized it couldn't have been Hope, at least not in her corporal form.

Had that been God's comforting arms? Or an angel sent to collect her? Could it be that his father, her "Pops", had come, acting as a loving escort on her next journey? The only thing he knew was that after four long years of testing, pain, surgeries, painful recuperations, awful treatments, and exhausting struggle, his daughter was finally in the place she needed to be.

She was at peace.

Something told him he might never be again.

Saturday, December 15th
3:03 a.m.

Clay lay in the quiet darkness of his bedroom, too heartsick to move, or to make a sound. How many times had he dreamed of that night? How many times would he have to relive losing his daughter? He waited until he thought a full minute had passed before checking the time on his alarm clock. His impatience earned him a split second of seeing 3:03 before it changed to 3:04.

He reached up with one hand, knowing before he touched his face it would be wet with tears. He wiped them dry and climbed out of bed. After a trip to the bathroom, he shuffled to the kitchen area and started the coffee brewing, then the fireplace to take the chill from the air. His phone, set to silent, vibrated from its spot on the charging station.

He lifted it, held it before his blurry eyes, and squinted to put the text into focus.

Are you okay?

"What the hell?" He slipped on his reading glasses, stunned to see the message was from Allie.

He shot a text back.

I'll live. Thanks.

A full minute passed before she sent another. *I'm sorry I was a bitch.*

He frowned and answered her. *You couldn't be a bitch if your life depended on it.*

Her comeback: *Don't be so sure.* She sent an evil looking, wild-eyed emoticon. *Whatcha doing?*

He chuckled and checked the pot before answering. *Waiting for first cup of coffee. You?*

The same. Want some company?

He held his breath. Would she drive out here to meet him?
Absolutely...
He waited, his heart pounding, for her reply.
R U dressed?
He looked down at his flannel loungers. Was she playing some kind of game? If so, it'd help if he knew the rules.
Yes. He then added a belated, *somewhat . . .*
Clay stared at the screen, trying to imagine what her comeback to that would be.

A loud knock at the door had him juggling his phone to keep it from hitting the marbled work surface of the island. He opened the blind on the door, astonished at the sight of Allie standing at the bottom of the steps holding an empty mug.

He opened the door and stared, open-mouthed. Her gaze moved from his face to his bared chest.

"You said you were dressed." Her phone dinged and she checked his addendum. "Somewhat", she snorted. Her gaze raked over his bare chest again. "Sorry".

He reached down to offer her a hand up the metal steps. "No problem. Careful, it's probably slippery right now."

"Y-you want to go put some clothes on first?"

His mouth tightened on the threatening grin. "You worried you won't be able to keep your hands to yourself?"

"Oh, brother." She grabbed his hand and stepped into the trailer. "Is this the thanks I get for worrying about you?"

His heart swelled at her confession. "You were worried about me?"

She nodded. "I was . . . the anniversary and all." She scraped her teeth along her bottom lip. "I woke up around two o'clock and felt guilty. I couldn't make myself go back to sleep. I started to call you a dozen times, but I was afraid to wake you." Her gaze found his chest again. "Next thing I knew, I'd driven here."

"How long were you parked out there?"

"About ten minutes, I guess. I remembered what you said about the time, how you wake up at 3:03." Her gaze found his again. "Your lights came on at 3:04."

He nodded, passed a hand over his face. "Tell me about it." He cocked one eyebrow at his early morning visitor. "You scared the crap out of me, you know."

Allie made a big show of checking the floor. "Where? These shoes are new."

He placed a hand on the top of her head and gave her a playful push. "Aren't we witty at three o'clock in the morning?"

"Did you scream like a little girl?" She grinned at him.

"I'm sure I would have if I hadn't been trying so hard not to drop my damn phone." He performed a fair imitation of a juggling act.

"I kinda wish I could have seen your face."

His skin prickled with goose bumps at the sound of her low chuckle resonating in the air. Maybe she hadn't meant for it to come off sounding all sex-kitten-sexy-as-hell, yet somehow, it did. "I'm gonna go change."

"Please do. I could throw myself at you any second now." Spirited sarcasm oozed from every word.

"The cream and sugar are in the cabinet above the coffee pot, smartass."

"All righty."

He walked to his bedroom, amused at Allie's wicked sense of humor, but somewhat disappointed at her self-control. If he was being honest with himself, he could handle an out-of-control Allie right now.

Clay slipped into a pair of socks and jeans he'd left folded on a chair, and then turned toward his closet for a shirt. He paused to consider his reflection in the mirrored doors. He flexed his biceps and tightened his abs, frowning at the memory of the less-than-flattering tone of her parting comment. More diligence during workouts wouldn't hurt.

He pulled a navy blue, long-sleeved Henley from a hangar and slipped it over his head before heading back to the kitchen area. He froze at the sight of Allie, leaning against his kitchen island and sipping from a mug of coffee.

Her brow furrowed as she lifted her gaze to his. "What's wrong?"

"Not a thing." He forced himself to approach her, rested one hip against the lower cabinetry. "I'm not used to seeing a woman in this place, other than occasional visits from my daughter." He turned to fill his mug, realized she already had. "Thanks," he said, lifting it to his mouth to sip the dark, rich brew. "Ah coffee . . . it's my one, true addiction."

He lowered the mug and studied her. From what he could tell, she wasn't wearing a spit's worth of make-up. Even without it, her skin was creamy, even-toned, and her eyes glittered with mischief.

She blushed under his perusal, tucked her hair behind her ear. "What? Quit staring at me."

"How the hell can you look so good this early in the morning?"

She placed her mug on the island's surface and used both hands to smooth down the front of her sweater.

A frown tugged at the corners of his mouth. "I didn't mean to make you uncomfortable."

"I'm not."

"Yes, you are. You always fidget with your clothes when you're uncomfortable. You pull your blouse, smooth it down, things like that. I swear you have no idea how good you look to others."

"Don't exaggerate. I'm not a teenager who'll believe whatever any man says to me. My body has serious flaws. I need to lose—"

"Nothing! You need to lose nothing, Allie. Your body is curvy and soft, the way the majority of men like women to be."

"That's not true."

"Are you a man? Do you hang around other men? Are you privy to what guys tell other guys they find attractive on a woman?"

Her lips pursed in an adorable pooch. "I guess not."

"That's right. I am, however, and everything about you is just right for ninety percent of the heterosexual male population. You're too thin for about five percent and too heavy for the other five percent who've bought into the anorexic movie star and model images."

"That's not been my experience."

"By your experience, you mean your marriage to a sexist bastard for, what, twenty years or so? Let me guess, he spent his time perfecting his flirting technique on other women, but never his own wife, re-living his glory days as a football jock, insisting his spare tire was 'all muscle', all the while slapping your ass and making snide comments." Her silence proved him right.

"Let me tell you about guys like that, Allie. Guys like that lie. They lie to their wives or girlfriends, and they lie to themselves. And they do it for two reasons . . . to feel better about their own crumbling, sagging bodies, and to suck the self-confidence right out of the women in their lives."

He gave his head an adamant shake and ran one hand through his hair. "Bruce needed you to feel bad about your body, he needed to keep you down, lacking in self-esteem, or any sense of self-worth. If he hadn't, you'd have walked away years ago, and he knew that."

Her hands stopped their fidgeting. She stared straight ahead, as though considering his reasoning.

"Believe me, your ex *knows* how good you look, how good you've always looked." He continued, hoping to hammer his point home. "He'd just rather die than to admit it to you, or anyone else."

"You know what?" Her mouth contorted in a half-smile.

"What's that, Allie?" His insides warmed at the look of determination on her face.

"He *was* a football jock, and he *does* have a spare tire . . . and a board-flat ass that did nothing for a pair of jeans." One hand moved in a self-conscious manner to rest on her butt. "And he always called me jelly-butt."

"You do not have a jelly-butt."

"I know I don't. I do twenty-five squats a day, dammit. And they're perfect squats."

"How does a perfect squat look?"

She widened her stance and stuck her arms out in front of her. "The trick is to push your hips back and keep your weight on your heels."

A few repetitions had him nodding in agreement. "That's as perfect a squat as I've ever seen." It also had him taking two casual steps over to stand behind the island. "Do, uh . . ." he reached down to adjust the erection caused by her perfect squats. "Do you ever use weights?"

"No." Her eyes widened. "Do you think I should?"

He cocked his head sideways to eye her butt. "I don't see the need to change a thing. It's apparent that whatever you're doing now is working exceptionally well for you." When she opened her mouth to speak, he raised one finger in silent warning. She seemed to reconsider any negative statement she'd been ready to spout.

"Thank you, Clay. I appreciate that."

He nodded. "Well done, Allie. *That's* how you take a compliment." Her smile warmed his heart. "How's that coffee?"

She lifted her cup and took another sip. "It's good."

He craned his head toward the double reclining love seat. "Let's sit a while. Tell me about your plans for the holidays. How'd you spend your Thanksgiving?"

"I spent most of it with Cynthia, John Michael, and his bunch at Mr. J.D.'s. He's got that big old place out in the country. Cynthia's kids skipped it so they could be in for the wedding."

"And your daughters?"

"They chose to spend Thanksgiving with their dad this year. They'll be with me for Christmas."

"That's only fair."

"I'm sure they'll complain. Cynthia keeps telling me not to lose hope with them. She barely had a relationship with her daughter, Trini, until recently."

"I think she's right. There are enough of your qualities in those girls and they'll eventually appreciate all you do for them." He cleared his throat. "Now what I want to know is how you feel about the other hot and heavy romance in your family."

Her eyes sparkled with laughter. "You mean my mom and your Uncle J.D.?"

"Of course!"

"It was strange at first. Mom is, you know, she's *mom*! But those two . . . they're adorable together, don't you think?"

"They appear to be compatible. I guess time will tell."

"Yeah. New love always feels like it'll last forever. Then real life happens."

"Sometimes it's death that happens." He met her gaze, guessed she'd swallow her tongue rather than risk upsetting him by asking him to explain. "For clarification's sake, my daughter's impending death ended my marriage."

She blinked several times, her face awash in uncertainty. "Impending? I'm not sure what to say. Would you like to talk about it?"

He settled back into the recliner. "In Margie's defense, although she was never the hugs and kisses type of woman, she was a decent mother to our two older children. When we got married, I was twenty-five, and she was twenty-seven. She wanted two kids right away, even though I worked away from home for weeks at a time. She said she didn't care, as long as she got her two kids before the age of thirty, because she planned to shut down the baby-maker after that."

Allie frowned. "Somewhat of a flawed concept, I gather."

"I had a vasectomy, and although it did take, it didn't take soon enough."

She nodded. "Those little swimmers can survive up to six months, I hear."

He nodded. "Margie was thirty-five and finally where she wanted to be, career wise, teaching French and Spanish at the university in Lake Coburn. As you can guess, she was not thrilled with the idea of being pregnant." He took a sip of warm coffee and lowered the cup. "As a matter of fact, it took some heavy duty talking to convince her not to abort our baby girl."

To Allie's credit, she kept her silence through the admission.

"I told her I'd work solely in the states and would be around more. I insisted I'd be super hands-on with this one if it was at all possible."

"And she agreed."

"She did. That's when I went into business for myself. I tried to work only near home, but sometimes it wasn't possible. I did a lot of driving, a lot of diaper changing, and midnight feedings, baby-proofing cabinets, and bandaging boo-boos. Later, it was tee-ball and soccer practices and games, then girls' soft-ball, and more soccer. Hope was so much more into sports than her older sister."

"You think it had something to do with you being around more?"

"Nurture over nature?" He shrugged. "Who knows? Hope could hit a homer and catch fly balls like nobody's business, and she took it as a personal insult the few times anyone scored when she kept the goal.

Then one day she got hit in the face by a softball. I brought her to the hospital and while examining her, the doctor found some unusual bruising on her outer thigh and some swelling of her abdomen. When the bruise on her cheek wouldn't go away, we realized . . ." He stopped and took a deep breath. "They ran tests and discovered the leukemia."

"That must have been awful for you and your wife."

"God, I felt like it was the end of the world. It took everything I had to hold it together for Hope. Margie . . . well, she and Hope had never been close. Hope resembled her mom in physical traits. She had the same curly, dark hair, and brown eyes, tall and thin build, and she tanned rather than freckled in the sun. Despite that, the two of them never bonded. After Hope's diagnosis, they seemed to grow even further apart. The thing is, it bothered me more than it did either Margie or Hope. I always hated seeing that gulf between them."

"Maybe it was some kind of self-preservation mechanism. Margie distanced herself to keep from having it hurt too badly to lose her. Maybe Hope sensed it, and only gave her mom what she needed to survive. I don't know, of course. Personally, as a mother, I would have spent every second .

. ." She waved off the remainder of the comment. "I've never been in her shoes, so it's impossible to know how I'd have reacted." Allie reached out to cover his hand. "I'm so sorry, Clay. It's not enough but it's all I can ever think of to say."

He took a deep breath and clutched her fingers. "Thanks, Allie. It's enough, believe me." Her yawn had him checking the time. "It's almost four o'clock. Why don't you close your eyes for a while, try to get some shut eye before you have to go to the shop later?"

"Mm . . . these chairs are so comfortable, I might do that. I love leather furniture."

"You haven't seen comfort yet, lady." He felt around for a button on her side of the console. In an instant, her chair was on its way to a full reclining position.

"Electric recliners? Fancy-schmancy Mr. Andrews." She adjusted her position and closed her eyes. "Mm . . . I like . . . I like a lot."

Clay reached over to turn off the lamp, careful not to break the tenuous hold he still had on her fingers. He sat there in the quiet of the space, staring into the silent, flickering flames of the fireplace. His eyelids grew heavy but rather than close them, he turned his head to stare at Allie's profile. Her soft, even breathing told him she was already asleep. In a whisper, he repeated the last words she'd spoken. "I like . . . I like a lot."

Chapter Five

December 15th – Saturday, 9:00 a.m.

Clay picked up his ringing phone, frowned at the unfamiliar number appearing on his screen.

"Hello?"

"Clay, is that you?"

He cringed at the sound of his ex-wife's voice. "Last I checked." Margie laughed, but he didn't crack a smile.

"How are you? I've been thinking about you."

"What do you want, Margie?"

"Must you be so gruff?"

Here we go . . . the same old Margie, putting him on the defensive within thirty seconds. "Is there a specific reason for this call?"

"I-I called to tell you I'm moving back home."

"Okay."

"Back to our home."

"It's your home, Marg. I signed it over to you, remember? Along with nearly everything in it." He swallowed the rest of his bitter retort. *The one you wanted no part of while our daughter lay dying for the last several months of her life.*

"Well, we had so many good times, made so many wonderful memories of all of us as a happy family."

"What. Do. You. Want?" He managed to grind out the question through clenched teeth.

"Is it in decent shape?"

"How the hell would I know that? Last I heard from Brian was that you'd rented it to someone."

"Yes, but they didn't renew the lease. They've been gone for two months, and it's been closed up since then."

"Did you leave the utilities on and ask your renters to leave the unit running?"

"I'm not sure, but I think I did."

He clenched his jaw. Houses sitting empty in south Louisiana with no power turned into oversized Petri dishes for mold and mildew. "If you didn't, you'll go home to a huge mess and a ton of work and expense to get it back into living order."

"I called Brian, but he and Sean are recovering from the flu this week. I hate to ask, but—"

"I'll go check it out for you."

"Thank you so much. I'll owe you one. You'll have to come over one day and I'll cook your favorite meal . . . a big ole batch of crawfish etouffee."

"That's not my favorite meal, Margie. It's yours."

"Oh, well, it used to be. I'm surprised you remembered."

"Are you? I'm not surprised at all you don't remember mine."

"Clay—"

"I'll go check it out for you. I don't need you to cook a meal for me."

"I wouldn't mind."

"Okay then, I don't *want* you to cook a meal for me." That shut her up for a few seconds.

"Couldn't we talk?"

"You passed on six months of opportunities to talk when you left me and our daughter. I had nothing to say to you then, and even less to say today."

"Despite what you think of me, I loved my daughter. I couldn't handle it. I couldn't watch her suffer. I couldn't watch her die."

"I've heard it all before, Margie. You know my stance. I couldn't have walked away from her if my life depended on it. It's what a father—a parent—does." *Or should do.* "I'll check out the house for you. Is the key hidden in the same spot?"

"Yes."

"I'll go in a few minutes. I have plans later this morning."

"Thank you."

He ended the call without another word.

Clay pulled into the driveway, let the truck idle several minutes as he stared at the last place he'd seen Hope alive. He finally turned the key and sat there in silence as he replayed the last day he'd stepped foot inside the place on that cold and rainy day two years ago.

He'd made the final drive to the funeral home with his bags tucked into the extended cab of his truck, along with an armful of photo albums and a box of items from his kids. After the graveside service, funeral attendees gathered at the church hall. He'd stayed long enough to show his appreciation to everyone who'd come to offer support. After the last straggler left, he'd handed over a set of keys for their Lake Coburn home to Margie.

"It's yours," he had told her.

Her big brown eyes had widened. "What do you mean?"

"The house and everything in it. I'll sign it over so you'll be sole owner. All I want is the rural property west of Jennings."

"Are you asking me for a divorce?"

"I'm not asking. We've been separated for six months and I just buried our only minor child. I don't need to ask. I'm done."

"You can't mean that."

Clay had walked away from her then, her cries of protest still ringing in his ears. He'd stayed in a hotel while looking for another place. The bartender at the hotel's club area mentioned he had an RV for sale. Within two days, he had completed the necessary paperwork, and he owned his like new, temporary home.

He had taken two weeks off, and buried himself in preparations at the pond, getting friends to help him pour the slab, then building the roof with enough clearance to pull the camper in and out, as necessary. Not that it had moved since he'd parked it on the cement slab two years ago, but if he needed to move it, he could.

By then, Margie had recovered enough to get a lawyer and ask for more than her share of the savings and IRA's. She hadn't bargained on the female judge's critical opinion of her abandoning her husband and child at such a crucial time. Despite the judge's generous ruling in his favor, he'd given her half of their savings, along with the house. They had offsetting IRA accounts, so his remained intact.

Here it was, two years later, and the prospect of entering this place still threatened to suck the life right out of him.

He grabbed his truck's door handle. "Suck it up, and get it done, bub."

He stepped out into the cold, clear, December day and trudged around to the back door. The front yard was in decent shape but the back yard looked like shit. The renters must have had dogs. Big ones, judging from the size of several holes they'd dug in the exact spot his kids' jungle gym had sat for fourteen years.

He shook his head, muttering low curses at the inconsideration of people, but concluded with an adamant "Not my problem".

Clay found the loose brick and located the spare key to enter through the back door. The interior looked fine, with no sign of dampness. The electricity was on and he checked the thermostat—on and set to sixty-eight degrees. Marge must have rented the place furnished, because all the furniture was the same.

Clay pivoted in a slow circle, checking out the interior of the home where he'd raised his family for the last fourteen years of his marriage to Marg. They'd moved in without a minute to spare, one short week before Hope was born. Brian had already turned seven and Terri, nearly six.

This place had been part of the negotiations he'd come to think of over the years as Phase I of project *Hanging On To Hope*. Margie had insisted all three of their children should have their own bedrooms, and that they have a spare as a guest room. It hadn't been easy to find a five bedroom home that wasn't outrageously priced in this area east of Lake Coburn. They'd nearly given up and had purchased the property between here and Jennings for the purpose of building when this place finally became available. It had been enough of a bargain that they'd kept the undeveloped property with the pond for family camping expeditions.

About ready to escape this museum of memories, he paused when something on the dining room table caught his attention. Clay approached the table and focused on the large scrapbook laid out on the surface, opened about midpoint. He reached out to flip to the front cover, sucked in his breath at the familiar multicolored letters spelling out *Book of Hope*.

He let the cover drop onto the table again, his heart pounding in his chest. His gaze landed on the open page and some type of list highlighted with star-shaped bullets. The words blurred until he slipped on the pair of cheaters he carried in his pocket. Clay leaned over the table and read from the list that his daughter had entitled "Hope-fuls". Too engulfed in memories, her approach took him by surprise.

"She wanted us to reconcile, you know."

He spun around, swearing as his gaze landed on his ex-wife. "What the hell are you doing here?"

Margie pointed to the scrapbook. "It says it right there. It's number five on her list of "Hope-fuls".

He turned back to the book, read another line before slamming the thing shut. "It says she kind of missed having a mom."

"It's a reasonable deduction. She wanted me here, with her, and with you. She wanted us together." She stepped towards him, a one-piece sweater dress clinging to her thin body. Her dark hair cut in a short style and her make-up applied flawlessly. Other than being far too thin, she looked good.

He wasn't affected in the least.

"You lied to get me here . . . for this?" He indicated the scrapbook.

"It wasn't a lie."

"Wasn't it? You claimed you couldn't remember if you'd paid to leave on the utilities."

"I couldn't. I got here a few minutes before you did and realized I had."

"Just stop, Margie. I don't know what kind of game you're playing, but there will be no reconciliation."

She sidled up to him, ran her long nails down the front of his shirt. "We could spend some time together, see how things work out."

He grabbed her hand and pushed it away. "Do you even know what today is?" He continued at her blank expression. "It's the two year anniversary of our daughter's death, and you had no idea." He stopped to shake his head. "No reconciliation. Not today. Not ever."

"Are you seeing someone?"

"I'm interested in someone. We're talking right now."

Her eyes widened and she made a show of looking around the room. "Funny, I don't see her here."

"I've had enough of this shit. Don't call me under false pretenses again." He took a step toward the door, and stopped. As an afterthought, he made a grab for Hope's scrapbook, tucked it under his arm.

"That book should stay here in her home," she said.

"It stays with me."

He made it to the door before she tried again.

"Hope would want her Mommy and Daddy together, Clay. She would!" Her tone held more than a trace of desperation.

He swiveled, and sent her one last glare. "The only thing Hope ever said to me was to try to be happy. Now that I think about it, she never once mentioned you." He smiled. "I think our daughter knew you better than I did."

"My daughter loved me!"

He frowned at her wild-eyed expression, wondering if she was on some kind of medication—or needed to be. "I've never questioned her love for you, Margie. Hope was the most loving, generous, and forgiving kid on earth. It was your lack of feelings for her that always bothered the hell out of me." He pointed a finger at her. "Don't even get me started on your lack of compassion during the end of her illness. And if you think I was the only one who noticed, you're mistaken."

Somehow, he made it to his truck without blowing a gasket. How in hell did that woman have the nerve to pull something like this? Why was she even back here? Had something happened in Paris that caused her to lose her grip on reality?

Instead of going home to get ready for his 'date' with Allie, he pointed his truck in the direction of Brian's apartment complex in downtown Lake Coburn. He picked up his phone and hit a programmed number, couldn't help but smile when he heard Allie's cheerful greeting.

"Hey, I'll pick you up a little later than planned. I've got to make a run to my son's place in Lake Coburn."

"No problem. When I called the tree farm, the owner assured me they still have a good selection of fresh trees. More people are turning to artificial. I have one up in the attic, but I'm in the mood to decorate a fresh-cut tree."

"We used them too until Hope got sick. She made an announcement after that—only real Christmas trees. I just haven't had the heart, much less the square footage to put one up since . . . then. I'm kind of excited to help pick yours out though."

"Maybe it's not my place to suggest this, but have you thought about planting a real tree in her honor? You could plant a beautiful spruce, one you could nurture and shape and even decorate every Christmas if you felt up to it. It would look lovely next to your pond."

His mind filled with memories of his three kids decorating their trees when they were young. Then he thought of the week they'd spent at a cabin in Tennessee about ten years ago, and how much fun he and the kids had decorating the huge outdoor Christmas tree on the property the first night. They'd sat outside every evening the rest of the week with hot chocolate just to admire their handiwork.

"I'm sorry, did I hit a nerve?"

Her question jarred him from the memories. "Yes, but a good one. Do you have any idea where I could get a live potted spruce?"

"I think they sell them at the tree farm. We'll ask when we get there."

"Thanks hon, I owe you one."

"Nah . . . keeps me from feeling guilty about using you for your truck."

When it came to putting a smile on his face, this lady ran a tight race with his grandkids. "So that's why you invited me to come along with you?"

"Pffft, of course! I sure as hell don't want to spend an hour vacuuming tree needles from the trunk of my car."

He laughed. "Is that all you see when you look at me—four tires and a truck bed?"

"Oh, stop it. Don't forget the drop-down tailgate for easy access. Give me a call when you leave Brian's place, smartass."

"Will do, sassy pants."

He parked next to Brian's silver Jeep Cherokee in the parking lot and walked up to the second story apartment at the end of the complex. He knocked, heard his son's baritone giving his grandson a gentle reprimand.

"Sean Patrick, don't you *dare* open that door until I get there . . ."

He stood back as the door opened a second later. "Hey Pop, what pulled you away from Andrews' Pond to the big city of Lake Coburn?"

Sean threw himself at Clay's legs as he called out in a perfect imitation of his father. "Hey Pop!"

Clay lifted his grandson in his arms. "Hey short stuff! I'm gonna have to quit calling you that soon. You're growing too dang fast. I think your dad needs to quit feeding you so much."

The child's hazel eyes widened. "No! I like food. 'Cept for veg-a-bals. But daddy says I have to eat them so I can grow big like him."

He carried his grandson into the apartment. "Your daddy's right. Even yucky stuff like spinach and broccoli will make you grow big and strong."

"Can I show you my tent, Pop? Me and daddy builded it after I waked up this morning."

"We *built* it after you *woke* up," Brian corrected his son.

The boy released a tortured sigh. "Yeah. That!"

Clay set him on the floor. "Sure thing, Sean. I need to talk to your daddy for a minute first, okay?"

"Okay! I'm'a get it ready for you, okay, Pop?"

"*I'm going to*, not I'm-a," Brian called out to his son.

"Yeah. What he said, Pop," Sean said.

"You do that, short stuff." Clay shook his head as the boy darted out of the room at the speed of light. "Man, I wish I had that kind of energy."

"He's something, ain't he?"

Clay leaned forward. "He's something, *isn't* he?" He used the same tone his son had used to correct Sean seconds earlier.

Brian burst into laughter. "Point taken. Now what are we discussing?"

"Have you seen your mom since she got back?"

Brian seemed confused. "When did she fly back into town?"

"I don't know. She said she asked you to check on the house but you and Sean were both recuperating from the flu."

"I haven't spoken to her in two weeks."

"What the hell is going on with her? She lured me to the house and came on to me like she expects some kind of reconciliation." He filled Brian in and waited for his reaction.

"That sounds crazy-desperate, even for Mom. Hell, she abandoned you and Hope in that house. It's difficult enough for *me* to look at her and not think of that. It's got to be worse for you."

Clay sat on one end of the couch. "I can't even think about her without remembering the day Hope asked me if I thought she'd ever see her mom again. Margie used Hope's scrapbook to try to guilt me into moving back in with her."

Brian shook his head. "I can't think of Hope without remembering that scrapbook of hers—"

"The Book of Hope . . ."

"For a while she was always writing things down, and then she stopped, seemed to lose all interest in it. I asked about it once and about that list of Hope-fuls." Brian lowered himself on a large ottoman across from his father.

Clay leaned forward, rested his forearms on his thighs, hands clasped. "What did she say?"

"She said . . ." Brian faltered, stopped to clear his throat. "She said she already knew that some things were beyond hope. It was July 1, my birthday. Remember, the two of you had just made it back from MD Anderson?"

Clay nodded. "I do remember that day. Up until then, Hope seemed defiant about her condition, determined to beat it. She grew so quiet on the drive home, and she was different after that. She'd brought a Science report to keep her busy during her treatment but said she was too tired to finish it. Until then, she'd never missed an assignment." He tunneled his fingers through his hair. "Dammit. I knew going into that house would bring this shit to surface."

"As for Mom, I'm as clueless as you are. I thought she and Jacques were getting along fine."

"Is that the fiancé in Paris?"

"Yeah, his name is Jacques Bessette. I've only spoken to him a couple of times over the phone; he sounds like a decent guy. I have no idea what happened between them to send her running back to the states this way. We both know it's useless to ask Terri if she knows anything. She hasn't spoken a word to mom since the funeral and has no plans to, as far as I can tell." He splayed his hands. "Sorry, Pop. I haven't been much help."

"No worries." Clay looked at his watch and stood. "I've gotta go. I'm taking someone tree shopping."

"Gramma Jane decided to get a tree this year?"

"No, not your Gram." He tucked in his shirt and grinned at his son. "A lady friend of mine."

Brian seemed to consider it before nodding at his dad. "Good. It's about time you get back out there." He froze. "Oh, shit, does Mom know? Maybe she heard about it and came back to claim you as her own."

Clay cocked his head and thought about it. "I don't know how she could."

"Is this friend anyone I know?"

"I doubt it. She owns a hair salon on Academy Street in Jennings called Allie's Cut Above. Her ex has a car dealership on Highway 26, Sarver's Auto Sales. She's a real sweet lady."

"Hmm, I'm not familiar with the salon but I know a few people who've had bad experiences with that dealership. They said the owner's kind of a jerk."

"That seems to be the consensus, so far." Clay walked into his grandson's room to inspect the blanket and sheet tent Sean had built with his dad. "Are you in here?"

Sean stuck his head out from under a blanket. "I'm wight here, Pop! How do you like our tent?"

"I think it's about the best looking tent I've ever seen. I wish I could stay longer to visit with you but I can't today." Clay lifted the boy and wrapped him in a bear hug. "I love you, short stuff."

Sean coughed. "I can't bweathe!" He laughed after Clay loosened his grip. "I love you too, Pop!"

"You know, you can call me Paw Paw, or Grampa, or Poppa even."

The boy shook his head. "Daddy calls you Pop. I wanna do just like Daddy."

Clay nodded and threw his son a look. "You hear that, huh? Your work is cut out for you."

Brian ran a hand through his own short-cropped hair as he addressed the little boy. "Let's hope you don't do exactly like your daddy."

Sean's brow scrunched. "Why not?"

"Well, because your dad has done some stupid things from time to time."

The boy stared at his father. "You did?"

Brian scooped his son out of Clay's arms. "Yep, but the smartest thing I ever did was decide to keep you with me. I love you, little man."

Sean gave him a cheesy grin. "I love you too, Daddy."

Clay left them, pondering on how becoming a single dad at twenty had changed his son. Brian had been marginally rebellious as a teen, but had managed to avoid any real trouble. No matter how many various warnings he'd drilled into his son's head over the years— *think* before you act, be careful, be safe, don't drink and drive, watch the other driver, respect women, and always wear protection—Brian had impregnated a twenty-one-year-old with no interest in marrying him nor raising a child. She'd called him soon afterward asking for the money to pay for an abortion.

Brian had convinced her to have the child, volunteered to pay for everything, give her the support she needed, both financially and emotionally, so that she could finish college, and after that, as well. When Sean was six days old, his mother signed papers to give up all legal rights to her son. So began Brian's journey as a full-fledged, full-time, single-dad.

No matter how it had happened, no matter how many worried, disheartened phone calls and visits Clay had received from his son, he'd never been more proud of him for hanging in the way he had that first year. Not a day went by that either of them regretted Brian's decision to raise Sean.

During the first dark days and weeks after Hope's death, Clay had been the one making the calls, the unexpected visits in the evenings. At twenty-three months old, Sean Patrick Andrews had always found a way to put a smile on his grandfather's face, bringing him to a level of joy he hadn't expected.

A year later, Everly Hope LaBleu had come along to Terri and her husband, Ryan, adding another bulb to brighten Clay's world.

He couldn't help but repeat what he'd admitted many times over the past two years . . . thank God for his grandchildren.

Chapter Six

"This one looks damn near perfect." Clay called Allie over to the latest in the long selection of trees she'd examined.

Her eyes lit up at his discovery. "Oh, that is a beauty. Do you think it'll be too tall for my eight foot ceiling once we put it on the stand?"

"It's six foot and has plenty of exposed trunk for trimming if you need." He walked around the tree. "I don't see a bad side, do you?"

She made two laps around the tree, stood back and nodded. "This is it. I believe we've found my tree." She reached over and pulled the tag to keep anyone else from taking it.

He took the tag from her. "I'll let them know for you."

"Thank you, Clay. I'll stay right here, and don't forget to ask if they have any potted trees to sell."

He lifted a finger to let her know he'd heard and headed for the owner of the place. Clay had just finished his business with the man when he turned around to see Johnny Ferguson approaching.

"Clay! You're about the last person I expected to see here."

"I could say the same for you. I thought you and Cynthia were still on your honeymoon."

"We got back on the tenth, and figured we better get a tree up this weekend or it wouldn't happen at all. She'll be at the hospital a lot for the next week and a half. You know how it is. Somebody worked over so she could take off a week. Starting Monday she's returning the favor."

"Where'd y'all go?"

"We spent a week in Nashville at the Gaylord Opryland Hotel. I'm telling you, neither one of us wanted to come home. The hotel was beautiful, with everything decked out for Christmas. They provide shuttles back and forth to downtown Nashville and all kinds of tours every day."

"Cuts back on the stress level when you don't have to fight traffic."

"You've got that right. We toured the Grand Ole Opry, the Ryman, attended a concert at Bridgestone Arena, and danced in clubs up and down Broadway Street. We can't wait to go back."

"I'm glad y'all had a good time." Clay searched the area around them. "You come here alone?"

Johnny held up a ticket stub for a tree. "Cyn's back there guarding the tree. Pickings were kind of slim today."

Clay nodded. "I know what you mean. It took us a while to find one Allie liked."

Johnny's brow shot up. "You're here with my sister-in-law?"

"Relax, Johnny, we're just friends."

"Oh?"

Clay sent his cousin a warning look. "Yeah. That's it, for now. I'm interested in more, but we haven't discussed it. I don't think she's ready for that."

"You'll have to earn her trust."

"I know."

"And once you do, don't do anything to make her regret it."

Clay frowned at his cousin. "I know."

Johnny raised one hand. "I'm protecting my own interest here. You make trouble with my sister-in-law and I'll sure as shit feel the backlash."

"I understand." He waited until Johnny finished his business and the two of them walked back to where Allie and Cynthia stood talking at the halfway point between the two trees. "They found each other."

Allie greeted him with a smile. "I looked over about five rows and saw her." She hugged Johnny. "Big sister was just telling me what a fabulous time you two had in Nashville."

"We did. On the way home, we were saying how great it would be to go back. It'd be a blast to go with another couple." He looked from Allie to Clay, then back to Allie.

Cynthia's amused snort broke the uncomfortable silence. "John Michael, if you're trying to be subtle, you need to work on your skills, sweetie."

He pulled his wife in front of him and wrapped his arms around her middle. "I wasn't aiming for subtlety. I look at these two and see people who deserve to be as happy as we are. Why waste time when there are so many better things to do with it?" He punctuated his statement with a tender kiss to his wife's neck.

Clay grabbed the back of his neck and looked uncomfortably at Allie. "I thought about asking if the three of you would all want to come over to my place later this evening. It'll be a great night to sit out by the fire pit, play a game, or two of washers while we listen to music and drink a little beer, or wine, if the ladies prefer." He faced Allie, his mouth tightened in a grimace as he thumbed at the other couple. "I'm not sure they're ready for mixed company, though. What do you think, Al?"

Allie grinned and played along with him. She spoke behind her hand, but loud enough for her voice to carry. "I know what you mean. They may need a few more weeks for the newlywed bliss to wear thin."

"Hmm, that could take a while", Cynthia purred, leaning into her husband's embrace. But I suppose we could restrain ourselves for one evening if the offer still stands."

Clay waited until Allie's gaze landed on him. "What do you think?"

"Sounds like fun to me. I could cook us a big pot of chili and cornbread, how's that sound?"

"Only if you cook it at my place so I can watch you," Clay insisted.

She placed her hands on her hips. "Do you plan to steal my recipe?"

"The thought crossed my mind, but once I learn to cook it myself, I'd be glad to return the favor."

She laughed. "Okay, Mr. Andrews. You've got a deal."

Cynthia pulled her sister close for a one-armed hug. "This is fun, isn't it? I can't remember the last time you and I spent an evening together like this."

"I don't think we ever have. Kind of difficult with you up there in Oklahoma with 'Golden Boy' as Bruce used to call Gene."

"Gene was far from golden", Cynthia snorted.

"Compared to Bruce, he was. At least you didn't find out about his affair until after he died. I'm not trying to lessen your pain, believe me, Sis. But it's different than knowing it's an on-going thing and having to live with it."

Cynthia's gaze turned icy. "You knew about his affair from the beginning?"

Allie chuckled. "I could always tell when he was sleeping around on me over the years. Bruce wasn't nearly as intelligent as Gene, or as creative at lying, either."

"What the hell is wrong with us, Allie? How did we both get sucked into marriages with men who manipulated us the way they did?"

Allie gave the chili one last stir, covered it, and turned off the burner. She sipped from her glass of wine before setting it on the counter. "I think you got married too young. You met Gene right out of high school, married him a year later. That's too young to know what you want."

Cynthia sighed. "Yeah, sounds about right."

"I, on the other hand, was a green twenty-two when I met Bruce, and still naïve enough to believe all men were as good as Dad was to Mom. I was shy and didn't date much. You'd been married for three years by the time you were my age, so I was sure I was old-maid material. It took three years for Bruce to marry me, and he waited until after the honeymoon to tell me he didn't particularly want children. He said kids were only good for two things: to make a woman's ass bigger and a man's bank account smaller. It took three more years for me to accidentally get pregnant."

"What'd you do, skip a couple of pills?"

"I've never been on the pill in my life. Bruce wouldn't have dared leave that choice up to me. He wore condoms. Always. The two times I got pregnant were because the condoms broke when I was ovulating."

Cynthia's mouth gaped open. "You're not serious."

Allie chuckled, remembering the temper tantrums Bruce had thrown each time she revealed her pregnancy. "I couldn't have timed those better if I'd tried. Two kids, three years apart, exactly what I wanted."

Cynthia managed to close her mouth. "I remember now that you mentioned using condoms, but I thought you only used them occasionally. You're telling me every single time?"

She nodded. "I should have bought stock in the damn things, knowing how much money we spent on them. I always resented him stopping to put them on, but considering all his . . . indiscretions . . . I'm sure it saved me from contracting an STD or two."

"Allie . . ." Cynthia paused. "Was Bruce your first?"

"Bruce was my first, my last, and my only."

"Are you telling me that you've *never* had sex without a condom?"

"I guess I am. Why?"

Cynthia paused. "Did you enjoy sex?"

Allie met her sister's gaze. "Not particularly, no."

Cynthia covered her mouth with one hand. "Oh, Allie, if this thing with you and Clay is headed where I suspect it is . . ."

"What?" Allie straightened, stepping away from the cabinet.

Cynthia's mouth spread in a wide grin. "If that man is anything—*anything*—at all like his cousin, I'm thinking you're in for a future of exceptionally pleasurable experiences. I have two bits of advice for you. First, accept that there are truly good men out there, and from what I hear, Clay is one of them. Second, learn to relax, sit back, and enjoy the ride."

Allie tried to concentrate on the conversation going on around her. Her thoughts returned to Cynthia's prediction. She and Clay were only friends, weren't they? He may think he was interested in more, but she wasn't kidding herself.

Or was Cynthia right about him? Was he one of those rare men like her father, and according to her mom and sister, Mr. J.D. and John Michael, as well? *Relax, sit back, and enjoy the ride.*

She closed her eyes, tried to imagine what that would feel like with Clay. A soft touch to her arm jostled her back to her surroundings. She looked up to find Clay's blue-eyed gaze on her, his brow furrowed with worry lines.

He leaned closer. "Anything wrong, Al? Are you getting cold?"

"Oh, no, I'm fine, thanks. I was just thinking about something Cynthia and I discussed earlier," she said, her voice lowered to keep their conversation private.

"Oh oh . . ." He sucked in air through his teeth. "It sounds serious. Should I be worried?"

"I don't think so. I'm the one who should worry." *That I'll fall far short of your expectations of me.*

He reached out, threaded his fingers gingerly through her hair, and then leaned in to place a tender kiss on her temple. "You, my girl, should never have to worry about another thing in your life." He released her and sat back, smiling. "Now stop borrowing trouble."

Allie caught her sister's amused gaze on her. She turned away and stared into the flames of the fire as they caught at the log.

Frigid.

She winced, remembering Bruce's last words to her before walking out with his packed bags: *"You couldn't please a man if your life depended on it. You're frigid and you've got a fat ass. I did you a favor by marrying you when I did. Nobody else wanted you back then, and nobody will want you now."*

Something's off.

Clay walked Johnny and Cynthia to their truck, reflecting on how quiet Allie had been during the tail end of the evening. They'd laughed so much earlier when the two of them joined forces in his tiny kitchen to cook a big pot of chili. After the arrival of her sister and his cousin, the four of them had eaten and spent a couple of hours outside under the stars. However, Allie's mood had gone off-track during the last two hours.

He frowned as Allie left his camper carrying her purse. "Where do you think you're going?"

She shouldered her purse strap. "I thought I'd save you the trouble of driving me home. Cynthia and John Michael can drop me off on their way back to Lake Erin."

"I don't mind bringing you home, Allie."

"I know, but I'm trying to save you the trouble."

"You're no trouble. Besides, I thought you could help me pick out a spot near the pond for my tree."

Clay would have had to be blind to miss the look Allie shot at her sister, but he let it go, pretended he didn't notice the concern on her face. He gave a gentle tug at her wrist until she stood before him out of earshot from the other couple. "What'd I do, Allie? Talk to me".

"What do you mean? You didn't do anything."

"The last couple of hours you've avoided eye contact with me, and now you're running off to keep from being alone with me. Aren't we past this stage?" He tucked a finger under her chin to lift her face to his. "Aren't we?"

"I don't know what you mean. I'm trying to save you some gas in that tank you drive. I'm . . . I'm being green, you know, conserving energy."

He cupped her face in his hands and pulled her close, her mouth tantalizingly near to his own. "Stay with me, Al. I'll bring you home later."

"I-I have to get up early tomorrow. I'm attending eight o'clock mass in the morning."

"It's not even nine yet. I'll get you home in plenty of time. Stay with me." He lifted his face to the sky. "We have a sky full of stars and plenty of fire left in those logs."

Gently, she pulled his hands from her face. "They'll all be here another day. I have to go."

Resigned for the moment, he nodded and tugged her close for a hug. "Call me when you get home so I won't worry, okay?"

"I will. The chili is in a plastic container in your fridge and I put the pot soaking in the sink."

"Thanks, I appreciate it."

He waved them off, and walked toward the cluster of chairs, overwhelmed by the quiet solitude of the night. He dropped into the one nearest the fire, spent the next ten minutes staring at the stars while he waited for her call. Anything was better than facing the emptiness of his camper. Funny how he could tolerate the tiny space easier when it was crowded with people, rather than when he was alone in it.

His phone dinged and he read the text.

I'm home. Thanks for a great evening.

Call me, Al. Let's talk.

We don't need to talk. Everything's fine.

Please...

His heart nearly pounded out of his chest when the phone rang in his hands. He hit talk and brought it to his ear.

"I'm glad you called."

"I knew you'd come to your senses, Clay."

He pulled the phone away from his face, realized the caller was Margie. "I thought you were someone else."

"Sure, you did."

A muttered curse rolled off his tongue as he hit the end call button. As usual, her timing was unbelievably horrendous.

He checked to see if Allie had sent another text. She hadn't. He called her number, and it went straight to voicemail. He took a second to get his thoughts together before leaving her a message.

"What are you so afraid of, Allie? I told you that day in the diner, I don't bite." He grinned as he pictured her listening to the message. "Oh, by the way, I hope you weren't fibbing about going to mass in the morning. I'll be there around 7:45 to collect your cute butt." He chuckled to himself as he ended the call. That'd give her something to think about. If she wanted out of it, she'd have to buck up and call him.

He wasn't too surprised when his phone rang a few minutes later. He checked the screen this time, making sure he saw Allie's name before answering. "I figured that would kick you into action."

"Don't you dare show up here at seven forty-five in the morning."

"Fibbing about going to church has got to border on sacrilege in somebody's bible."

"I'm going to mass with my girls. Kayla has to be there with her confirmation class."

"At eight o'clock?" Her silence was answer enough. "You didn't want to be alone with me."

More silence followed.

"What are you so afraid of, hon?"

"I'm not ready for any of this." Her tone was tight with unspoken emotions.

"For what? Friendship? Talk to me, Al."

"Is friendship all you want from me?"

"If you want me to be honest, I want a lot more."

"I'm not ready for more. I'm not equipped to . . . to . . ."

"To what?"

"I'm just not good at it, Clay. I think there's something wrong with me."

"There's nothing wrong with you."

"That's not what my ex-husband used to say."

"What did he used to say?"

"He-he said I was frigid."

He clamped down on his jaw. "Did he now?" He took some comfort in the fact that she'd even admitted something like this to him. It indicated some level of trust, although he doubted she could have spoken the words face to face.

"Yes, he did. On many occasions."

He stifled a groan, along with the giant-anaconda-length string of profanities he'd love to hurl. He prayed for the chance to plant his fist in that son of a bitch's face one day. "Yeah, guys who screw around on their wives love to use that one. Just so you know, to the rest of us that translates to them not having the equipment, or know-how, or *consideration* to get the job done. And by that, I mean making sure the wife gets hers . . . first."

"First?"

"Well, yeah."

Allie's snort carried to him before her muttered reply. "Try never."

Clay slapped a hand over his face. "Oh man, here I was, wishing for the opportunity to punch him in the face, when I should shake his hand and thank him when I see him."

"Why would you do that?"

Allie's unexpected reaction had him smothering the chuckle forming deep in his chest. "He's making this way too easy for me."

"You think I'm easy?"

"No, hon. You'll see what I mean one day."

She gave an indignant huff. "I'm not sure I want to if you think this is at all humorous."

"Well, Al, that's what I'll be doing from here on out."

"What's that?"

"Getting you to 'want to', with your permission, of course."

"You're asking my *permission* to let you try to get me to want to have sex with you?"

"Yes, I am." He waited patiently, his mind focused on an image of her pondering his proposal, weighing the pros and cons of discovering what she'd missed during her marriage to that ass hat of a husband. Step one complete: Stimulate her curiosity.

"Question!" she blurted.

"Shoot."

"What happens if you succeed?"

"If I succeed in making you want me?"

"Well . . . in making me want sex."

"With me."

"Well . . . yeah."

"So, what happens when you decide you want *me*?"

"Okay. . . yeah."

Step two complete: Make it personal. "It depends on you, beautiful, and how far you want to take it. That's not to say I won't have a few requirements of my own, but you'll be in complete control if and when it happens. I'll take care of the where and how."

"What kind of requirements?"

Clay relaxed his head against the chair back, enjoying the evening sky as much as Allie's willingness to question. Even then, he suspected she wouldn't have been this chatty about this particular subject matter face to face. "I'll require some kind of commitment, for one thing. I've only had a handful of sexual partners in my lifetime and there's been nobody since my wife."

"Are you serious?"

"Does that surprise you?"

"It does."

"What did you think? That I was some kind of man-whore?"

"No, but I didn't expect you'd lived like a monk for two years, either."

"Two and a half years. Marg left me six months before Hope passed away." He waited through the pause in conversation, until she worked through however she chose to interpret his statement.

"I still find that hard to believe. I mean, I believe you, of course, but . . ."

"How could a mother leave her sick child behind to live in Paris?" he finished for her. "I'm not sure, Al. I can't be certain her reaction would have been the same with either of our first two children or not. Margie never doted on or pampered our kids. She's more of the academic type, you know? While other mothers were perpetuating the Santa Claus, Easter Bunny, and Tooth Fairy theories, Margie sat our kids down at five with an encyclopedia or a computer print-out full of facts de-bunking the myths."

"Oh, wow . . ."

"Yeah, try explaining that to the irate parents of other kindergarten students. When I came in from work, I had to sit our kids down again, and tell them to keep their mother's opinions to themselves. And then I made sure they knew it was okay to believe in Santa, the Easter Bunny, and the Tooth Fairy."

"Oh, my gosh. That is so awesome of you!"

"I told you Marg never wanted a third child, and as a result, there'd always been something missing between her and Hope. From the second she was born, I was my daughter's primary care-giver. Thank God Brian and Terri were around to love on her when I was gone during the day. If I had to leave for any length of time for work, I'd pack up Hope and take her to my parents' place, and that was fine with Margie. I didn't trust my wife enough to . . ."

"You didn't trust your wife with your daughter's welfare?"

"Not in the sense you may be thinking. I knew Hope would feel physically safe with her mother. I just didn't think she'd feel loved."

"I can't even imagine what that must have been like for you, as an adoring father."

"I knew going into that third pregnancy with her what I'd be dealing with, and it sure as hell beat the alternative. On the pro side, I got to experience everything I'd missed out on with my first two because of my work. I let my older children know how much I regretted that, too. I didn't want them resenting me for being so hands on with their youngest sibling. As a result, I developed stronger bonds with Brian and Terri as well as with their little sister."

"I can see it."

"What?"

"I can see how your wife distancing herself turned into a blessing for you. Can I just say how much I admire you?"

"Don't be so quick, Allie. I wasn't kind to Margie after Hope died. I told her at the funeral I planned to divorce her."

"Didn't you say she'd been in Paris for . . . how long?"

"Six months."

"Well, I'm sure she must have expected it. I mean, did she think you'd welcome her back with open arms?"

"That's exactly what she expected."

"Interesting . . . for someone who refused to believe in Santa, the Easter Bunny, or the Tooth Fairy, it sure seems like she'd have had a tighter grip on reality."

His laughter began as a chuckle deep in his belly, progressed until it burst forth in a loud guffaw.

"I didn't think it was that funny."

He gasped, trying to catch his breath. "That's why you're so wonderful." He groaned and wiped tears of laughter from his eyes. "You don't think you're funny, but you've got a hell of a sense of humor. You don't think you're intelligent, but you're crazy sharp. You don't think you're pretty, but you're gorgeous. You see yourself as too heavy rather than the bodacious, curvy woman you are."

"Stop, Clay—"

"And finally, you don't think you're desirable." He released a long, drawn-out sigh. "And that's the kicker, Al, because I'm sitting with my eyes closed, imagining you over there with your phone in hand, talking to me. I swear to God, all I can think about is how badly I wish you were here so I could prove you wrong."

Silence greeted him . . . deep, heavy, and so prolonged Clay checked the phone to make sure they were still connected.

"Allie?"

"I'm here. Thank you."

"Now, don't you wish you'd have let me bring you home tonight?"

"Maybe."

"I bet you'd still be here."

"Good chance."

"Maybe you'd still be here tomorrow morning."

Her lighthearted laughter reached him. "I guess it's possible I could be there in the morning, but only in a stay-up-all-night-talking kind of 'be there'. No way in hell would I have slept with you."

"Hold on, now. Have you forgotten the two hours of fabulous sleep we shared in my recliner just last week?"

"My apologies, sir! Please allow me to rephrase. No way in hell would I have taken my clothes off to have sex with you in your bed, or recliner, or couch, or next to a roaring campfire, or even next to a cozy electric fireplace with 3-D flames to warm our bare tushies."

"I'm not sure how you can be so confidant of that."

"It's simple. I have not shaved my legs since the wedding. I wouldn't take my jeans off for you, Blake Shelton, Trace Adkins, or Toby Keith." She paused. "Well, maybe for Toby Keith—but *only* if he asked me twice and begged me pretty please."

Clay burst into laughter. "There's that wicked sense of humor again. You are quite mistaken if you believe hairy legs would scare me away. Besides, sometimes I think *I* should have been a cowboy."

"Very good, Mr. Andrews. You're quicker than I thought you would be."

He chuckled. "So, Ms. Sarver, are you ready to be wooed, flattered, and otherwise bombarded with messages that will send you into a sensual overload?"

"Are you ready to hear I told you so?"

"You're a cruel woman. Next time you see me, I'll have my game face on."

"If you say so. Thanks for the lovely evening. Good night, Clay."

"Good night, Al."

Chapter Seven

Sunday, December 16th

Allie shook herself mentally, as images of striking blue eyes invaded her thoughts. She should be concentrating on the word of God, not fidgeting and daydreaming about six-foot-plus of sexy. She tried harder to follow along with the service, without much luck.

"What's wrong with you?" Cecily's irritated hiss reached her, and Allie reacted with a hard glower. After a few more minutes, the priest's call to offer each other the sign of peace was a welcome break from trying to keep thoughts of Clay from her mind. She forced a hug on her daughter, whispering "Peace be with you, Cecily." She shook the hands of several people in the row in front of her, then to the right, before turning to reach those behind her.

"Peace be with you, Allie."

Her gaze travelled from the large hand he extended, to the handsome face, taking a few seconds to register. She swallowed and took it. "Peace be with you." He held it several seconds too long, covering their clasped hands with his left. His mouth twisted in a one-sided grin that said "Game On". She pulled her hand from his and faced the front.

Damn . . . damn . . . damn! If she'd had a gnat's chance of concentrating on the service before discovering his presence, that had all been blown to hell. She could practically *feel* the heat from his gaze burning her backside. Thankful she'd chosen a tunic with some length to it, at least she didn't have to worry about her butt being exposed.

Cecily elbowed her and hissed. "Who is that?"

"He's a friend," she whispered. "Now, shh . . ."

Cecily leaned close to whisper in her ear. "He keeps staring at you."

Allie pulled away and turned a glare on her daughter. Dear Lord, would this service never end? She shook her head, overwhelmed with guilt, and so badly flustered she couldn't remember a word of today's homily.

After the service, she and Cecily waited for Kayla to separate from her confirmation group to join them. They'd just rounded the corner of the church when Kayla's announcement grabbed Allie's attention.

"Why's that guy from the wedding reception standing by our car?"

"That's where I've seen him!" Cecily gasped. "He wasn't all Cowboy-ed up like he is today, though. He was in the pew behind us in church. Dude kept staring at Mom like he wanted to eat her for lunch."

"Ew. . . that's disgusting."

"He's a friend. Both of you hush, now." Allie glanced at her daughters. "I mean it, too."

They approached the car and Allie took a deep, calming breath. "Hello, again."

"Good morning." He touched the brim of his brown, felt Stetson, and turned his warm gaze on her daughters. "Ladies, how are you this beautiful morning?"

Allie blinked as Cecily and Kayla murmured what sounded like *polite* responses to him. Then again, she shouldn't be surprised. Clay certainly poured on a healthy dose of masculine charm with a side dish of contemporary cowboy sex appeal. It was a hell of a good look for him, and apparently, its effectiveness crossed all age barriers.

Sometimes I think I should have been a cowboy . . .

His comment from the previous night came back to her. Toby Keith, shaved legs, how he wouldn't have let that stop him. Heat crept up her neck, encompassing her entire face. Score one for Cowboy Clay.

"Where are you three lovely ladies off to this morning?"

Cecily looked at her sister and shrugged. "Home, I guess, for a long, boring day with Mom."

"I wondered if I could treat the three of you to brunch this morning." He turned his gaze on Allie. "What do you say, pretty lady? Want to join me?"

She tore her gaze from him to question her girls. "Either of you have plans . . . or objections?" she threw in as an afterthought. Surely, they would, and it would get her out of this. She couldn't think of anything more uncomfortable than sitting at the same table with Clay and her daughters, and waiting for them to say something to shame her in front of him.

"Can we go to Shoney's?" Kayla asked.

"Or Denny's?" Cecily added.

He faced her, his gaze smoldering with unspoken words and hidden messages. "We have a split-decision. Your lovely mother can be the tie-breaker."

She glanced from one girl to the other, her mind working at a furious pace. They'd have to order at Denny's, which meant a longer period of painful waiting for the two of them to embarrass the hell out of her for the pure enjoyment of it. Shoney's had the buffet, so they could get in and get out of there quicker.

"Shoney's is fine with me," she said. Her stomach fluttered at the handsome smile he flashed their way. The man was out and out dangerous with that thing. Yeah, a quick buffet brunch would be her salvation. The girls would get their usual pancakes topped with whipped cream and strawberries. They'd finish in ten minutes flat and be out of there in record time.

"You. Dog!" Allie hissed at Clay as soon as her daughters left them alone at the table.

He flashed her 'the smirk', knowing she wanted nothing better than to slap it off his face right about now. Clay had imagined the wheels turning in her head. Shoney's . . . breakfast buffet . . . in an out in twenty minutes. Yeah. No. He'd nixed that by working her girls with talk of ordering steak and eggs from the menu.

She shook her head. "They *always* have the buffet when we come here. I can never get them to eat anything but those damn pancakes. You show up and only sirloin will do?"

"Maybe it's the hat. You know. Real men eat beef kind of thing?"

She sat back, her mouth puckered in a cute little pout.

"Or maybe it's the boots." He stretched one boot-clad foot along the aisle. "I hear ladies love country boys." If he couldn't impress her with Toby, maybe Trace would work.

She leaned in close. "Maybe it's the line of bullshit you've been feeding them since we got here."

He slapped both hands over his ears. "Hey, now, watch the sensitive ears."

"Oh, please."

He laughed and pulled her close in a one-armed hug. "Don't you think this is going well? Just relax and enjoy the time with me and your girls."

"I'm afraid they'll run to their father and tell him all kinds of things."

"Like what—that a friend of yours took them to brunch? Scandalous!" He placed a finger on her lips before she could protest again. "Don't worry about your girls. I've got this."

She took another deep breath. "You won't be around to feel the backlash, you know. It'll just be me and them at home once we leave here, and I'll have to put up with the snide remarks."

"There won't be any. If I do my job properly, they'll be eating from your hand."

She quirked one brow. "Don't you mean *your* hand?"

"Hell, no, they've already seen one man steal the respect you deserve. My plan is to remind them that you're the one who deserves their respect." He trailed his fingers along the side of her face. "But I can only do part of that, Allie. You have to believe it yourself before they will. Once you do, they'll fall in line."

One eyebrow rose in curiosity. "How do I do that, Clay?"

He leaned in, lifted her chin, and kissed the tip of her nose. "I'm going to help you see yourself through my eyes."

The food arrived at the table seconds after the girls returned.

Kayla clapped her hands. "Oh, that looks yummy. Who knew we could have steak for breakfast?"

Allie placed her napkin on her lap and picked up her utensils. "All you had to do was ask, hon. How many times have I tried to get you two to eat something besides pancakes?"

Kayla opened her mouth to say something but stopped as Clay nodded in agreement with Allie.

Cecily gave her a nudge. "She's right, you know. Every time we come here, we always eat the same thing."

Kayla thought about it, and nodded. "Yeah, I guess you're right, Mom. But from now on, I'm going to order different things on the menu." She cut a bite of steak and popped it into her mouth.

Cecily swallowed a bite. "Me, too. I never knew steak and eggs could taste so good together."

Allie smiled at her daughter. "Glad to hear it. It's good to try new things every now and then."

"So why didn't you order a steak instead of an egg-white omelet and fruit?"

"Because I'm older, and I'm not as active as you two still are. I have to make sacrifices whenever and wherever I can."

"It's because Daddy always called her jelly-butt", Kayla chortled while Cecily joined in on the laughter.

Allie's fork clattered to her plate as she scooted back from the table. "Excuse me, please."

Clay watched Allie's retreat, and whistled low under his breath. "I don't know whose bottom your dad was looking at, but all I see is a gorgeous woman with a few well-proportioned curves." He looked from one girl to the other. "How old is your dad, anyway?"

Cecily looked at her sister. "He's two years older than Mom, isn't he?"

"So that puts him at forty-eight? I'll be fifty in a couple of weeks. I guess he must be in a heck of a lot better shape than I am, right?" He turned his attention back to his steak.

Kayla burst into laughter. "God, no! Dad's got a big beer belly and a comb-over."

"Trust us, you're in way better shape than he is," Cecily added.

Clay turned his gaze on the girls again. "Go figure, and he didn't carry babies in his belly for eighteen months, either." He returned to cutting his steak, all the while shaking his head. "I sure hope you girls choose husbands who find better ways to show their appreciation once you've had children."

Kayla looked contrite but kept her silence.

"You know, my last two boyfriends told me I had a hot mom," Cecily admitted.

Clay swallowed a bite of steak and used his napkin to wipe his mouth. "I've got to agree with your last two boyfriends. The fact that she's as beautiful on the inside as she is on the outside . . . well, that's what you call *lagniappe*. Not an ounce of conceit in her." He used his fork to point at Allie's oldest daughter. "The thing is your mom doesn't feel good about herself at all." He rested one elbow on the table. "Now why would a woman as beautiful as she is think so badly of herself?"

Cecily pushed a piece of steak around on her plate. "I attended a seminar for extra credit a couple of weeks ago on domestic verbal abuse." She put down her fork and reached for her glass of lemonade. "We watched a video, and parts of it sounded a lot like how our dad treated Mom."

Kayla's jaw dropped. "Seriously?"

Cecily nodded. "The wife in the video had low self-esteem because of it, too. She . . . she reminded me a lot of Mom." She set her glass on the table and pushed her plate away. "I've kind of lost my appetite."

Kayla placed her fork next to her plate. "I'm kind of sick to my stomach."

Clay stared at both girls. It would have been too easy to tell them what they needed to do from here on out, but he stopped himself. He'd helped them to see the problem. The solution had to come from them or it wouldn't stick. He looked up as Allie approached the table.

She sat and glanced from one girl to the other. "What's wrong with you two? Did someone die when I was in the ladies room?"

Cecily played with her straw. "No. I'm just full already."

"Me too," Kayla added.

Allie eyed them for a second before changing the subject. "You know, I thought I'd schedule the three of us for a mani-pedi afternoon when school lets out for Christmas break."

"Can we go see that new Scott Eastwood movie one day, too? Lanie and her mom went and they both loved it."

"Sounds good to me." Allie pointed at their plates. "Now eat. It's the least you can do when Mr. Clay was generous enough to treat us."

Once the girls dug into their meal with gusto, Allie turned a curious gaze on Clay. He shrugged and popped another forkful of steak into his mouth.

"It was wonderful meeting you girls. Thanks for accompanying me to brunch."

Kayla's head popped up from the couch. "You too, Mr. Clay. Thanks for Shoney's."

Cecily emerged from the kitchen. "Thanks for the movies you rented and popcorn this afternoon, too. It was fun."

"Sure thing." He waved and walked out Allie's front door, pulling it closed behind him. She stood waiting for him at the end of the porch, arms crossed and head tilted. "What?"

"Why do I feel like I'm in a Debbie Macomber novel?"

He frowned. "I'm sorry. I don't know who that is."

"She wrote those Mrs. Miracle books that were made into movies. You know, a family is in shambles until this wonderful Mary Poppins type nanny comes along and makes everything all right. Except this one is wearing a Stetson and Tony Lamas."

"These are Justin's. Tony's don't work for my feet. Was that Doris Roberts in those movies?"

"I believe so."

"I saw those. Hope loved Christmas movies on the Hallmark channel. We watched them all through the month of December, and then again when they had the Christmas in July." He chuckled. "So you think I possess some kind of magical powers?" Clay edged closer to her.

"Maybe magical is too strong a word—persuasive? Did you perform hypnosis on them when I left the table at Shoney's?" She wiggled her fingers in front of his face. "Look into my eyes while I count backwards from ten . . ."

"If I could do that I wouldn't have to work so hard at convincing you how wonderful you are, would I?"

"Well, something happened. That's when they started acting civilized."

"I didn't do anything special. What happened in there today," he pointed to the house. "That was all your daughters."

She took a step closer to him. "Well, thank you, Mr. Miracle. That was the best afternoon I've had with my girls in years."

He nodded. Step three complete: Conquer from within.

Clay shuffled closer to narrow the gap between them. He placed his left hand on her waist, dragging his thumb across her ribcage. Her subtle intake of breath told him to stay this particular course. He used his right hand to brush a stray lock of hair back from her face. "You have the most beautiful eyes I've ever seen, Allie. They're green, but ringed with dark blue, and you've got all these little amber specks . . . they're so unique."

She blinked then looked away. "Thank you. I have my father's eyes."

"Ah, that coloring is genetic?"

"No, I have my father's eyes. Corneal transplants."

He stood for a moment, dumbstruck and confused. It wasn't impossible, of course. He opened his mouth to ask why she'd needed a corneal transplant just before he noticed the "tell" . . . the barest spark of amusement in her eyes. "And you accused me of feeding your girls a line of bullshit?"

In seconds, she was snorting with laughter. "It was good, right? I nearly had you believing it?"

"You're something, you know that?" Edging backwards to the darkened end of the porch, he tugged her closer. He brushed his lips against her forehead, then lower against her cheek. She didn't push him away, didn't crack a joke, or turn her head. She needed to be kissed, and he suspected she wanted to be kissed. He'd just decided to act on it when a late model black Camaro blaring classic rock turned into her driveway.

"Oh, crap," she hissed. "When Cecily posted those picks of us to social media, I had a feeling he'd call asking questions, but I didn't expect him to pay us a personal visit."

Clay didn't need to ask. Allie's reference pointed to the ex, the verbally abusive role model, the daddy of the freaking year, "Bruce the Bastard". He chuckled deep in his throat, welcoming the challenge. "Oh, this is so perfect."

"Don't confront him, please. You don't know him."

"I don't plan on confronting him, but I sure as hell won't back down if he does."

Within seconds, Clay caught sight of a man resembling a heftier version of the character James "Big Jim" Rennie on that Stephen King-novel-turned-TV-series, "Under the Dome". Come to think of it, "Big Jim" was a used car salesman, too. Bruce pulled himself belly-first out of a car built for a much smaller person. He stood there adjusting the sagging waistband of his khaki colored slacks and re-tucking his shirt, unaware of their presence on the darkened porch.

Allie waited until he strutted up the steps and placed his hand upon the brass door handle, without the courtesy of a knock, before speaking. "What do you think you're doing?"

He stiffened and looked up, without stepping away from the door. "What the hell are you doing out here?"

"I'm standing on my front porch."

"It's only yours because I paid for it."

"It's mine because we both paid for it, and because a judge said you lost your rights to it. What do you want, Bruce?"

"Who's that hiding behind you?"

"I'm talking to a friend."

Clay imagined the guy's head as a huge Geiger counter, and this nosey bastard's needle did an immediate spike to the far right.

"A friend, huh?"

Clay stepped up, front and center into the glow of light from the door's transom window. "That's right, an extremely good friend." He turned to face Allie. "Until I can convince this lovely lady I'm worthy of much more." He approached the man, dwarfing him vertically by a good four inches, despite the jerk's considerable bulk. "I'm Clay Andrews." When the ass hat ignored the hand he'd offered, he retracted it and burst out in a hearty laugh. "You're shorter than I imagined, Bruce. But I have to admit, you've exceeded my expectations of obnoxiousness, even for a car salesman."

"Who the hell do you think you are, talking to me like that?"

Clay raised his hands. "Hey, I *tried* to be friendly. You set a different tone and now you get to live with the consequences of your actions. Something tells me you're not used to that."

"I'll ask you one more time, Bruce. What do you want here?" Allie's tone remained calm but serious.

"I came by to ask *my* daughters what they want for Christmas."

Allie snickered. "At eight o'clock on a Sunday evening when the girls have school in the morning? You should have come up with a better story before you came snooping around here. I know you saw Cecily's social media posts, Bruce. You're only here to satisfy your nosiness."

"I have every right to check out whatever strangers you're bringing into the house with my girls."

"Oh please. They spend weekends with that dipstick who smokes pot on the balcony of your condominium. You *do* realize she's offered to share it with them on more than one occasion, don't you?" She raised her hand to stop his counter attack. "You know what? Don't bother." She opened the door and stuck her head inside. "Girls, your father's here and he wants to ask you both a question."

Her daughters migrated to the front door and stood there, waiting through Bruce's hemming and hawing before he finally spoke.

"I just wondered why you girls haven't finished your Christmas lists for this year, that's all. I got a partial list with a couple of items on it for each of you." He held up two slips of paper. "Neither of these equals the generous amount I'd given you to spend." He lifted one brow at Clay as though gauging his reaction.

Cecily turned a confused gaze on her father. "Is this a joke, Dad?"

"No."

"Yesterday Summer asked us to cut back our lists," Kayla added.

"What do you mean, cut them back?" Bruce bellowed. "I gave you each a generous price limit, didn't I?"

The girls exchanged another uncomfortable glance. "Well, yeah, but Summer told us you couldn't spend more than a hundred bucks each on us, this year. We know about the procedure."

"What procedure?" Bruce asked.

Confusion etched into the teens' two faces. Cecily spoke up first. "She said you didn't want us to worry, Daddy."

Kayla stepped forward. "Is it your heart or something?"

Bruce did an excellent imitation of one of those bug-eyed, bobble heads. "What the hell are you talking about, Kayla?"

Allie stepped forward. "Based on what I heard at my salon the other day, I don't think it's your father that's having the medical procedure."

His gaze narrowed. "What do you mean?"

She glanced at Clay then back at Bruce. "Maybe we should talk about this inside."

"Just spit it out," Bruce growled.

Allie released an exasperated sigh and crossed her arms. "All right. Word around town is Summer is scheduled for a boob job. Didn't you know?"

Clay came close to feeling sorry for ole Bruce. The look on his face revealed this was the first he'd heard about it. And hearing evidence of how he was being used for his checkbook from his two daughters, in front of his ex-wife and her new 'friend', well damned if that wasn't just about the most humiliating thing that could happen to a guy.

He turned, grumbled all the way down the steps. "You girls get me your lists tomorrow—your *full* lists. I'm about to take care of some business right damned now."

The four of them watched until he peeled out on the roadway, no doubt heading back to the condo he shared with his little gold-digger dipstick of a girlfriend.

"Poor Daddy," Kayla remarked.

Cecily shook her head and herded her sister back inside the house. "Poor Daddy, my butt."

Allie gave her a quiet reprimanding. "Watch your mouth please, Cecily."

"Well, it's true, Mom. He's got nobody to blame but himself."

Clay waited until the girls disappeared into the house before speaking. "It's a hell of a thing when a man realizes all his scapegoats have up and disappeared. He's left with nothing more than the man in the mirror to blame."

"You think so?" Allie said. "That particular man is a master at blaming everyone else and believing his own lies."

"I defer to your expertise. After all, who would know better than you?" He approached her again, slipped his hands around her waist. "And I've gotta say, you handled that extremely well. I didn't see a woman who'd let a man bully her into having his way. I saw someone taking control of a situation."

"Any other time, I'd shield the girls from that kind of display. But I've decided it's time my daughters see the man's true nature." She placed her hands on his forearms. "It may have helped a little having you here."

He moved one hand to the base of her skull, threading his fingers through her hair, and pulled her close. "I'm glad to help, so long as you realize I'm not here to take control. You call the shots, remember?" He lowered his mouth just shy of tasting her lips and held steady.

She rose to her tiptoes and brushed her lips against his for a feather-light kiss. "Thank you, Clay."

His fingers tightened around her silky hair, wanting to take control, wanting to crush his mouth against hers. He held himself back, needing that to come from her.

Allie reached out, cupped the back of his head in her hand. She tunneled her fingertips through his hair, massaging his scalp and paused, as though weighing the choice to either follow through or abandon the cause. Finally, she pulled him down, brushed her lips against his, and again, and a third time. Her breath mingled with his and her tongue darted out to taste his lips.

He nipped at her lower lip. She did the same and he nearly lost his mind, his breath, his control. An involuntary hiss escaped his lips at the tightening across his lower mid-section.

Allie released a throaty chuckle. "Am I hurting you?"

"No. Yes. But damn, it's a good hurt. Hurt me some more."

"I would, but it appears I've misplaced my riding crop."

"You're not planning to go all fifty shades on me, are you?" He wanted to cry when she pulled those plump lips from his reach. "Ah, no! Where're you going with that luscious mouth?"

"You know about fifty shades?"

"I'd have had to live under a rock not to."

Her eyes widened. "You do realize that was a joke."

He pulled her close, smothered his laughter in the silken softness of her sweet-smelling hair. "It's okay, hon, you can be your kinky self with me. Your secret's safe."

"What?" She pulled away from him, eyes frantic, body tense, relaxing only when she noticed his shoulders shaking with laughter. She slapped at his arm. "That's just mean."

"You're right, and I'm sorry." Her furrowing brow and tightening mouth concerned him. "What's wrong?"

"It's been a while since a man has spoken those words to me."

He studied her. "You're serious, aren't you?"

"You just met my ex. Did he look like the type of guy to ever admit he was wrong or apologize?"

He reached around to scratch the back of his head. "A valid point if ever I heard one." He pulled her back into his arms again. "Now where were we?" The door opening behind him had them putting a good two feet between them.

"Mom!"

"No need to yell, Kayla. I'm right here."

"Oh. Your phone just rang, but I didn't get to it in time." She handed Allie her phone. "What are y'all doing out here?"

"We're only talking, sweetie. Thanks for bringing me the phone, now go on inside, please." Her mother shot her a warning look as she pulled up her phone's call list. "Oh, Mom called. She's usually in bed by this time. I better call her back." Within seconds, Mr. J.D. had picked up her mom's landline.

"Allie, your mom fell, and I tried to pick her up but she says it hurts too much. The ambulance should be here any minute, but I thought you should know."

"I'm on my way, Mr. J.D." She ended the call and faced Clay. "I have to go to Mom's, Clay. She fell."

"I'll drive you," Clay said.

"Are you sure?" She pushed open the door to let her girls know before turning back to face him.

He took hold of her elbow. "Positive, now let's go."

He pulled into her drive a few minutes past midnight and shifted his truck into park. "Well, at least you get to sleep late in the morning."

She rubbed her tired eyes. "I'll have to make sure the girls get up for school, but Cecily can drive them. I never sleep past eight a.m. anyway." She gave him a tired smile. "Thank you for being there with me. You could have left once Cynthia and John Michael got there, you know. Someone could have dropped me off here."

"No way would I have left you to deal with that alone. I'm just glad it wasn't serious. A fractured wrist is still inconvenient for someone her age, but it could have been much worse."

"True, but thanks anyway."

Clay walked her to her door. He cupped her face in both hands and touched her forehead with his. "You go in there and get some rest now, do you hear me?"

"Yes sir and you go home and do the same."

"I will," he said, giving her a quick kiss and heading toward his truck.

Allie closed the door and leaned against it. She turned her head toward the sound of someone stirring on the couch. A sleepy voice called out to her.

"Mom?"

"I'm here, Cec."

"How's Maw Maw Bess?"

"She's back home with a hairline fracture of her left wrist. Go to bed now, sweetie. You have school in the morning."

"Can she take care of herself?"

"Mr. J.D. is going to spend the night in the guest room to take care of her. You should have seen those two trying to comfort each other, Cecily. They are so sweet together. Poor man feels so bad because he was there when it happened, even though he couldn't have prevented it. She just tripped. It's what happens when people get older."

"I don't want Maw Maw Bess to get older. Old people die, and she can't die, ever. The world wouldn't be the same without her, or her blackberry cobbler."

Allie smiled. "I'm sure she'd be thrilled to know how much you'd miss her cobbler, Cecily."

"And her red velvet cake with that special cream cheese frosting and filling she makes. Maw Maw Bess bakes the best goodies in the world."

Allie rubbed her exhausted eyes and dropped onto the sofa next to her daughter. "She loves baking because she loves pleasing people."

"That's not the only reason I'd miss her, you know. I'm crazy about Maw Maw."

She smiled as Cecily sniffed and wiped at the corner of one eye. Despite how bratty her girls had always been towards their mother, they had always adored their grandmother. Bruce's mom passed away when they were both too young to remember much of her. She hadn't been the kind of hands-on, cookie-baking, grandchild-hugging grandmother that children like to be around, anyway. No, her daughters had recognized early on which grandparent would give them unconditional love. She reached out to touch her daughter's face. "She knows how much you love her, Cec. We'll go pay her a visit tomorrow, but you need to get to bed now."

"Did daddy say something to upset you or Mr. Clay earlier?"

"Mr. Clay can take care of himself, honey." She thought about how she'd put Bruce in his place and nodded. "And I can too. I think your dad got more than he bargained for tonight."

Cecily nodded. "So did Summer. He kicked her out of the apartment tonight. Put a hold on all his credit cards and made dang sure she didn't have any checkbooks. He said he's calling the doctor she'd scheduled the surgery with tomorrow to let them know he wouldn't be paying for a dime of it."

Allie tried to work the kinks out of her stiff shoulders. "I can't say I'm surprised by any of it, but I'm sure your dad's upset about all this."

Cecily's mouth tightened. "How can you still be so nice to him? You should be doing cartwheels, or a happy dance, or something. He left you for a younger woman, Mom."

"And he's paying for it now. I've decided to take the high road, honey. It's more difficult to show compassion to people who've hurt you, but it's the right thing to do. Would you respect me more if I was the kind of person who'd kick someone who's already flat on his face?"

Cecily dropped her gaze to her hands for a moment. When she looked up, her eyes were moist with tears. "I'm sorry, Mom. All this time, Kayla and I thought you were weak. We thought you should have fought harder to keep daddy. And we kind of blamed you for the divorce."

Her daughter's revelation hit her like a punch to the throat. "You blamed me?"

"I know. It was stupid, so stupid. I thought Summer was so cool at first. She'd take us shopping, using daddy's credit cards, of course. Said she wanted to be the best, coolest stepmom in the world. When she offered Kayla and me a joint, it got me to thinking . . . what kind of mother would do this? Mom would never do this."

"No, I wouldn't. I'm not here to be your best friend. I'm here to stay on your butts to do your chores, your schoolwork, to mind your curfews, your manners, and to be the best young women you can be."

"I told Mr. Clay and Kayla today that I saw a film on verbal abuse at school."

"You did?"

Cecily nodded. "I think Dad was verbally abusive to you, and you have low self-esteem because of it."

Her daughter's observation took Allie by surprise. "Yes, he was, and I do have issues because of it, Cec. I'm trying to change my way of thinking about myself."

"It's not fair, Mom. Daddy treated Summer way better than he treated you. He didn't bark at her or order her around like he did to you. A couple of weeks ago she started bragging to Kayla and me about how she and daddy used to sneak around behind your back, and how clueless you were. They'd have sex in the restroom at the dealership, long before he left you. Daddy overheard what she was saying and blew up at her."

It irked her to hell, hearing how much her girls knew about their father and Summer's adulterous behavior. Since they did, she may as well do some damage control. "Is that the weekend the two of you came home early?"

She nodded. "It's been different since then. Kayla and I stay in our room when we're there. Summer gets all pissy and then she and Daddy get into big arguments."

"I always suspected she'd be temporary, and I was never clueless, you know. I knew everything."

"Why didn't you do something about it?"

"What could I have done, ask him to stop? He wouldn't have. I could have left or ordered him out, but at the time, I didn't think I could make it on my own. Now, I know differently." She contemplated the place she was in now. "When I think about it, your dad and Summer did me a huge favor. I wish I'd been strong enough to walk away on my own, but I wasn't. Despite the humiliation, they forced me to be stronger than I thought I could be."

"I never thought about it that way."

"Well, I didn't for a long time, Cec. Sometimes you need to lose everything to find your own strength, and sometimes you have to view yourself through another person's eyes before you can see what's been there all along."

Cecily's face stretched in a knowing smile. "So, whose eyes have you seen yourself through lately, Mom?"

Allie faced her first-born child. "Most recently, my beautiful daughter's."

Cecily beamed at her mother. "Thanks, Mom. I thought sure you were going to say a certain fine-ass dude with blue eyes."

Rather than act shocked at the comment coming from her seventeen-year-old, she grinned. "He is that, isn't he?" She laughed at Cecily's adamant nod.

"I hope he's as wonderful as he acts, for your sake. I mean, we thought Summer was great at first, and now we know she was always just a tramp looking for some married guy to pay for a set of 44-Double D's."

"There may be more to her than that. You never know what someone's been through before they've come into your life. Even Summer used to be someone's innocent little girl."

Cecily shook her head. "All I know is she's out of a boob-job, for now anyway." She released a long disgusted sigh. "But, I bet she'll find some other clueless man to latch onto soon enough."

"I hate to say this, but there's a good chance you're right." Allie cocked her head to the side. "As for Clay, he's my new brother-in-law's first cousin, so your Aunt Cyn and I both got the inside scoop on him."

Cecily's mood lightened. "So, Aunt Cyn's husband knows what kind of man he is. He'd know if the dude's got any fetishes he keeps hidden away, right? Like if he wears women's underwear, or if he's a girl trapped in a guy's body, or if he's got pedophilia tendencies . . . or if . . . if he's just like Dad?"

Her daughter's questioning brought a grin to Allie's face. "I'm thinking Clay is fetish-free, hon. He came with a good recommendation. You know, he lost his fourteen year old daughter to leukemia a couple of years ago."

"Oh my God! That's so awful. If he was here right now, I'd want to give him a big ole hug."

Allie stood and gave her daughter a sad smile. "And if you did that, I'm sure he'd appreciate it." She reached out to her. "Now, go to bed. I've still got to shower." She smelled her dress. "Ugh. I smell like a hospital."

"Mom? Are you and Mr. Clay going to live together like Dad and Summer did?"

Allie studied Cecily's face. "You mean, would I let him move in with us?"

Cecily nodded.

Here was her chance to instill her own values upon her daughter. "No way, sweetie. You know, Cec, I'm not sure what the future holds for the two of us as a couple. I have some issues I have to work out for myself before I transition into any kind of physical relationship with a man. But, I'd want to wait before doing that."

"For how long?"

"Well, until marriage, if it's at all possible."

Cecily's eyes bulged. "You're going to marry Mr. Clay?"

"No, I'm saying that whether I end up with him or any other man, for that matter, I can promise you there will be no moving in together before marriage."

"Would you sleep with him?"

Allie sucked in her breath. This wasn't a subject she would have broached, but since Cecily did, she decided to tackle it. "Look, if it gets to that point, I can't swear we won't. But I can promise you I'll try my best not to, if it's at all possible."

Cecily smiled and gave her a slow, thoughtful nod. "If you want, I bet Kayla and I can help you out with that."

Thinking of all the interruptions her girls would likely plan for them had Allie chortling with laughter. "I may hold you to that."

Before her daughter walked away, Allie pulled her close for a hug. "I love you a lot, Puddin' Pop. Thanks for waiting up for me."

Cecily giggled at the nickname her mom had given her years ago. "It's not nice to make fun of a kid's addiction, you know."

"I'm not making fun. I loved Puddin' Pops too." She pulled away and patted her butt. "No doubt, they contributed to this."

Cecily's face wilted into a somber expression. "Don't make fun of yourself, Mom, and . . . I'm sorry for all the times that I made fun of you with daddy. You look great just the way you are."

Allie took a shocked breath. Were her insecurities over her own body affecting her daughters in a negative way? Did she want them growing up thinking that "dipstick thin" was the only acceptable way to be? "Okay, I'll try not to do that anymore."

"Good."

As she parted ways with her daughter in the hallway, she couldn't help wondering if she'd awakened in some kind of alternate reality this morning. Things were off-kilter, but in a good way.

She grabbed her nightclothes from a drawer and closed herself up in her bathroom to shower off her seventeen-hour-day exhaustion.

Clay Andrews.

Allie caught her own reflection in the bathroom mirror. Funny how a single thought of him could put a sappy smile on her face.

Chapter Eight

Wednesday, December 19th

Allie walked through the door Clay held open for her. "That movie was fabulous! Don't you think?"

Cynthia followed, trailed by her husband, John Michael. "I loved it! It's a definite contender for an Oscar. Or it should be, anyway."

Allie's gaze travelled first to Clay, then to John's. "What did you guys think?"

The look that passed between them said they'd rather be beaten to a bloody pulp as soon as contribute their opinions.

"It—it was okay," Johnny said.

"It was good," Clay volunteered, ignoring his cousin's glare.

Allie bit down on her lower lip. "You two hated it, didn't you?"

Clay opened his mouth then snapped it shut. "I just said it was good. Not great, just good."

Her shoulders slumped. "Oh, I'm sorry. I thought sure you'd like it."

"Allie, I did like it. I just didn't love it like you and Cynthia did."

"I think my husband liked it somewhat less than you did, Clay." Cynthia laughed at the face Johnny made. "But that's okay. Next time we'll choose something with less singing and a few more cars blowing up to satisfy that violent nature of yours."

Johnny pulled his wife close. "Now babe, you know I'm a lover, not a fighter. I don't necessarily need to see cars blowing up to be happy—"

"But less singing would be a step in the right direction," Clay admitted.

Johnny used his index finger to point at him. "I concur, cousin."

"Clay!"

The four of them turned in unison toward the sound of the feminine voice. Clay's gut clenched as his ex-wife ran up to the four of them. Instinctively, he placed a hand on Allie's lower back.

"Oh hell," he spat.

"I didn't expect to see you here." She cast a shrewd glance in Allie's direction. "Hello," she said. "I'm Margie Andrews, Clay's *wife*. And who are you?"

"*Ex*-wife, and that didn't take long," Clay growled, swing himself and Allie away from her. "Let's go."

Allie leaned in close as they were walking away. "What didn't take long?"

"For her to piss me the hell off," he grumbled.

She took his hand and pulled him to a stop before turning to face Margie. "Hello, Margie. I'm Allie Sarver, a good friend of Clay's."

Cynthia stepped forward to flank her sister. "And I'm Allie's sister, Cynthia Ferguson. I'm John Michael's wife."

"Oh . . ." Margie looked around them both to peer at John Michael. "Hello there, Johnny. I'd heard you remarried. Congratulations . . ." She straightened, glaring at the two women in front of her. "I guess," she added.

Allie snorted with laughter as she lifted a finger to point at her. "I've heard a *lot* about you, Margie." Her chin lifted and she scrutinized the woman before her. "Lots and lots about you."

Cynthia tapped her sister's arm. "Come to think of it, so have I, and not a damned bit of it was good."

"No. I've heard some unflattering things, as well," Allie agreed. She stepped forward, and her sister took her place beside her. "Now, what is it you wanted?"

Overwhelmed by the sisters' successful double-teaming, Margie took several steps back then turned in full retreat mode.

Johnny whistled under his breath before turning to his cousin. "Bet she didn't see that coming."

Clay shook his head and snickered. "Ol' gal never had a chance."

Allie blinked her big green eyes. "She seemed frightened. Did she appear frightened to you, Sis?"

Cynthia cocked her head. "Why yes, she did, Al. What do you think scared her off like that?"

Allie placed her index finger on her chin. "Why, I'm sure I don't know, Cynthia. I'm as puzzled as you are."

Clay and Johnny burst into laughter as the two women gave each other a well-synchronized high-five.

Clay caught his breath enough to gasp in response. "Teach her to mess with our girls."

"Hmph," Allie said. "Teach her to mess with sisters."

Friday, December 21st

Johnny plopped down in the Adirondack chair on their deck. "So whose turn is it?"

Cynthia grinned at her husband. "You know what they say sweetie. If you have to ask, it's your turn."

Clay rose from his chair and kicked a log back into place in the fire pit situated in the center of the Ferguson's deck. "I believe it is John Michael's turn."

"It is," Allie said, once he returned to his spot beside her.

Johnny's chest rumbled with laughter. "Okay. This goes back a ways. I remember playing spin the bottle at somebody's birthday party. I can't remember whose or what year it was, but I remember being so nervous about my turn I was nauseous. I swear, when they locked me and Betty Ann Bertrand inside that closet, I thought I would throw-up on her."

"Oh no. Did you?"

"No. But I didn't put nearly as much effort into that kiss as I should have. A single thought kept running through my mind: Don't throw up, dammit, don't throw up . . ."

Cynthia straightened in her chair. "Wait a minute. I was at that party, too."

"Did you play?" Allie asked.

"Yes. I remember wishing the bottle would land on Ronny LePretre but it never did. That was the end of sixth grade year party. Only a couple of weeks before this guy, here, accosted me between the stacks of hay at his daddy's feed store."

"I had a good reason," he said.

She batted her eyes. "You were crazy in love with me even then?"

"Afraid not. I was desperate to counteract my poor performance with Betty Ann." He adjusted his collar. "A reputation like that could follow a guy around for life."

"So, that was damage control?" Clay offered.

"Yeah, a self-promotion campaign, or it started out that way, anyway. I didn't fall crazy in love with her until after the kiss."

"Well that was a promotional bust for you then, because I never told a soul about that incident," Cynthia said. "I wanted to keep you all to myself." She leaned toward her husband for a kiss.

Allie shook her head. "Oh boy, here they go again."

"I know, right? And after they assured us they were ready to mix with polite society." When Allie shoved her hands in her pockets and shivered, he stood. "Let me move your chair over here where it's warmer."

She settled into the spot next to his. "It is much warmer here."

"I told you." They sat in silence for several seconds until she glanced at him then faced the fire again. "What is it, Allie?"

"I'm wondering about your ex. Maybe I'm reading too much into it, but she seems a little desperate."

"There's something wrong, for sure. She lured me to our old place under false pretenses the other day."

Allie kept her silence as he explained the circumstances of his house visit, but her sister wasn't so calm.

"Is that normal behavior for her?"

"Not at all, and that's what bothers me. Something's out of whack, even for her. I visited my son, and called my daughter later, to see if they knew anything. Neither of them had a clue. It's disturbing."

"Do you . . ." Allie paused and took a deep breath. "Do you need to tend to her, somehow?"

"Tend to her, how? You mean talk to her, or try to reason with her in some way? Hell no."

"She is the mother of your children."

"Would you feel the need to 'tend to' Bruce because he's the father of yours?"

"Good point. I guess it depended on the circumstances."

"You know, I'm kind of glad it happened, though. I left with the scrapbook Hope had started. It took a few days before I could go through all of it, but I'm glad I did. It brought back a lot of good memories for me."

"Aw, that's great, Clay. Do you still have it?"

He smiled at the thought of it. "She was extremely creative. It's still in the back seat of my truck. I keep forgetting to bring it to Brian's so I can show Sean."

Her facial expression changed; a softening of the eyes and slight tilt of her head accompanied her reply. "I'd love to see it, if it wouldn't bother you too much."

"Not at all."

He retrieved the book and sat beside Allie, whose softhearted reaction to the images and writings touched him. She turned the pages, stopping to ask questions often, wiping her eyes occasionally.

"Was this book a gift from you, Clay?"

"No. Her big sister, Terri, gave it to Hope on her thirteenth birthday. She was so sick by then, but she loved collecting anything that inspired her. Between her weakened condition and her immune system being shot, she couldn't attend school anymore. She insisted on keeping up with projects and assignments. They all ended up in her book."

Allie examined page after page of handwritten poems, inspirational quotes, and other musings. She skimmed through papers, all produced as homework assignments or for extra credit: the fall of the Roman Empire, the study of solar activity and its relation to climate change throughout the ages, and the revolutionary war. Allie paused at a family tree dating back eight generations. "She did this all by herself?"

Clay reached out to touch the drawing of a large tree with a massive array of branches. "Terri's the true 'artist' in the family. She offered to draw it for her, but Hope wouldn't have it. She said it was her grade and she wanted to do it herself. So Terri did a few sketches to show her the techniques and Hope did what she could." His finger skimmed over the tree's root system. "The assignment was four generations, but Hope wanted to dig deeper. She scoured the Internet and different sites until she got to these ancestors. She stopped when she saw this." He pointed out the name and waited for Allie's reaction.

"Oh! She found another Hope." She tore her gaze from the page to stare at him. "Was this intentional?"

He smiled and shook his head. "Not at all. When she was born, Terri insisted on the name, because she'd hoped all along for a sister. Anytime I'd ask her what she wanted, she'd show me her crossed fingers and say, "I hope it's a girl, Daddy." He laughed and used his sleeve to wipe at his eyes. "So, of course when she was born, and Terri's hopes came true . . .""

Allie's eyes moistened with tears. "What a sweet story." She turned the page again and frowned as she studied Hope's last assignment, noticeably unfinished. "And here's where she stopped."

He nodded, his heart growing heavier as he examined the unfinished chart. "Yeah. She was so weak, so disheartened when it got to be too much for her." He shook his head. "That girl loved school. She loved learning new things . . . thrived on it. So when she gave up . . ." He felt the weight of Allie's hand on his back.

"I'm so sorry for asking. Please don't talk about it if it's too painful for you."

Her concern for his feelings comforted him, giving him the strength to continue. "I didn't want to face it at the time, but it signaled the end. Just after Margie left the country, Hope quit working on this." He shrugged. "Would it have changed anything if her mom had stayed? I don't know, but I can't help but connect the two occurrences in my mind."

Allie lowered her head over the chart listing Hope's genetic descriptions and blood type. Body type, bone structure, hair color and type, eye color, skin tone, size foot, shape of nose, ears, mouth, distinguishing features like shape of eyebrow and hairline—Hope had barely begun to fill in the chart on herself for her school Science assignment. "Her blood was AB, the same type blood as both my girls."

"I wish you could have met her, Al. She was such a cool kid. You know, Terri's little one, Everly, resembles her Aunt Hope in some ways. Her middle name is Hope."

"Terri and Hope were close, weren't they?"

He nodded. "As difficult as it was on me, sometimes I think it was worse for Terri. Hope was her shadow for so long. Terri was devastated she didn't get to say goodbye to her sister." He shook his head. "She hasn't set foot in that house since she died. Not even during the funeral process. She's bitter towards her mother." Clay took a deep, cleansing breath and released it, along with the tension that always accompanied those heartbreaking memories.

"Where do your children live, Clay?"

"Brian is in Lake Coburn and Terri and her family live in Natchitoches now. They'll be here the weekend before Christmas. Maybe you'd like to meet everyone then?"

"I'd love to, at some point, but we'll be spending Christmas Eve at Mr. J.D.'s. Cynthia's kids will be in for that, and Kyle and his family may be coming in from Houston."

"We're having something on Sunday, the twenty-third. Do you think you can make it?"

"I'd like that. My girls will be with their dad that day at his sister's place in Lafayette."

"I'll see you there, then." Clay pulled his ringing phone from his pocket and groaned when he saw the number. "Aw, give me a damn break."

"Is it work?"

"I wish. It's Margie, again." He lifted his phone. "She's left eleven messages on my phone in two days." They all seemed to hold their breath until the ringing stopped. A follow-up ding signaled she'd left message number twelve.

Johnny sat forward. "What the hell does she want, man?"

"I don't know. I haven't listened to any of them."

"Don't you think you should?"

He shook his head. "I can't imagine needing to hear anything she has to say."

"But—"

"Okay!" Clay held up his phone. "I'll play them right now. That way we can all hear her craziness at the same time." He got to his messages, pushed a button and put the phone on speaker.

Message 1: *Clay, we need to talk. I want you to call me.*

Message 2: *Clay, I've got a problem with the water heater at the house. Do you think you could come over to check it out for me?*

"I'm betting there's not a damn thing wrong with the water heater," Clay barked. "Even if there was, she knows how to call a repairman."

Message 3: *Please Clay, you know she'd want us to be close again. Can't we try?*

Clay glanced at Johnny. "See what I mean?"

His cousin grinned. "She must have fixed it herself."

"Not likely. She's always been of the opinion that hiring someone else to do it was better than breaking a nail. She knows how to pick up a phone to call someone."

Message 4: *Please don't ignore me, Clay. It would be best for our children if we reconciled.*

Message 5: *Call. Me.*

Message 6: *What do I have to do to get you to listen to me?*

Message 7: *Hope wanted her mommy and daddy back together, Clay, you know she did. Would you break her heart this way if she were still alive?*

Allie gasped at that one. "Where was that concern when she left her sick daughter?" She waved her hands. "I'm sorry. Forget I said that. That's none of my business."

Clay reached out, placed a hand on hers. "Don't be sorry, Al. That's what I've been saying since she flew back into town."

"Was it first class or on a broom?" Cynthia's question had the rest of them breaking out into uneasy laughter.

Message 8: *I've tried everything to get you to speak to me. You're forcing my hand, Clay.*

Johnny looked up, his face etched with concern now. "Forcing your hand? What the hell does she have up her sleeve, an ace of spades?"

Allie paced a nervous path across the wooden deck. "I don't like this, Clay. She sounds so desperate."

"She sounds deranged," Clay added.

Message 9: *Don't make me beg. I need you to come home to me.*

Message 10: *This house is too big for one person.*

"So sell the damn place," Clay growled at the phone.

Message 11: *I never stopped loving you, Clay. Quit trying to act like you don't feel the same way.*

Clay lifted the phone. "Honey, this isn't an act, I assure you."

And finally . . . Message 12: *Dammit Clay! Don't make me do something you'll live to regret!*

The four of them stared at the phone, each face registering its own expression of shock.

"She's . . ." Johnny wiped his mouth. "She's losing it, Clay."

Cynthia sat back hard against the chair. "I think she's already lost it."

Allie looked at Clay. "She needs help."

Clay met her gaze. "That may be, but what do you want me to do?"

"I don't know, but you can't just let her continue like this. You have to find a way to help her."

He stood. "Like she helped Hope by walking away?" He pointed at his chest. "I don't have to do a damn thing for her. She's not my wife, anymore. She's not my problem."

"But she's the mother of your children, and she's becoming more and more . . ." She flailed her hands, as though trying to find the word.

"Delusional," Cynthia volunteered.

"Yes, delusional and unbalanced."

"A few of those sounded threatening, if you ask me," Johnny said.

Clay gave him a serious glare. "What do you think the police would say if they heard these recordings? What do you think they'd do?"

Johnny nodded. "I doubt they'd do anything, but at least in would be on record that it happened."

Cynthia pointed at the phone. "Do not delete those messages. You may need them as evidence if she ever does something desperate."

"Good point," Clay said. A deep repetitive buzzing cut through the air and four sets of eyes gazed at the phone in his hands.

"It's her . . . again."

Allie placed a hand on his arm. "I think you should take it, Clay. Try to talk her into getting some help."

"I'll speak to her, if you'd like," Cynthia added. "Maybe she'd listen to reason from a medical doctor?"

"I don't think she's in a frame of mind to listen to reason from anyone, but here goes." Clay got to his feet and lifted the phone. He hit the button to answer then hit the speaker. "Margie, you've got to stop this. You need help."

"I do, Clay. I need help from you. This place, this place is a mess. There are so many things I could use your help—"

"Stop it, Marg. You know as well as I do there's nothing wrong with the water heater, and if there is, call a freaking repairman. I'm not going back there. Ever. Do you understand?"

"You're not being reasonable, Clay. Hope would want—"

"You listen to me!" he snapped. "You lost the right to tell me what Hope would *want* when you abandoned her. Don't you ever . . . *ever* say that to me again, you got that?"

"I'm—I'm—yes—of course. I won't . . ."

He rubbed his forehead with one hand. "Margie, get some damn help, would you? Talk to someone. Make an appointment with a therapist to deal with our daughter's death. I've had two years to deal with it. But you . . . you ran away from it. You ran all the way to Paris, France so you wouldn't have to deal with it."

"I love you, Clay."

"No, dammit. You don't. I don't know what happened over there with Jack, or Jacques, or whatever the hell his name is, but it didn't happen because you still had any feelings for me."

"I never stopped loving you, and I know you feel the same way."

"No, Marg. I don't love you." His gaze raked over the other three witnesses. Deciding he had nothing to lose by unloading his feelings, he continued. "If you want to know the truth, I started falling out of love with you the day I had to bargain for the life of our child. You remember that, don't you, Marg? That I had to beg and barter so you wouldn't abort a child we created together?"

"You . . . you don't understand, Clay."

"Oh, I understand. A third pregnancy wasn't in your neat little plan, and when Hope came along . . . beautiful, perfect Hope . . . everyone fell in love with her. Brian, Terri, and I . . . we all fell hard for that baby girl; all of us except for you. You never did. You never could love her."

"I tr-tried, Clay. I tried to love her."

He paced the deck while his laughter approached the level of hysteria. "Do you hear yourself? How screwed up do you have to be to force yourself to love the beautiful child who never gave us the slightest bit of trouble? But that was okay, because *we*, including Mom, Dad, and the rest of my family . . . *we* all loved that sweet, brilliant, creative, talented little girl plenty enough to compensate for your total lack of feeling where she was concerned. And then . . ."

Clay stopped, covered his mouth to hold back the painful sob building in his chest. Once more, his gaze connected with Allie, and he found the compassion, the strength he needed to continue. "And then she got sick, and you spent the next three and a half years pulling even farther away from her before walking away completely. But, you know what, Marg? Through it all, Hope never gave up on you. She always loved you. She overlooked your lack of love and loved you anyway. God forgive me, I couldn't. I still can't." He stopped to wipe his eyes.

"Clay, I couldn't bear the thought of seeing her die—"

"Don't! Don't you dare use that as an excuse, as an acceptable reason to abandon your child! It doesn't fly with me, and you want to know why?" He continued when only silence greeted him. "Because I . . . I *know* the truth. I *know* that you *never* had her in your heart. Not from the moment she was conceived."

He took a deep breath and released it. "So you find some other way to deal with your emotional breakdown. I don't give a rat's ass if you're hurting, or if you're lonely, or if you're feeling regretful. You *should* be feeling all of those things. It's the least you could do for our daughter. If you have no one to share your life with, it's not my fault. It's yours. Deal with it. But do not expect me to participate in this, and do not call me again. Not ever."

"Cl—"

Clay ended the call, cutting off any useless nonsense she was about to spout. He used his coat sleeve to wipe his eyes and surveyed his audience. Johnny stood there, his mouth a hard, grim combination of anger and sympathy, his arms wrapped around his visibly upset wife. Allie stood alone, with one hand over her mouth as tears streamed down her face.

He reached out to her and she came to him, burying her face in his chest, overcome by quiet sobbing.

"I'm sorry, Clay. I'm so sorry." Her words and sobs muffled by layers of clothes and outerwear.

The four of them stood there in the quiet of the cold, December evening, each of them dealing with the situation in his or her way.

Clay took another deep breath. "There's your cold, wet blanket to ruin a perfectly fine evening."

Allie pulled away from his arms to wipe her eyes. "I shouldn't have pushed you to answer that call."

"I think she needed to hear it. All of it," Cynthia said, as she and her husband stood to join them near the fire.

"I agree," Johnny said. "Maybe she needed to hear that in order to get some help."

That earned his cousin a curious glance. "You believe that?"

Johnny shrugged. "No, but there's always hope."

Clay released a low chuckle. "Yeah, I guess you're right, Johnny. There's always hope." He nodded, a slow smile spreading across his face.

"Always . . . Hope." His throat constricted, and he fought to regain control of his speech. "I must have a hundred cards and letters from my baby girl for birthdays, Father's Day, and for no damn reason at all. From the day she could spell and write the words, that's how she signed them. Always, Hope." He shook his head. "God, I miss that kid."

"Why don't you tell us some funny Hope stories, Clay?" Johnny smiled at the two women. "Ever since she was little, Hope would keep us in stitches at the annual Ferguson reunions. The kid had a crazy sharp sense of humor."

Clay wiped his eyes again and laughed. "You remember the fart contest?" His gaze clashed with Johnny's and they both burst into laughter.

"Tell us!" Cynthia urged them.

"Hope couldn't have been more than six," Clay said, glad to remember happier days. "She saw one of her older cousins, one of the boys, trying to make those fart noises—you know, using his hand under his armpit. It fascinated her, of course, as it would any angelic little first grade girl. When she tried to do it herself, the kid laughed at her."

Allie's eyes crinkled with laughter. "Whose kid was it?"

"Hell, I can't even remember, but Hope ran up to me, all serious. She said, 'Daddy, I'll be in the bathroom for little while.' I asked her if she had a bellyache and did she need to go home. She looked at me with those big, brown eyes, and she was all business. 'No, Daddy, I'll be in there practicing, but don't ask because it's a surprise. I just didn't want you to worry about me.'" He grinned at Allie. "Yeah, she was *that* kind of kid."

"That's too sweet."

"I know, right?" Clay said. "She'd been wearing a cute little pink overall short set, you know, the kind with the two straps over the shoulders that buckled, with a short-sleeved shirt under it. So, she decides her shirt is in the way and removes it. Then she spends a while perfecting her technique. She even figures out she could amplify the sound if her pit was dampened."

"Hey, I'm telling you, the kid was sharp," Johnny insisted.

"After thirty minutes or so, she comes walking out of that restroom in her little pink overalls, shirtless, and carrying a wad of wet paper napkins in one hand. I asked her, 'Hope, where's your shirt, honey, and what's with the paper towels?'"

Clay paused in the story-telling long enough to explain. "Now every year we set up a bandstand so that some of the musically inclined family members can have a jam session. She walks up to Johnny's boy, Zachary, who had been playing the guitar at the time, and grabs the microphone from the stand. She challenges her older cousin," he raised one finger . . . "and anyone else who thought they can make a better armpit fart noise than she can."

Johnny continued amidst the snorts and chuckles from the ladies. "She asked everyone to 'gather round the bandstand' which we did, and had us vote, by applause, who had the loudest armpit fart."

Allie clapped her hands together. "Oh, my goodness! Did she win?"

Clay grinned, still remembering the pride he'd felt for his youngest daughter's spirit of determination. "Of course she did."

"My son, Zachary, conducted an 'interview' afterwards," Johnny explained. "Zach kneeled next to her with the microphone. He asked her what she attributed to her success. She got this serious look on her face. I swear to you, no one made a sound." He pointed to Clay to conclude the story.

"She picks up the wad of wet paper towels and looks out at the crowd. 'Well, Zach,' she said. 'It's all in the amount of wet you use. It can't be too dry, but it can't be too wet. And you *know* when you find it, because then . . . it sounds *just* the right amount of *nasty*.'"

Both women collapsed in their chairs, howling with laughter.

Clay joined in on the laughter. "My daughter knew how to work a crowd."

"It was the highlight of the reunion," Johnny said, as his and Clay's laughter filled the air. "Zachary still talks about it to this day."

"Oh my gosh, that's so funny." Allie wiped tears of laughter from her eyes. "It's too bad y'all didn't have some kind of trophy to give her."

"But we did. The reunion committee always gave out little trophies for different things: travelled farthest, youngest attendee, oldest attendee, and best entertainment. She won, hands down, in the entertainment division."

"That's a great story, Clay. Do you have more?"

Allie's eyes, still puffy from tears cried earlier, were wet with tears of laughter now. It was a good look for her, and Clay, determined to keep it that way, shared other humorous stories about Hope and his kids.

Two hours later, he walked his girl to her front door. He leaned one shoulder against the porch column and smiled when she turned from unlocking the door.

"I had a wonderful time tonight, Clay, despite the thing with Margie."

"I did too." He nodded toward the door. "Are the girls home?"

"No. They both spent the day in Beaumont with friends for the night." She paused, her face a study of hesitancy. "I'd ask you in, but . . ."

"Say no more, I understand." He flexed his arms and struck a comical pose for her. "It must be excruciating, trying to keep your hands off of all this masculine virility."

Her mouth formed a twisted grin. "I'd ask you in, *but* I haven't had a chance to pick up the place. The girls and I all left in a rush this morning. I had some last minute Christmas shopping to do after spending all day in the salon today." She shrugged. "All I had time to do was change my clothes before you picked me up this afternoon."

He hung his head. "Wow. Not the slightest attempt to preserve my bruised ego; I'm so humiliated."

"Stop it."

He laughed and pulled her close. "Thanks for spending the evening with me. In case you haven't noticed, I'm becoming addicted to you and our time together." Contentment embraced him like a warm blanket when she laid her head on his chest and wrapped her arms around his waist.

"Thank you for allowing me to be a part of this evening. All of it, the happy and the sad."

He rested his chin on her head. "You're welcome. Besides, it all fits in with my plan to make myself irresistible to you."

"Oh, yeah?" She pulled away to peek at him. "How's that coming?"

"It's a work in progress," he admitted. "When you can't keep your hands to yourself, then I'll consider it a complete success."

She grew pensive before her posture stiffened, as though she'd just found herself on the precipice of being happy . . . then remembered she wasn't supposed to be.

"Thanks again, Clay. Good night."

He latched onto her hand before she could get completely away from him. "Talk to me, Al."

"I'm not ready to talk about it. I'm not comfortable talking about it. It's too personal." She pulled away again. "Good night."

Allie couldn't take a deep breath until the door was shut and locked and he was on the opposite side. She leaned against it, willing her heart to calm itself. Was he already in his truck? She waited for its engine to roar to life, but jumped at a soft bump against the door's exterior.

He called out to her. "Like me baring my soul to three people tonight wasn't personal?"

Oh God, he's still out there. "I never said it wasn't. I only said I'm not ready for that."

Something brushed his side of the door, sliding down the side. When he spoke again, his voice sounded from near the lower portion, closer to the porch surface.

"Allie, don't push me away."

She closed her eyes, slid to the floor, before resting her head against the thick wood panel. "Stop doing this to me, Clay. Stop making me feel bad about not wanting to bare every little part of myself to someone else's eyes."

"You mean emotional, like baring the soul, or physical?"

"Both, I guess, but mostly on a physical level."

"Are you still worried about that?"

"It's a big part of it, yes." His chuckle sounded from the opposite side, grating on her nerves. "Can I say how comforting it is that you find humor in this situation?" Her tone roiled with cynicism. *I sure as hell can't.*

"I'm not laughing at you. I'm just thinking I need to work on my skills."

Surely, he can't think . . . Ah, hell no, hadn't the man suffered through enough for one night? She took a deep breath. "Clay?"

"Yes?"

"If you're wondering whether your mission to make me want you is succeeding, just stop."

"Why?"

"Because it is, I do, I want you." She left the rest unsaid. *I want to do things with you, and to you. I think about you all the time.* She waited through his prolonged pause.

"I'm sensing a *but* in the works . . ."

"But that doesn't change the facts. I'm not comfortable with my body." *And I have no idea how to please a man in bed.*

"There's nothing wrong with your body."

"You haven't seen it."

"I've seen enough of it to know that I find every inch of you desirable."

"You can't possibly know that until you've seen every inch of it. Besides, I've seen your tall, willowy ex, remember? I'm nothing like her."

"Thank God for that."

"You know what I mean."

"So do you. If you think I'll be comparing you to her in bed, you're wrong. So wrong, it's laughable. Do you think I could ever again be attracted to a woman who's done what she's done?"

"I guess not."

"Damn straight." He paused. "You know, earlier, when I had her on the phone, I nearly couldn't say what I had to say. I struggled to complete it because it hurt so bad to talk about it, to come out and admit some of the things I wanted to tell her."

Allie turned so that her right side was up against the door. She placed her left hand against the panel, hoping to give him some small bit of comfort. She sensed him moving on the opposite side. This was ridiculous. Surely, he had to be freezing. She rested her head against the door. "But you got through it."

"I did. Now ask me how."

She swallowed. "How?"

"I focused on you, Allie. Your compassion, your kindness, your empathy for me, and it gave me strength. *You* gave me strength to finish what I started."

She played back a scene from earlier in the evening—Clay, choking on painful memories of the most horrific time of his life, and him turning that broken-hearted gaze on her. She'd stood there, frozen in place, unable to move or to speak any words of comfort to him. Unable to do anything but meet the painful look in his eyes head-on to let him know she understood what he was going through. She sat up, realizing that he *had* seen it. He'd known she was there for him, willing him strength.

Allie got to her feet and turned the deadbolt. By the time she opened the door, Clay was standing, his gaze centered on hers.

"I get it, Clay."

He nodded, relief washing over every nuance of his features. "It's about damn time."

"Am I trying your patience beyond normal endurance?"

"No, but my ass is numb." He rubbed his hands over his butt as validation.

"Do you want to come inside?"

His left brow rose in a devilish display of tantalizing mischief. "Do I want to? Hell, yes! Should you let me inside?" He cocked his head to the side. "I'm not so sure."

Allie considered her options. She could continue to let the threat of intimacy intimidate her for the rest of her life. Or . . . she could begin a new chapter in her life tonight. She opened her mouth then closed it, her mouth too dry to form words. Swallowing, she licked her dry lips, deciding to invite him into her home, maybe even her bed.

Before she could act, he spun around, and hauled ass back to his truck.

"Clay?"

"I can't go in there."

She stepped out onto the porch. "Why not?"

He opened his truck door and called back to her. "I'll call you when I get back to my place." He paused long enough to look back at her, the interior light illuminating a face etched in pain. "After I take a cold shower." He winced. "Or two."

"Oh." She smiled as she caught his meaning. She closed the door and leaned against it, "Ooh."

Chapter Nine

Sunday, December 23rd

Clay ushered Allie and her girls into the farmhouse his father and uncles had built for his family somewhere around the mid-1950s. "It looks like we're one of the last ones here." He held one hand up to stop Allie from uttering the apology she had brewing. "We're still early, so stop. I remember what it was like living with teenage daughters too, you know."

"Hey, look who finally decided to get here! Let me take this off your hands" Brian grabbed the casserole from Allie's hands, peeked under the lid. "Yes!" he crowed. "Finally, someone who puts marshmallows on the sweet potatoes, the way God intended them." He winked and placed the dish on his grandmother's kitchen counter, but returned, followed by his sister and brother-in-law.

Clay took a deep breath. "Everyone, this is Allie Sarver, and her daughters, Cecily and Kayla. Ladies, this is my son, Brian, father to Sean Patrick, here." He placed the roasting pan full of cornbread dressing on the kitchen counter and turned to grab his daughter in a bear hug. "And this is my daughter, Terri, whom I've missed, as you can see."

Terri hugged him back. "Hey, Daddy. I've missed you, too." She pulled back and turned to Allie and her girls to introduce her husband, Ryan. Her gaze lit on the teenage girls. "Finally, someone I don't have to speak to in baby talk."

"Speaking of which," Clay said, as Sean entered the room, holding his toddler cousin's hand. "Here are the other lights of my life. This is Brian's son, Sean Patrick, and Terri's little Everly Hope." He lifted his grandchildren and held them each in an arm. "Hey Ev, you got a kiss for Paw Paw?"

The one-year-old gave him a toothy grin and puckered her mouth for a kiss. Clay laughed as he smacked her on the lips.

"Oh, look how cute they are!" Cecily gushed.

"They're adorable!" Kayla shrieked.

"Oh, do y'all like babies?" Terri winked at Allie. "Wonderful . . . built-in baby-sitters. We can negotiate on your hourly wages."

"I love kids. I'd watch them for free!" Kayla added.

"Oh, honey. You only say that now because you haven't tried to keep up with the little tornado. Everly went from crawling, to walking, to running in less than a month and leaves a mess wherever she lands."

Clay lowered the children to the floor. As if trying to prove him right, Everly went straight for a huge dictionary on her great-grandmother's end table.

"There she goes. Book pages are her preferred snack." Ryan moved the book to a safe spot.

All eyes turned to the room's entrance as Jane Andrews appeared. "I leave the room for a few minutes and y'all start the party without me."

"Hey, Ma. I want you to meet someone."

Once Clay made the introductions, his mother stood eye to eye with Allie, nodding her head. "The eyes are the window to the soul, and yours show great kindness. It's wonderful to meet you, Allie."

"Thank you, Mrs. Andrews. It's wonderful to meet you, also."

"Oh, *pshaw*! Dispense with the formalities, please. Just call me Jane, and these two lovely young ladies must be your girls. Welcome, all. Welcome to my home!"

It took another hour for the dinner's completion, which progressed much easier since the teenage girls were keeping the little ones occupied. They gathered for a short blessing and dug into the scrumptious meal of juicy roasted turkey with all the appropriate and delicious side dishes.

Halfway through the meal the front door banged open, and all activity came to a screeching halt. Everyone gaped at the woman carrying a bag of gifts in one hand, and balancing a clear bowl of red gelatin in the other.

"I hope I'm not too late, I brought a dessert."

Clay pushed away from the table. "What the hell, Marge?"

Margie blinked her wide eyes, trying to appear innocent, no doubt. "I wanted to see my children and grandchildren, Clay."

"Then you should have set something up with Terri and Brian for another day, and surely another location."

Terri snorted from the opposite side of the table. "Like that's gonna happen. I don't want that woman anywhere near my daughter . . ." She looked up, her eyes hard and defiant. "Or me either, for that matter."

Jane raised herself from her chair at the head of the table. "You know, Margie, if you and I were here alone, I'd ask you in, if nothing else other than to give you a piece of my mind. I will not have you barging into my home and making a scene. You should have called first if you wanted to visit."

"Well, I would have, but I misplaced your number, Jane."

"It's the same number I've had for well over forty years. Please, leave now."

Margie lifted her chin. "I see. Well, at least let me leave the dessert. *Our* kids always loved strawberry gelatin when they were young, Clay. I'm sure *our grandchildren* will enjoy it, too." She approached the table, her gaze landing on Allie.

Before Clay could stop her, Margie faked a misstep and dumped the entire contents of the bowl onto Allie's lap with a single, pronounced *plop*.

Amid a chorus of horrified gasps, his ex-wife stood there holding the empty bowl. "Oh, I tripped." She placed a hand over her mouth to stifle her mean spirited laughter. "I am *so* sorry." Bypassing all attempts at sincerity, Margie's mouth twisted in a scornful grin.

Clay grabbed the bowl from her and scooped the jelled conglomeration back into its container. Too furious to speak, he shoved it at Margie then dragged her by the arm to the door, her heels clipping rapidly on the surface of the oak planks. He yanked her across the porch, down the steps, and all the way back to her vehicle. Clay pulled the door open and shoved her inside her car. "Get the hell out of here and don't let me find out you ever set foot on this property again."

She opened her mouth to speak.

"Now!" he bellowed.

He stood watch until she backed out of the drive and disappeared from sight. A string of under-his-breath curses poured from his mouth as he re-entered the house. He'd expected to be greeted with a chaotic bout of embarrassed tears and furious name-calling. Instead, he encountered something quite different.

Allie stood in the dining room, surrounded by her girls, Terri, and his mom, all of them picking off pieces of gelled dessert and bits of fruit from the front of her suede skirt.

"Oh, here's another piece of grape for you Sean. Let's see, are there any cherries left? I love the cherries. There are never enough of them in cans of fruit cocktail, don't y'all agree?"

Terri nodded, choking on her laughter but caught her breath enough to speak. "I have to agree with you, Allie. I usually add an extra jar to mine. Personally, I prefer ambrosia salad. Oh!" She stopped and placed both hands on Allie's shoulders. "Aren't you glad she didn't bring *that* instead of gelatin salad?"

Allie's eyes grew big. "Oh, I don't know. I love ambrosia. If she had, I'd still be sitting there with a big spoon in my hand, and I wouldn't be sharing it with any of you."

Clay shook his head as everyone at the table dissolved into laughter. Allie's gaze found his, her eyes crinkling with pure joy.

Allie.

His Allie had single-handedly turned a potential disaster into something lighthearted and funny. He approached the table and stood in front of her. She didn't protest when he took her face in both hands. He dipped his head, and kissed her . . . a long, leisurely, open-mouthed kiss, with just enough tongue to show her he was serious. He didn't give a damn who watched. The best part, the absolute best part, was that Allie kissed him back.

"Whoa! Way to go, Mom!"

"Outstanding execution, Pop."

Clay broke the kiss, and touched his forehead to Allie's, his mouthed widened with a huge smile. "Surely you would have shared that ambrosia with me."

"After that kiss?" She pulled back to give him a wink. "Good chance."

"I'm crazy about you. You know that, right?"

Her smile turned softer, more serious. "I'm beginning to see that."

He gave her one final smack on the mouth and stepped back to scan the small but attentive crowd. "Everybody okay?"

"Hunky dory . . ." Ryan coughed an added "Stud" into his hand.

"All right, that's enough," Clay grumbled. He faced Cecily and Kayla. "I bet you two thought there'd be no entertainment."

Cecily snickered as she took her seat. "Please, Mr. Clay. You should have been to our Dad's this past Thanksgiving."

Allie turned to her daughter. "What happened on Thanksgiving? Neither of you mentioned anything to me."

"That's because Dad gave us each a hundred bucks not to say anything," Kayla volunteered.

Allie leaned in closer to her daughter. "You're not serious, are you?"

Kayla nodded. "Oh, yeah."

"Yeah, I guess that's a moot point since he kicked Summer out of the apartment," Cecily admitted. "Dad went to the trouble of buying this whole Thanksgiving spread from some deli, because he says Summer can't cook for sh . . . uh . . . Dad says she can't cook."

"Dad even invited her parents. I've gotta hand it to him; at least he *tried* to make it enjoyable for everyone," Kayla said.

Clay nodded, thinking nobody could argue with that reasoning.

"Anyways, Summer had been pouting in the bedroom ever since her parents got to the condo," Cecily continued.

Allie frowned. "And why had Summer been pouting?"

"Because her mom said Summer's see-through blouse, with no bra, wasn't appropriate dress for Thanksgiving dinner. Her dad said it wasn't appropriate for any time, if his opinion counted for anything. Summer said it didn't, but she locked herself up in the bedroom. She came out during dinner, dressed in sweat pants and an old T-shirt, and stoned out of her mind."

Kayla raised both hands for emphasis. "Mom, I swear, she attacked that turkey like she hadn't eaten in a *month*."

"But . . ." Cecily looked around to make sure she had everyone's attention. "She climbed up on the table to do it. Yep, she's sitting up there in the center of the table, her legs crossed, and chowing down on some grub. She's got a turkey leg in one hand and a bottle of wine in the other. And then . . ." She looked at her sister.

"The table broke!" Kayla crowed, before bursting into laughter.

"Oh come on, girls." Allie stared at her daughters. "This can't be true!"

Clay tried to choke back laughter, but failed. "Honey, you can't make up something like that."

"Mom, I swear. Summer sat there, on the floor, covered with food," Kayla snorted with laughter.

"But, she *never* let go of that turkey leg!" Cecily finished.

Allie doubled over with laughter, along with everyone else. She used napkins to wipe tears from her eyes. "I see a talk with your father in the near future . . . and you two! You took his money to keep quiet?"

Kayla beamed at her mother. "But we pooled it and got you an awesome Christmas gift with it, Mom."

Clay shot her a grin as he held up both hands and dropped them, before shrugging. "Aw leave 'em alone, Mom, as long as it went to a worthy cause."

Allie clucked her tongue as she pointed at both her girls. "From now on, there will be no acceptance of bribery money from your father."

"Oo-kaaay," Cecily said. "But Mom, what's it worth to you to keep the 'Jello incident' out of the Jennings Daily News?"

Clay spewed a mouthful of wine, spraying the pristine white tablecloth with the dark liquid. He followed the act with a round of coughing, mixed with bawdy laughter.

"Oh my God!" Brian slapped the table. "You have got to bring these two to the next family reunion, Pop."

Clay met Allie's gaze and nodded. "I'll see what I can do."

Cecily climbed out of the truck's rear passenger door. "Thanks for bringing us to meet your family, Mr. Clay."

"Thanks for coming, Cec. I hope you weren't too bored."

"You're kidding, right? That was like the best time I've had in forever."

Allie stopped herself from being offended. Truth was, it was the best time she'd had in forever, too.

Kayla bounced out of the passenger side behind Clay. "Oh my God, I had so much fun with Sean and Everly. Your mom is awesome and your kids made us feel right at home, Mr. Clay. Thanks for bringing us with you."

"You're welcome, Kayla."

She took several steps toward the house then doubled back to throw her arms around his waist for a hug.

Allie sucked in her breath, wondering what his reaction would be to her daughter's unusual show of affection. She needn't have worried. A huge grin spread across his face as he returned Kayla's hug.

"Thank you, Kayla. That means a lot."

She backed away and gave him a sad smile. "I thought you might be missing hugs from a kid my age right about now."

He nodded. "I was, and anytime you have one to spare, I'll take it."

Cecily approached him, her movements hesitant. Allie recognized the question in her daughter's eyes. Could she trust this man? Would he be around long? Would it be worth putting forth the effort to get to know him? All reasonable concerns and she had no concrete answers for her. Sure, it looked good, now, but life didn't always provide happily ever after endings. Anyone who's ever read a Nicholas Sparks novel knew that.

Clay opened his arms and Cecily went to him, gave him a hug, and then got on her tippy toes to whisper something in his ear.

Clay's smile broadened even more and he nodded. "Me too, Cec. Thank you."

Allie approached, holding out the empty casserole dish. "Bring this inside, please, Cecily."

"Sure, Mom." She grabbed the dish and sent Clay one last wink before following her younger sister into the house.

With the girls inside and out of earshot, Allie studied Clay. "What did she say to you?"

"It's a secret," he said, without a single trace of smugness on his face.

She frowned. "Oh . . . okay."

He grabbed her hand and pulled her to him for a hug. "Nothing bad, I assure you. As a matter of fact, it reflects my own feelings."

She shrugged. "I guess that'll have to suffice."

"Yep."

"So, I guess you'll be spending Christmas Eve with your family at Jane's?"

"We all got invited to your shin-dig", he said.

"Oh, yeah? How'd you manage that?"

"You remember that phone call Mom took just before we left?"

She remembered Jane stepping out to answer the phone. "Yes."

"That was Uncle J.D. inviting us all over for Christmas Eve lunch at his place in the country. Mom accepted the invite for all of us. She didn't tell me until we were leaving, though."

Allie feigned a horrified expression. "Without asking? What if y'all didn't want to spend another dull, boring day with me and my girls?" Laughter rumbled through his chest, creating ripples of warmth throughout her body.

"No chance of that, lady." He looked toward the house then back at her. "Those are two great young ladies, Al. You did good with them."

She sent him a curious look. "They've always had the potential. They were wonderful children, but as teenagers . . . ugh, I've had my doubts." She raised one brow. "You've been a positive influence on them. I'm not sure how you did it. I'm still leaning toward hypnosis."

"It's nothing that far-fetched." He sobered. "I missed out on those years with Hope, so they're a much-welcomed blessing. They're like the free prize in the box of your favorite cereal as a kid, you know?"

"Oooh . . . Captain Crunch!" she said.

"Mine was Coco Puffs."

"Wait a minute, if they're the prize, what does that make me?"

"You, lady, are the sweet, crunchy, chocolatey goodness inside the box. And moreover, you're the full box, not the bits you have to shake from it to get one last bowl."

"Wow. That's a flattering analogy."

"It was meant to be. I was a cereal connoisseur as a kid, you know."

Laughter bubbled up at the thought of him spouting an eight-year-old's version of praise over a bowl of Cocoa Puffs.

He pulled her closer. "Don't laugh at me."

"I'm not—just trying to picture it, that's all."

"Yeah? Picture this."

He dipped low for a toe-curling kiss that had her wrapping her arms around his neck for more. His hands wrapped around her waist to pull her close. A minute into it, the door opened and Kayla's head appeared.

"What are you two doing out there?"

"We're talking." Allie pulled away to put some space between them, and immediately missed the warmth of his body next to hers.

"I haven't heard any talking in the last minute or so. Don't make me repeat the question."

Clay hung his head. "I'm making out with your mom."

She walked out on the porch, arms crossed, eyebrows raised. "Excuse me, but I don't see a ring on that finger yet."

Once Allie recovered from shock and got back her power of speech, she shook her head. "Sweet baby Jesus, Kayla Brianne, I can't believe you said that. I've only dated Clay for what, a week and a half?"

Cecily joined her sister on the porch. "Our point exactly. Less than two weeks and already you can't keep your hands off of each other."

Clay cleared his throat and shoved both hands into his pockets.

Allie crossed her arms and frowned, dropped her voice several octaves. "I had no idea when I made the promise that they'd come down so hard on us."

"What promise did you make?"

"I'll tell you later." Allie lifted on her toes to kiss him goodnight. When she pulled away, he followed, adding another kiss or two, until Kayla's cough from the doorway forced them to separate.

"Well," Clay growled. "These two have sucked the fun right out of this night."

"I know, right? Before you know it, we'll be forced to hit the back roads looking for a good place to park."

He grinned at her. "Or we would if I didn't have a good size piece of land down one of those back roads." He leaned forward to whisper in her ear. "It comes with a fully furnished RV."

She covered her ears. "Oh, hush . . . now that's all I'll be thinking about, dammit." She laughed and pushed away from him. "You'd better go home before the guard dogs attack. Thanks again for a wonderful day."

He pulled one hand from his pocket to give her a salute. "Yes ma'am. Thanks for coming." He took two steps backward toward his truck and saluted the girls, as well. "Good night, girls."

They responded with a chorus of "Good night, Mr. Clay!"

Allie waited until he'd backed out of her drive to turn toward her door. Her daughters stood there, both wearing grins that said they were dying to say more. She lifted one finger. "I'm still your mother. Not a word. Not one word."

The girls exchanged a meaningful glance but followed her into the house in silence. She'd nearly made it to her bedroom before Cecily called out to her. She turned and found both girls standing at the end of the hall. "Yes?"

"Just so you know, Kayla and I have decided he meets our high standards as boyfriend material for you."

"Yeah, in other words, we approve," Kayla added.

Allie smiled at her girls. "Well, that's good to know. I'll tell him he's passed your test. Unless . . ." She narrowed her gaze. "Unless he already knows? What did you whisper in his ear, Cec?"

Cecily smiled. "He didn't tell you?"

"No, he kept your secret."

Her daughter nodded, as though adding one more item to the "PRO Clay" column.

Allie's gaze followed Cecily's trek to the bathroom. "Aren't you going to tell me?"

Cecily aimed her somber expression at her mother. "I said, 'I hope she keeps you.'"

Clay stepped under the steaming shower and stood there, head down, eyes closed, with one hand propped against the back wall of the shower for support. Water pounded on his neck muscles, easing the day's tension from his upper torso.

A lost cause, as it turned out, because in a flash he remembered the reason for his tension. What in hell were his poor kids going to do about their crazy mom? Just because she wasn't his problem, didn't mean it wouldn't leach into his private life. He cared what happened to his kids. Even he could see that Terri's refusal to deal with her mom could turn into a potential disaster. He didn't want his daughter twisted up inside with mother issues for the rest of her life.

He shivered as a cool draft hit his backside. Damn, this had been one frigid winter.

Frigid.

The word brought an image of Allie to mind . . . soft, pliant, smiling, so damn beautiful, and he'd bet his life on her being far from frigid. Just the thought of her had him in full arousal. He turned toward the shower head, letting the spray hit him in the face to run down the front of his body. He turned again, letting the spray hit his back and shoulders.

He had to wonder if Allie thought about him as much as he did her lately. The last several days, he thought of her constantly. God, he wanted that woman in his life; and not just for a night or two but as a permanent fixture. He faced the back wall again, so hard he wondered if he'd have to resort to something he swore he'd never do.

Another strong draft sent shivers down his spine, this time preceded by a pair of soft hands on his waist. He gasped, thrilled that Allie had come to meet him. He reached down to cover the hands with his own, felt the long tapering fingers with short nails, a pair of small breasts pressed against his back. His eyes flew open and he spun towards his intruder.

"Get . . . the hell . . . out of here!"

Margie stood there, unashamed, unrepentant, and wearing nothing but a determined look on her face.

Clay shut off the water, grabbed the towel he'd hung over the stall and wrapped it around his waist. "You've got some damn nerve. Get the hell out of my house before I call the friggin' law on your ass!"

"But Clay, you love my ass, don't you? You left the door unlocked . . . I knew you wouldn't mind."

"I do mind, and I guaran-damn-tee my door will be locked from this day forward." He shoved her aside and grabbed another towel. He threw the towel at her, along with her pile of clothes on the floor. "Dry off, put on your damn clothes, and get the hell out of my house. I'm calling the Sheriff's department right now." He slammed the door shut, and leaned against it to keep her from coming out until he could boot her fully clothed ass out the door.

He reached for his phone on the shelf where he'd left it. His wallet, keys, and a small pile of change was still there, but no phone. He found it on his bed and mentally scratched his head. He could have sworn . . .

An uneasy feeling rolling around in his gut, he picked it up and found the text app opened, then cussed long and loud at the naked image of himself that Marg had sent to Allie. That sudden draft he'd felt had apparently been created by his ex-wife opening the door just enough to snap a picture of him in the shower—in a full erection profile, no less. More disturbing was the text she'd sent along with the image:

I had him first. Looks like I'll have him last. Better luck next time.

Clay didn't have to think twice about what to do. He called Allie immediately. She answered on the second ring.

"Hey sweetie, I'm just stepping out of the shower. Can I call you back?"

"Listen to me, hon. While I was in the shower Margie trespassed into my home. Apparently, I didn't lock the door. Trust me when I say that it won't happen again. She found my phone and took a picture of me in the shower, and she sent it to you in a text with a nasty little message. I'm begging you not to believe it. I had no idea she was even in my home when she sent that." He waited for her response, praying she'd believe him.

"What picture?" she asked, finally.

"It's kind of a side view of me in the shower. I'm-I'm-I had my mind on you when she took that shot, dammit. Please, baby, you've got to believe me. I was thinking of you."

"And where is she now?"

"I've got her pinned in the bathroom with her clothes and a towel. As soon as she's dressed, I'm booting her ass out of here."

Icy silence preceded Allie's next words. "As soon as she's dressed?"

Clay squeezed his eyes shut realizing that his next words would most likely make his situation worse. "She got in the shower with me while my back was turned. I didn't know until I felt her hands on my waist, and then I thought it was you. I hoped it was you. But when I turned around, it . . . wasn't."

"No, of course not."

"I grabbed my towel and got the hell out of there." He slapped his hand over his pounding head. "I swear on my children and grandchildren . . . that's all there was to this. I grabbed my phone to call the Sheriff's Department first to report her, but then I saw she'd sent you a text and image from my phone."

"And she's still locked in your bathroom?"

"Yes."

"Keep her in the bathroom. I'll be there in ten minutes. And Clay?"

"Yes?"

"Don't let her know I'm coming."

"I won't." Before he even said the words, she'd ended the call.

"Clay?" Margie called from the bathroom.

"I'm not talking to you."

"I'm dressed."

Bullshit.

She pushed against the door. He wouldn't budge.

"Are you going to let me out of here?"

Not yet.

"I'm sorry, Clay."

Sure you are.

"I-I shouldn't have come here. I know that now. I'm so ashamed."

I can think of a few more things that should shame you, but they don't.

Clay waited a full five minutes before he remembered he had a towel around his waist. He'd be the one ashamed if Allie caught him in nothing but a flimsy-ass towel. He eyed his dresser, out of reach on the opposite side of the room. He looked at the bathroom door and growled. Just his damn luck, he'd leave it unguarded for two seconds to grab something to wear, she'd come waltzing out buck-ass-naked, and Allie would catch him trying to wrestle her back into her tiny bathroom prison. Hell, her finding him in his towel would do less damage.

"Shit . . ." He had to wonder how many other guys had ex-wives who were as big a pain in the ass as his was. Keeping one foot jammed against the door, he stretched enough and finally managed to reach the stack of folded laundry on the foot of his bed, thankful he hadn't taken the time to store it in his closet.

"Ah ha! Score one for procrastination." He'd just pulled the stack to him when she decided to renew her efforts to escape.

"Let me out, Clay! I've learned my lesson."

I don't think so, but you're about to. Allie didn't sound particularly amused by the situation.

He leaned all his upper body weight against the door and managed to finesse his ass into a pair of jeans. The sweatshirt he pulled from the stack was the easy part. Satisfied for the moment, he turned his attention back to his captive. Margie droned on and on, spouting her insincere apologies about everything. Everything but what she should have been apologizing for . . . abandoning her daughter. By the time the front door opened, he'd had about all he could take. When Allie entered his bedroom seconds later, Clay put a finger to his lips, hoping she'd hear some of Margie's confessional.

"Clay, are you there?"

"I'm here. Are you dressed, Marg?"

"I'm dressed. How many times do I have to apologize to you?"

"You know, Marg. It's not me you should be apologizing to, it's Allie."

"Oh . . . well . . . you're right. Next time I see her I'll do just that."

Allie's gaze narrowed and he stepped away from the door. "She's all yours."

She jerked open the door. "Let's hear it, Mar—good Lord! Oh, now that is unfortunate for you, honey. It's as cold as the dickens outside and that's where you're going this instant, clothed, or unclothed."

Margie's eyes widened. "It'll just take me a minute to throw on my clothes!"

"Oh, no! You've had more than enough time to do that." Allie snatched the clothes from Margie's grasp in one hand and grabbed her by the hair with the other. "Avert your eyes, Clay. All kinds of Boney Maroney ugly is about to come through here."

"I've seen it, and it does nothing for me."

"Ouch! Claaayy!" Margie shrieked, as she tried to pull Allie's hands from her hair.

Allie jerked hard on Marge's hair. "If you'd stop fighting and walk, it'd be a lot less painful."

Clay cleared out of the way to let the strange grouping pass—Allie clutching a wad of Margie's hair at the scalp—Margie bent at a ninety-degree angle, shuffling behind her, and trying to cover herself. *Now* she's modest?

Allie continued jerking her all the way to the door, accompanied by a continuous series of yelps from Marge. She eased her way down the steps, pulling the captive's hair and scalp along with her.

"Watch your step, now. Wouldn't want you to fall on your way down and hurt that boney little ass, would we?" When they were both on the patio's cement slab, Allie released her with one, final, hair-pulling jerk.

Margie covered her scalp with one hand, her nakedness with the other, and shivered in the frosty air. "Oh my God, it's so c-c-old out here!"

Allie threw Margie's clothes in all different directions, making the bag of bones scuttle around collecting the items. "Yeah, it's close to freezing, but you knew that, didn't you? Bet you wish you'd have done that back in the bathroom when you'd had the chance, don't you? You need help, Marge. Start by eating something, would you? Thin may be in, but you make those winged underwear models look downright chubby." She stood at the top of the steps and shot a glance his direction. "Was she always that skinny?"

"No, and she wasn't always delusional, either. She's definitely unbalanced."

As soon as Margie was dressed, she got in her car to leave. Allie waved animatedly as she barreled out of the drive. "Don't come back, now, you hear? And go eat something!"

She turned and brushed her hands against each other as she stepped inside the RV. "That's how you take out the trash, Clay. Got any more hiding in there?"

"I hope not." He closed the door behind her. "But I have to admit, I kind of liked seeing you clean house that way. Was that a way of claiming your territory?"

"I guess it was. Why? Do you have a problem with that?"

"Nope." He pulled her into his arms. "It's just that I'm all kinds of turned on by you right now."

"That could be a problem, then. For sure, now that I've seen what "turned on" looks like for you." She waved her phone at him.

He cringed. "I can't help it. That's what happens anytime I think of you." He backed her against the wall. "Or when I kiss you, or hold you in my arms." He dipped his head to capture her mouth with his, finishing with a gentle tug at her lower lip. Somehow, Clay managed to release her when he seriously wanted to cart her off to his bedroom. "Before this goes too far, what's this promise to your girls I heard you mention earlier?"

She took a breath, releasing it with a slow tremble. "Oh. That. Cecily waited up for me the night of mom's accident. We got to talking, and she asked if you and I got serious, if we'd ever move in together like her dad moved Summer in with him."

He scratched his five o'clock shadow, already sensing the direction of this conversation. "You told her no, of course, because I'd never do that to you or to your girls."

"I told her no. I also said I'd *try* to wait before . . . sleeping . . . with anyone, because I thought it was the right thing to do."

"Wait for what?"

"Well—marriage, if it's at all possible."

He straightened and took a deep breath. "That explains the ring comment." He cocked his head to the side. "Should . . . should I start pricing diamonds?" Her lighthearted laughter put him at ease.

"I'd rather get to know you first, if that's okay. It's been a while since I've dated anyone." She made a face. "Even then I majored in bench-warming and minored in how to be a wall-flower."

Clay kissed the tip of her nose. "I'm rusty myself, but maybe we could tutor each other."

"Mm . . . You mean form a study group."

"Yeah, we could lie to our parents—"

"Or my kids . . ."

"Yeah, and make out when we're supposed to be studying."

"Ooh . . . that sounds naughty."

He pressed his lips to her forehead then wrapped her in a hug. "Hey, Al?"

She responded with something that sounded like a satisfied purr in the middle of his chest.

"Just so you know, I do think about us having a future together; I think about it a lot. Do you?"

She turned her face, resting her cheek against his chest. "I'm afraid to think about something like that."

"Maybe it's time to push that fear aside and consider the possibility."

She sucked in her breath.

"Do you hear what I'm telling you?"

"I hear you."

She lifted her face to his. The want he saw in those beautiful green orbs had him fantasizing about all the things he could do to her if she spent the whole night with him. He pushed away from her. "Good Lord, babe. You need to go. You need to go right now."

"Clay . . ."

He turned away from the pleading look in her eyes. "If you have any intention of keeping that promise to your girls, you'd better haul your sexy little ass right out that door in the next few seconds." He grabbed his keys and overcoat and slipped his feet into his boots.

"Are you leaving?"

"I'm following you home. Crazy Margie could be waiting somewhere to run you off the road or something."

Allie snorted. "I'm not afraid of her."

"Doesn't matter because I'm afraid enough for you, and I'm following you." He opened the door. "Let's go. Get in your car."

"Okay, but just follow me to the interstate. I'll be fine from there."

He walked her to her car, grunting as he gave her a soft pat on the butt. "You're fine from anywhere, but I'm still following you all the way home." The smile she sent him warmed his heart.

"See you tomorrow, Clay."

"You bet your sweet ass you will."

Chapter Ten

December 24th – Christmas Eve

John Michael stuck his head into the kitchen to make an announcement. "Make some room on the buffet, Ms. Bess. Aunt Jane and Clay are here with more food."

Allie's belly filled with butterflies at the mention of Clay's name. She removed the apron she'd worn to protect her clothes during the food preparation and hung it on a hook by the kitchen door. She smoothed down her blouse, pausing when her sister whispered into her ear.

"You look beautiful, don't worry."

She pressed a hand to her belly. "I always get so nervous before I see him, Cyn. This dating thing isn't for sissies, is it?"

"You'll get the hang of it. Until then it sure makes life interesting." She elbowed her sister in the ribs. "And so does what comes afterward. Now, go out there and greet your honey." Cynthia gave Allie a gentle shove toward the living room.

She took the tray of golden brown yeast rolls from Jane and gave her a one armed hug. "How are you? I'd hoped you would be resting from all that baking yesterday, but it looks like you've been at it again." She closed her eyes and breathed in the aroma of fresh baked bread. "These look scrumptious."

Clay's mother waved off her concern. "I can throw a batch of bread together in my sleep. I've been at it forever. Don't worry about me." Jane walked over to Bess. "Clay told me about your accident, Bessie. You should be resting, not cooking with one hand."

"Oh, pooh! I'm fine. I just fiddled when I should have faddled and tripped over my own two feet. I'm mad at myself for doing something so stupid."

J.D. placed an arm around Bess's shoulder and kissed her temple. "I'm mad at myself for not being quick enough to catch her before she fell."

Bess did a half-turn, and used her good hand to give his face a comforting pat. "That's just silly, J.D. Then we'd both be in a cast."

He caught her hand and kissed it just above the knuckles. "Well, I'm gonna make darn sure it doesn't happen again, sweet lady. Now what else do you need me to do in here?"

Jane placed one hand over her ample bosom. "You mean you got J.D. to work in the *kitchen*? Lord have mercy, it *must* be love."

"Oh, go on with you, Jane." J.D. gave his older sister a good-natured huff. "Now that the mouth of the south is here, I can go back in the living room with the men-folk." He turned away, letting his hand trail down Bessie's arm to give her hand a squeeze before walking away.

Her brow raised, Allie exchanged looks with Cynthia, whose mouth rounded in an exaggerated "O". "Mama's got a boyfriend," Allie chirped, in a singsong voice.

Bessie pointed one finger at her. "Allie Elizabeth, you mind your manners."

Allie's gaze landed on her own shoes. "Yes ma'am."

"Besides, what's that old saying about people in glass houses not throwing stones?" Bessie gave her daughter a gentle nudge in the ribs. "There's your stone right there, my girl."

Allie turned to see Clay standing at the doorway, his mouth twisted in a sexy half-smile and looking like he was sizing her up for his next meal. "Hello."

"Hello to you, too."

Allie returned to the buffet to find a spot for the rolls. She was still making adjustments when Clay made his presence known with a light kiss to her neck that produced a head to toe shiver.

"Mm . . . You smell good enough to eat." He clasped her hand and tugged her into the darkened hallway just off the kitchen.

"Clay, what are you do—"

His mouth covered hers, drowning out any more objections. He pulled away then went back for one last kiss.

She gave him a dazed smile. "Mm, good morning, Cowboy, and—what was it Brian said yesterday? Outstanding execution." His grin was contagious.

"I was inspired. Merry Christmas Eve, beautiful."

"You too. I don't know about you, but it just got merrier for me."

Kayla popped her head around the corner. "What'cha doing back here?"

Clay faced her with his hands up in the air. "Just saying hello, kiddo. Your mother's virtue is still intact."

"It better be," she said, giving them a wink before pulling them both back into the kitchen.

Allie looked down her nose at her youngest daughter. "You can tone this down a notch or two. We're in a house full of people. What could happen?"

Cecily stuck her face between them. "Excuse me, but what is it you always say, Mom? You can't be too careful."

Cynthia's snort of laughter kept Allie from reprimanding her daughters. "Wow, you've got your own little versions of the NSA there, don't you?"

Allie cocked her head at her sister. "Yes, but I think they've forgotten I hold the power to ground them for the rest of high school."

Cecily and Kayla's gazes clashed in a horrified exchange. "She wouldn't do that, would she?" Kayla asked her sister.

Cecily glanced at Allie then back at Kayla. "I'd say that's a possibility, but we'll persevere, little sister. I'm willing to sacrifice my freedom for the cause."

Kayla frowned. "Sure you are. You'll be graduating in five months. I'll still have three and a half years to live with her."

Allie rolled her eyes and pushed her daughters and Clay toward the living room door. "Stop! Get out of here, you three. It's getting too crowded."

"Come on girls. Let's go find some babies to spoil," Clay said, pushing her daughters ahead of him.

Cynthia laughed as Clay and the girls made their way toward the living room. "Cecily just called your bluff, you know."

"I think you're right."

"They're just looking after their mom. More proof of how much they love you."

Allie's gaze stayed glued to the back of Clay's broad shoulders, once more amazed at the changes in all of them since he'd come into their lives. Her daughters hadn't shown this much concern for her in years. She smiled as he turned at the door and sent her another wink. It was nearly impossible to find any fault with this situation.

Even so, once he disappeared through the door, a sinking feeling in her stomach replaced her joy. She sensed the bleakness of a looming catastrophe. No, it was best not to hope.

Clay settled onto the opposite end of the couch from Johnny and crossed one booted foot over his knee.

Uncle J.D. sat in his recliner, balancing a mug of coffee on the arm. "So, nephew, the scuttlebutt is that you and Bessie's youngest daughter are quite the item."

He nodded. "We've seen each other a few times."

Johnny rolled the newspaper he'd been reading and slapped his knee with it. "How's it going with my sister-in-law?"

Clay glanced toward the kitchen, caught a glimpse of Allie seated at the kitchen table and tearing lettuce for a salad. She happened to look up and catch him watching her. Her reaction was to give him a self-conscious half-smile and return to her task, her face a mysterious mixture of emotions. He'd hoped yesterday's kiss in front of everyone had sealed the deal, but what he saw there was more of the same old signs of doubt and insecurity.

"It's good. I think I'm more set on it than she is at this point, but I'm working on that."

His Uncle J.D. sat forward in his recliner. "You need some help with that? Johnny, didn't I tell you to give him the list—"

Johnny's groan drowned out the rest. "Enough with the damn list, Pop!"

Clay settled both boots on the rug and pulled himself to the edge of the couch. "What's this list you keep talking about, Uncle J.D.?"

His cousin snorted. "It's a list of cheesy li—"

J.D. cut Johnny off with one look. "Are you his Uncle J.D.?"

Johnny's mouth snapped shut. "No sir."

J.D. continued in a matter-of-fact tone. "It's a list of compliments for the ladies. I found them on the Internet and even came up with a few on my own.

"Compliments?"

"*Lines,*" Johnny insisted.

J.D. shrugged. "But they're good lines."

Johnny shook his head. "Cheesy-ass lines."

Clay wiped the grin from his mouth, tried to look serious. "Well, can you remember any of them, Uncle J.D.? I mean, I'm not above asking for help from someone with as much experience under his belt as you have."

J.D.'s face brightened as he turned on his son. "You see? My nephew can appreciate the benefits of experience and knowledge when it's staring him in the face."

Johnny gave his cousin a hard look. "You . . . Suck . . . Ass."

"Hey, I'm willing to try whatever works, man."

"All right, Clay," Johnny said. "Be sure and let me know Allie's reaction when you tell her she looks hotter than a Mexican tamale."

Clay smothered a laugh to keep from hurting his uncle's feelings.

"Or that her eyes are as blue as the deep, blue sea," J.D. added.

Clay cleared his throat. "I can't use that one. Allie's eyes are green."

"Oh, of course not." J.D.'s brow furrowed in concentration for a moment before his face illuminated with inspiration. "Her eyes are as green as a fresh-cut lawn."

"Then you can follow with "If you were a vegetable, you'd be a cute-cumber." Johnny sent Clay an exuberant nod. "Right?"

"Oh, man . . ."

"Your body is sixty-five percent water, and I'm thirsty," J.D. countered.

"Keep 'em coming, Uncle J.D," Clay urged.

"Was your dad a boxer? Cause you're a knockout!" Johnny volunteered. He looked at his dad. "What was the one with the vitamin, Pop? Can you remember?"

J.D.'s face stretched wide with a grin. "My doctor says I'm lacking Vitamin U. And my all-time favorite, if you were a banana, I'd find you a-peeling." He slapped his thigh. "And I've got plenty more of those, too."

Clay wiped the grin from his mouth and cleared his throat. "On the Internet, you say?"

"Oh, yeah. Zach hooked me up with his old laptop and showed me how to surf the net from the comfort of my recliner." J.D. leaned forward in his chair and gave Clay a serious look. "If you want to know anything about anything, just *Goggle* it."

"It's not *Goggle*, Pop, it's—"

"Whatever the hell it's called. I'm telling you, that's an amazing tool."

"You don't say." Clay held his breath as Uncle J.D. dropped his voice to a whisper.

"Do *you* know about the G-spot?"

After several seconds, Clay finally snapped his gaping mouth shut. "Wow! I've gotta admit, that one took me by surprise."

"I can show you an article that tells you exactly how to find it." He lowered his voice. "I hear it does wonderful things for the ladies."

Clay held up both hands. "I'm good, but thanks for the offer." He slapped one hand over his mouth and faced his cousin again.

Johnny sat there, his mouth stretched in a wide grin. "Welcome to my world, man."

"And you have Zachary to thank for this?"

Johnny nodded. "Yep, I figure I'll repay the favor one day. Maybe teach the twins the old *Name Game* song as soon as they can talk, and then have the kids ask their parents to do Chuck, Chuck, Bo Buck, Banana Panna Po Puck . . . you know . . ."

"Make sure it's in front of a room full of people," Clay added.

"It's the least I could do, don't you think?"

Clay gave him a hearty nod. "Oh, absolutely."

Cecily entered the room, bouncing Clay's granddaughter on her hip. She and Kayla sat on the floor, about six feet apart. Cecily placed the child on the floor in front of her. The baby girl, adorable in a red Christmas dress and tights, took turns running back and forth from one girl to the other. Each time she reached her destination she collapsed on them and erupted in contagious belly laughter.

"She's so cute!" Cecily said, smothering Everly's face with kisses.

"I know, I just want to take her home with me," Kayla countered.

At the sound of car doors, Johnny stood and walked to the door. "You girls are about to go into cuteness overload." He grinned at Clay. "Finally, I get to show off *my* grandbabies." He held the door open as his daughter-in-law, Cathryn, entered, carrying seven-month-old Caleb. Johnny's son, Zachary, followed carrying Caleb's twin sister, Cassandra.

"Oh, my gosh! Twins, Cecily!" Kayla screeched.

Cecily stood, taking Everly with her. "Look how adorable they are."

Cat handed Caleb over to his Poppa Johnny and stared at the girls. "Who are you two, where do you live, and do you babysit?"

John swung his grandson to one hip and made the introductions. "These are Cynthia's nieces, Cat, and they live in Jennings."

Cat gave a satisfied nod. "Jennings is close enough."

"I'm Cecily, and that's Kayla. She does more babysitting than I do, because mom won't let her date yet, but I might pass up a date for these two cutie pies." She cocked her head and pointed at Zachary. "I remember seeing him at the wedding reception, but not you or the babies."

Cathryn groaned. "That's because all three of us were sick with a horrendous virus. I wasn't about to subject anyone to that, and I made Zach go without me. So, you two are Allie's girls. Every time I've seen your mom, y'all were gone for the weekend." She faced her husband and clapped her hands. "We have babysitters in the family now, Zachary!"

He switched Cassandra from one hip to the other and laughed. "It looks like we've hit the mother-load. I'm Zachary, and since your Aunt Cynthia is my step-mom, that makes us step-cousins, right?"

Clay took Everly from Cecily. "Careful, Cec. I think Zachary's angling for a family discount already."

Within seconds, Kayla had lured Cassandra from Zach. It only took a minute longer for John Michael to turn Caleb over to Cecily.

"Keep a close eye on them, Cat warned the girls. They're both crawling all over the place, and they're fast."

"They're diggers, too," Zachary added. "Nothing is safe. Nothing is sacred. If they can reach it, it *will* go into their mouths."

The girls sat on the floor among an overabundance of baby cuteness.

Ten minutes later, Brian arrived with Sean, who turned out to be excellent at helping the girls round up the lightening-quick crawlers.

Lunch was a riotous affair, with parents doing their best to tend to small children before meals turned completely cold.

In the middle of the lunch, Brian stepped away from the table to answer a phone call. After several minutes, he re-entered the room, concern etched onto his brow.

Clay stood as the room quieted. "What's wrong, Son?"

"Mom has been in a bad wreck. She ran her car off the road and into a tree. The police officer said her blood alcohol level indicated severe intoxication."

Terri's mouth tightened. "I hope she didn't hurt anyone else."

"No, her vehicle was the only one involved. But your concern for her is touching, Sis."

Terri stiffened. "My concern for that woman ended the day she walked out on our dad and sister."

Clay turned to his daughter with a gentle reprimand. "She's still your mother, sweetie."

"I know that, Dad," Terri whispered. "But she made her choice, and I've made mine."

Clay knew better than to push his daughter on the issue. She'd washed her hands of Margie when she left for Paris. He turned his attention back to his son. "What's her condition, Brian?"

"She's in critical condition, Pop. She's lost a lot of blood and there's a severe shortage right now. The Jennings hospital asked if anyone in the family can donate as soon as possible."

Clay placed his napkin on the table. "I'm a universal donor. I'll go."

Allie thought she knew what a universal donor was, but wanted to be sure before jumping to conclusions. "You're—you're what?"

"I'm O negative. My blood is compatible to anyone's."

"Oh, that's . . ." She swallowed to keep the bile from rising in her throat. "That's great."

Heat infused her face as she struggled to regain her composure. O negative . . . it wasn't great. It was as far from great as it could possibly be. She placed one hand over her mouth until she could form a coherent thought. "Wh-what blood type do they need for your mother, Brian?"

"Mom is A. I'm O, like Dad, so I can give also."

For a moment, Allie's gaze clashed with Terri's. Years with a cheating husband had given her the ability to spot someone hiding a secret. Terri's secret had all the signs of being weight-of-the-world burdensome.

She knows.

Terri pushed away from the table, her entire body tense, and her eyes wide with panic.

Allie stood immediately. "I'm A. I'll be glad to donate if it'll help."

"You'd do that for her?"

Clay's question took her by surprise. "Of course I would." She placed her hand on Terri's shoulder. "I'm sure my girls would be glad to watch Everly if you want to ride with your dad and me to the hospital." She lowered her voice to a whisper. "I need to speak to you for a second, if that's okay." At Terri's nod, Allie followed her into the bathroom and closed the door. Clay's daughter stood before her, arms crossed tightly over her chest.

"Terri, if he learns the truth from this ordeal, I swear to you it won't be from me." Terri's curious gaze pushed her for an explanation. "I know Hope's blood type was AB."

Terri frowned. "How?"

"I saw her scrapbook . . . the abandoned Biology assignment. Hope knew, didn't she? I've helped two daughters with that same assignment. It's impossible for an O type parent to produce an AB type child. A girl as intelligent as Hope would have discovered that." Her heart broke for the teary-eyed young woman who'd kept her dying sister's secret.

Terri squeezed her eyes shut and nodded. "I knew she was bugged about something and finally got it out of her. In three and a half years of seeing Hope fighting for her life, I'd never seen her so crushed, so defeated as the day she told me she knew Dad wasn't her biological father."

Allie couldn't help but put her arms around Terri as the young woman's face crumpled in misery.

"That's why I can't forgive my mother. Poor Hope . . . that's when she quit. She believed the longer she lived and made trips to the hospital, talking to doctors, consulting with pathologists, the more risk of Daddy discovering the truth."

"Is Margie aware the two of you know the truth?"

Terri's gaze turned hard. "Hope asked me not to say anything, but she confronted Margie about it. Why do you think that woman ran off to France? She's a coward; a lying, cheating, coward, and if she dies because of her stupidity . . . God forgive me . . . I don't—"

Allie cut her off before she could finish. "Oh honey, don't say anything now you'll live to regret."

"I won't regret it. You weren't there to see how she treated my sister all those years. I never understood how she couldn't love her." Tears dripped from her chin onto the bathroom rug. "But now I do. I was so proud of Hope, Allie. Even when she was dying, my little sister had so much courage. She was so strong. If Daddy finds out . . ."

"He'd deal with it, Terri. You three kids got your strength from your father, after all." Allie grabbed some tissues and handed them to her. "Now dry your eyes and blow your nose. We need to get to the hospital. I don't know about you, but I refuse to let that woman die and leave me with a guilty conscience."

Terri dabbed at her eyes. "I hope my dad knows how lucky he is to have found you."

"Yeah, well, I consider myself lucky he even looked twice at me. Now, let's go."

By three that afternoon, Clay, Allie, Brian, and Terri had all completed their donations. Brian went into the ICU unit for a brief visit with Margie. Terri chose not to, but wanted to be there for her brother when he rejoined them. He returned, ten minutes later, his face pale and drawn.

Clay hugged his son. "Is it that bad?"

"I wouldn't have recognized her, Dad. There's so much swelling."

"That'll go down in a few of days," Clay assured him. "The doctor spoke to your sister while you were in there. If there are no signs of clots or leakages in the next twenty-four hours they'll downgrade her from critical and put her in a regular room."

Brian nodded and looked at his sister. "We can visit her two at a time. You want to come in with me? She's in and out of consciousness. She did manage to speak a few words, and asked if you were here."

Terri opened her mouth to speak, but after exchanging a look with Allie, seemed to change her mind. "I will for a few minutes, but then I want to go to meet my husband and daughter."

Clay nodded. "We'll take you back with us when you're done." He waited until his children had disappeared behind the double doors before facing Allie. "I don't know what you two talked about in that bathroom back at Dad's place, but I'm sensing you're somehow responsible for Terri even being here."

Allie gave him a half-hearted shrug. "I only said I understood how she was feeling, but urged her not to say or do anything she may regret later. In case her mother didn't—in case it's serious. It only takes a few kind words now to keep her from feeling guilty over this for the rest of her life."

"Well, that and a pint of blood, right?"

She nodded. "A little less than a pint, but I was still glad to do it."

He pulled her close for a hug. "Thank you, Allie. You have an exceptional soul."

"I struggle sometimes."

"Maybe so, but I think donating blood for my ex-wife goes above and beyond the call of girlfriend responsibilities—especially after Margie's class-act at Mom's place yesterday and again last night."

She pulled away and lifted her index finger. "This is going on the list of firsts, no doubt. In the spirit of full disclosure, I'll also admit the 'girlfriend' label takes the sting out." She straightened his collar before patting the front of his shirt. "As for Terri, she'll have to figure out on her own how best to deal with her mother, but I wouldn't push her if I were you."

"I won't, and thank you for being here for us. If my daughter feels comfortable enough to confide in you, I'm even more grateful." He took her face in both hands and gave her a firm but quick kiss before wrapping her in a hug.

Terri pushed through the double doors a few minutes later, her face paler than when she'd entered. "I'm ready to leave when you are, Dad. Brian said he'll stay another hour or so, but that we should go on home."

He took Allie's advice and didn't ask anything about Margie's condition. He decided that if Terri wanted to discuss it, she would. His daughter chose to sit in the back seat, even after Allie's encouragement to sit in the front with him.

"No, you belong up there with Dad," she'd said, before sending her a smile glowing with sincerity. "I'm fine back here."

He'd stolen several glances at his daughter from the rearview mirror and discovered nothing, but her silence during the drive home bothered him. Once there, he witnessed Terri clasping Allie's hand as she mumbled a quiet "Thank you".

He waited for Terri to go inside then tugged on Allie's arm to keep her from entering the house. She turned, her eyebrows raised in question. He pulled her against the wall and closed in on her, smothering her question with a kiss, and then another. He lowered his forehead to hers and took a deep breath before releasing it, along with all the pent-up tension from the last few hours.

"I'm not complaining, but what did I do to deserve that?" Her question, accompanied by a low purr, stirred feelings of need he'd ignored far too long.

"You astound me. You're a comfort to me, and now to my kids. You already know I'm crazy about you. I'm not sure how much more I can take before bringing out the big guns, you know?"

She blinked, confusion clouding her eyes. "The big guns?"

He nodded before lowering his lips to hers again for a soft kiss then a gentle nip that made her shiver. "You're making it impossible for me not to fall in love with you, Allie. Don't you know that?"

She tried to look away. He wouldn't let her.

"Don't be afraid of it." He sensed a protest coming, placed a finger over her lips to stop it. "You are. You're terrified of the physical part of it, for some reason. Even though I tell you how beautiful you are, and how desirable I find you."

She rolled her eyes. "And I keep telling you, I'm not good at the physical aspect of relationships. I *am* afraid. I'm afraid once you realize it's true, it'll ruin whatever feelings you have for me."

His rumble of laughter echoed between them. He kissed her again then slid his mouth lower to nibble at the delicate soft creaminess of her neck. Her reaction was a head to toe shiver proving that he'd affected her. "Lady, there's not a damn thing wrong with you, and I'm going to have so much fun proving it."

She sucked in her breath. "I hope I don't disappoint you."

He pulled away from her, skimming her face with the back of his hand. "I could say the same, you know."

"Mm, I doubt that," she whispered against his neck.

The door opened and Cecily's head appeared from the opening. "Found 'em! They're here on the front porch making out again."

"Oh look," Clay said. "It's the make-out police."

Cecily stepped onto the porch and clasped her hands as though she were holding a pistol. "Sir, please step away from the maternal unit. Don't make me use this on you."

Clay scowled at her. "That thing better not be loaded, young lady."

She struck a saucy pose, one hand resting on her hip. "I could say the same thing for you, Mister."

"Cecily!" Clay's bawdy laughter came close to drowning out Allie's cry of protest to her daughter.

"Well done, Cec. Well done." Clay used his hand to guide both women through the door before following them into the house. "I don't know about you, Al, but I'm still hungry. I didn't get to finish my meal."

"I didn't either, and I'm famished."

Bess called to them from the kitchen. "We covered your plates and kept them in the warmer for all of you. Terri's eating hers at the snack bar. We have coffee and dessert too, when you're done."

Clay and Allie joined Terri and the three of them spoke in hushed tones about the situation with Margie.

Terri sipped from her glass of sweet tea. "What's she going to do when she gets out of the hospital, Dad? What's going to happen if she doesn't have insurance? ICU alone can annihilate a person's life savings. Or even if it pays for that, will it pay for the around the clock care she'll need afterward?"

Clay had already considered these possibilities but kept them to himself. He focused his concern on his children. How would this situation affect them? As of yet, he had no answers.

"I knocked out my accrued leave when Everly was in the hospital with pneumonia six months ago," Terri continued. "Except for driving in on weekends, I won't be able to help Brian take care of her. This has all the potential of a freaking nightmare, and it all happened because she didn't have the sense not to drive drunk."

Allie gave her hand a gentle pat. "Finish your lunch, sweetie. There's no use worrying about it until you know how the situation unfolds."

Christmas day turned into a dream come true for Allie, despite Margie's hospitalization. It hadn't affected her time with Clay in the least. Eventually, he'd have to return to work and she wasn't looking forward to having him gone for two weeks at a time. Up until now, he'd been able to conduct most of his year-end business on his laptop or smart phone.

She sat cuddled beside him on her couch, both of her girls within sight of them. She fingered the necklace he'd given her as a Christmas gift. A beautiful heart-shaped pendant, covered in a layer of pavé diamonds, with matching earrings. No way had she expected anything so extravagant from the man. Although he'd been thrilled with his gift from her this morning, two tickets to a New Orleans Saint's game two days after Christmas, it paled in comparison.

The thought of getting away with him for the entire day had her stomach churning with butterflies, even though he hadn't mentioned taking her yet.

Allie threaded her fingers through his. "When are you leaving on Sunday?"

"I suppose we should leave around 8:00 a.m. Is that too early for you?"

She crooked her neck to look up at him. "You want me to go with you? I thought maybe you'd want to take Brian."

He leaned in to meet her eye to eye. "You're joking, right? You think I'd take the tickets you gave me for Christmas and go with anyone else?"

That's exactly what Bruce would have done. "They're your tickets. Technically you can take anyone you want."

"Well, that settles it. I want to take you with me. As a matter of fact, I've already booked a suite at my favorite luxury hotel for the night, Le Pavillon Hotel on Poydras."

"Le Pavillon?" Allie gasped. "A suite?"

"Yes ma'am. They had a last minute, one-night cancellation of the Art Deco themed suite. I hope you don't mind me taking it without getting your approval first."

Allie clasped her hands. "I've been in the lobby and the lounge area, but I've never spent the night in any of the rooms."

"The game starts at noon on Sunday, so it should end around 3:00 p.m. Even with horrendous traffic, we should have enough time for a lovely evening. We can dine in the hotel and find a club if you want to go dancing afterwards. Or we can stay in the hotel and . . ." He glanced at Cecily and winked. "Talk. Don't worry, Cecily, the suite has two separate bedrooms."

"Oh, thank you, Clay! That sounds fabulous. I don't have to work on Monday, so we can sleep late."

Cecily cleared her throat before giving her mother what she liked to call her stink-eye. "But, all of that sounds romantic, to me. What if you forget about your promise?"

Allie came back with an adamant "I won't forget."

"But, how will I know?"

Allie smiled as she considered her daughter's question. "I guess you'll have to do what I do every time you walk out that door. You'll have to trust Clay and me to behave ourselves."

"Oh." Cecily thought about it for a moment and her eyes grew large, as though she were revisiting everything she'd ever done behind her parents' backs without getting caught. "Oh!" She blinked several times and blushed at her mother's perusal.

Allie exchanged an amused grin with Clay before facing her daughter again. "Things aren't so easy once you see it from our perspective, are they?"

"Mom, I believe I've just gained a new respect for parenting," Cecily groaned. "But . . ." She placed her hands on Allie's shoulders and sent her a meaningful gaze. "I know when it comes down to you having to choose between right and wrong, you'll do the right thing."

Kayla stepped forward to add her two cents. "That's right, Mom." She spared an innocent look for Clay. "And you too, Mr. Clay. We trust the two of you *completely*."

The girls gave each other fist bumps as they left the room laughing amongst themselves.

"Hmm," Clay growled.

"I know. Did they turn that back on us, or what?"

"They did, but it doesn't matter. I'll be strong enough for both of us."

She kissed him. "What if I'm begging you to take me in front of the fireplace?"

He kissed her back. "I'll be stronger than that, for you . . . and your girls."

Neither of them had any idea how badly those words would come back to haunt them. The Saints game had been a close one, with the home team coming back in the last quarter to beat the Jags by ten points. Riding on the wings of a hard-fought victory, they were in high spirits upon their arrival at the hotel.

The Art Deco suite proved to be everything they thought it would be. Furnished with gorgeous period furniture and artwork paying tribute to the Roaring Twenties era, it had two luxurious bedrooms, and two marbled, private baths.

Up to her neck in a deep, claw foot tub filled with hot water and silky bubbles, Allie resisted the urge to pick up her phone and call Clay over to lather her back. As though he'd read her mind, he knocked on her door.

"Allie, the concierge brought us extra towels. Do you need some in there?"

She saw a couple folded on the rack. "Not at this moment."

"Do you need anything else?"

She bit her lower lip to keep from calling out to him.

"Allie?"

"Hmm?"

"Do you need anything?"

She took a deep breath and held it.

"Allie . . ."

She released her breath with a puff. "I-It'd be wonderful to have someone wash my back for me." Silence greeted her. She'd decided he'd already left when she heard the squeak of the handle turning.

"I don't think the concierge offers that service."

Her heart pounded like a jackhammer in her chest. "Would you do it for me?"

He cracked the door open. "Are you sure?"

She smiled, touched by his concern. "Yes."

The door opened and he stepped inside, bare-chested but still wearing his jeans. "You want me to put on my shirt?"

She soaked in the sight of him. Sweet Jesus, he looked good with no shirt. Well-defined pecs and the hint of six-pack abs had her stomach clenching. Somebody had been working out. Bruce had developed a paunch at twenty-seven and kept it, added more to its girth every year or two. "Don't you dare. It's only fair you should be as exposed as I am."

"Fair enough." He stood over her, his brow furrowed.

"What's wrong?"

"All I see are bubbles, dammit."

She blew some of the foamy suds away from her mouth. "You didn't think I'd let you in here any other way, did you?"

His mouth twisted in a grin as he rested his hands on his hips. "Hell's bells, you're up to your neck in suds, aren't you? I'm not sure I can even get to your back."

She chuckled and sat up, but not enough to give him a clear view of anything up front.

"Geeze, those things cling to you like a second skin." He clucked his tongue and grabbed a washcloth. "Which soap do you want me to use?"

She jutted her chin toward the metal rack across one end of the tub. "That bath bar smells fabulous."

Clay dipped the cloth into the water near her feet and grabbed the unwrapped complimentary bar of soap. He rubbed it on the cloth, working it up into a rich lather before returning the soap to the rack. He started with gentle circular motions on her shoulders, gradually working his way down her back.

Allie released a long sigh, luxuriating in the feel of his hand on her bare skin. As it dipped lower, she closed her eyes and let her head fall back. Clay's hand paused then trailed up her spine to the back of her neck. At some point, his bare hand replaced the washcloth. Fingers of his opposite hand lifted her chin a moment before he covered her mouth with a tender kiss.

She longed to touch him, but didn't dare. If she did, she wouldn't stop until he was in the tub with her, and that could only lead to one thing. She tensed at the old familiar thought, suspected Clay sensed it when he pulled his mouth from hers, moved it to her ear.

"Don't you dare," he whispered, sending a fresh wave of shivers through her body. His left hand disappeared into the layer of bubbles, trailing down the front of her neck. It made a slow path to her right shoulder, then her left before dipping lower to her cleavage.

The hitch of her breath brought him to his senses. He tried to remove his hand but she covered it with her own, holding him in place. Everything indicated she was ripe for some experimentation and he was up for that. He lowered his mouth to hers for another kiss, another nibble to her lower lip. He dipped his hand lower to her breast, watching for any sign of hesitation on her part, and finding none.

She sucked in when he circled her nipple with the pad of his thumb, uttered a small gasp when he gave it a light pinch. He moved to the opposite breast and did the same. Allie groaned, pulled him close for another kiss, tugging hard on his tongue, and threading her fingers in his hair.

She broke off the kiss. "That feels so good," she responded with a raspy whisper.

He tugged at the back of her hair, baring her throat to his mouth and drew another gasp from her. "Allie."

All she could manage was "Hmm?" between clamped lips.

He smiled. Having her too worked up to speak was a good sign. His hand made a slow trail down her belly, and past it. "If it's all right with you, I'd like to clear up that little frigidity issue once and for all."

Hiding behind a sheath of bubbles, she answered with a distracted "Mm . . . hmm . . ."

Within minutes he had her panting, reaching, straining for release. He found the sweet spot and she shattered, alternating between crying out and gasping for air. He worked her into a slow descent until she landed with a soft sigh.

Her face flushed a becoming shade of rose, and she opened her sleepy green eyes to gaze at him. "I have never, ever felt anything like that before," she whispered.

"Uh huh. I suspected as much. There's not a thing wrong with you, hon. It's always been operator error on your ex's part." He grinned. "Just so you know. I love being right about something like this." He gave her one last kiss. "We have reservations in the Crystal Room at 6:00 p.m. Think you'll be ready?"

She nodded her head drowsily. "I'll be ready."

Clay stood at the window, sipping on a whiskey and cola, with easy-listening music pouring from the television speakers. When the door to her bedroom opened, he checked his watch and turned, about to comment that it was still early.

The sight of her astounded him, stealing any meaningless message he'd been about to deliver. Dressed in a long sleeved, lace overlay version of the little black dress women always talked about, Allie glowed. Her Christmas gifts sparkled at her neckline and earlobes.

He swallowed, trying to bring moisture to the mouth that had gone dry. *Say something, idiot!*

"Damn . . ."

She gave him a shy smile, ran her hands down her sides, and then clasped them together. "Is that a good damn, or a bad one?"

He blinked and managed to close his gaping mouth. "I can't believe you'd even ask. You are stunning."

Her smile said she approved. "I'm glad you like it." She touched the diamonds that sparkled at her throat and earlobes. "They look good with it, don't they?"

He nodded. "They do."

"You've got good taste in jewelry."

"Well, it had to be something special; it was for you, after all." He downed the rest of his drink from the highball glass and approached her.

Allie held her breath as he approached with slow, deliberate steps. She released it when he stopped in front of her. Clay leaned in close and kissed her, his breath sweet with the taste of whiskey and cola. She barely resisted the urge to whimper, fought the compulsion to follow him when he pulled away from her.

Dabbing the corner of her mouth with her pinkie, she gave him an appreciative head to toe perusal. Sweet baby jeezus, the man looked scrumptious in a formal black suit. He accessorized with a crisp white shirt, and a gray and red silk tie. "Where's the GQ model?"

"Who?"

"The one whose suit you stole." She stopped to swallow. "You do it justice, Clay."

"I'm glad you approve." He adjusted his tie. "I had the suit already, but I bought a new tie for the occasion."

She reached out to pat the tie. "I like it—festive but classy."

He offered her his arm. "It's early, but you look too damn good and it's only fair to share some of that beauty with others. How about we go down to the lounge until they call us for our dinner reservation?"

She looped one hand and wrist around his muscled bicep, loving the feel of it. "Sounds like fun."

Allie drank in the sights of the entire hotel, luxuriously decked out for Christmas. Every step of the grand marble stairway held a pot of bright red poinsettias. Rich garlands of greenery draped every inch of the decorative scrolled iron bannisters. Everywhere she looked, she saw a decked-out Christmas tree or some other opulent decoration.

She inhaled the scent of fresh greenery. "I still can't believe you got a room here on such short notice."

"Pure luck. Someone had booked the suite and called a few minutes before I did to shorten their length of stay by one night. Being that we only needed it for one day, and I've stayed here several times before, they gave me the suite."

They found seats at the bar, staring at their own reflections in a huge mirror set inside an elaborate and massive backdrop of ornate wood, polished to a rich gloss. The time flew by as they listened to ghost stories from the bartender on duty. Before they knew it, the dining room called them for their dinner reservations. Clay had been bragging about their steaks, but Allie had to try a seafood pasta dish. It turned out to be every bit as good as it sounded. When their server asked about dessert, she had to pass.

"It's just as well," Clay admitted. "This way you'll have room for the PB & J social at 10:00 p.m. It's a great way to mingle with the other hotel patrons."

They left the Crystal Room, entered the elevator hand in hand. "Maybe we can take our hot cocoa from the social up to the roof; sit by the rooftop pool and look out at the view of the city." He smiled at her. "If you get cold, I'll be there to keep you warm."

She returned the smile but kept her silence, imagining all the ways he could accomplish that.

Back in their suite, she pulled up an extensive playlist from her phone with her favorite songs from the 80s until now, both contemporary and country. It didn't take long to discover they shared the same taste in music.

Clay offered his hand to her. She took it without question, letting him pull her close, one hand tucked into his chest. In seconds, he'd proven his worth as a dance partner. Why wouldn't he be as fabulous at that as everything else? They danced to the mix of ballads . . . "Angel Eyes", "One on One", and "Hello" by Lionel Ritchie. Allie braced herself when Kenny Chesney started crooning "You Save Me", one of her favorites.

"Mm . . . good song," Clay murmured, as it faded away. "I heard one yesterday that made me think of you. Do you mind if I find it?" He tugged at his collar. "Besides, I need a breather after that one."

Allie closed her eyes, sipping from a bottle of cold water as he searched his own phone. Within a minute, he found his choice. She released a groan as Little Big Town began harmonizing to "Bring it on Home to Me". "I guess we'll find out if we had a long enough breather." She cocked her head at Clay. "Can we can handle this?"

The corners of his mouth turned up in a provocative smirk. "You leave that to me, pretty lady."

They made it through the selection with minor damage, stopped to freshen their drinks during Foreigner's "I Want to Know What Love Is", thank goodness. She melted in Clay's arms as he proved he could country waltz to "Drift off to Dream" by Travis Tritt.

By the time The Cars started singing "Drive" Allie could barely resist pulling him to the sofa in their shared parlor area. She somehow resisted through "He Plays Piano in the Dark", but by the middle of Chris Isaak's "Wicked Game" he'd pulled her dangerously close. The end of the song had them both sinking, weak-kneed, to the couch. Hands everywhere, his lips hot on her skin, he finally pulled away from her, and Allie took a shaky breath.

He spoke in a voice thick with need. "This won't work, hon." He got to his feet, pulling her along with him. "We'd better stick to dancing."

They tried again, were strong through Faith Hill's "Breathe" and even Heart's "All I Wanna Do is Make Love to You". "You Shouldn't Kiss Me Like This" by Toby Keith produced a series of shivers but she stayed strong. Halfway through Ed Sheeran's soulful rendition of "Thinking Out Loud" she latched on to Clay's jacket lapels, on the cusp of tearing it and every shred of clothing from his body.

He grabbed her hands and stepped away from her. "Good grief, lady. How serious were you about keeping that promise to your girls?"

She fanned her heated face with both hands. "When I made it I was extremely serious. Now, I'm wishing I'd kept my big mouth shut. But . . ." she sent him a lust-filled gaze. "I told her I couldn't promise I wouldn't have sex if it came down to that . . . only that I'd try not to."

"Well," he groaned. "That puts a different spin on things, doesn't it?"

"I'm sorry. At the time I didn't think, I mean, I didn't know . . ." Memories of the earth-shattering orgasm she'd experienced at this man's hands had her wondering . . . no . . . had her wanting to know what other pleasures he could introduce to her. "Honestly, Clay, I'm ready for . . . more."

His perusal of her lasted longer than expected. Finally, he took a deep breath and released it. "I'll probably hate myself for this later, but I think we should wait." He gave her a sympathetic smile and a quick kiss. "I promise I'll make it up to you, but for now, grab your coat. We need to get out of this room until it's time to go to bed . . . I mean . . . time to go to sleep."

He escorted her to the rooftop to examine the pool and hot tub, along with the spectacular nighttime view of the city. By the time they descended from the roof just after 10:00 p.m., the wind-chill factor, somewhere in the mid-thirties, had cooled their internal thermostats to somewhere around the normal level.

They approached the designated area for the P B & J social to find it already in full swing. Conversations with other attendees revealed they were one of few couples from Louisiana. The majority lived in different parts of the country, with one couple from Brazil and another from Ireland.

All were as awed at the hotel's beauty, accommodations, and service as they were.

Allie passed on the sandwich, opting instead for a cup of delicious hot cocoa full of marshmallows.

"Mm, I can't remember a time when I didn't love marshmallows in cocoa." She flicked her tongue around the edges of her lips.

Clay reached out to wipe a spot of melted mallow from the corner of her mouth, stopped, and kissed her instead, using the opportunity to lick the sweetness away.

"You're not helping." She attempted to control the hitch in her breathing.

He grinned. "Sorry, I couldn't resist."

"A likely story."

"Listen, how about if one of us goes back to the room first?"

She nodded, unable to argue with the wisdom of that idea. "You go on ahead, Clay. I'll stay here for another half-hour or so."

He looked skeptical. "Please don't venture off on your own anywhere. I'm sure the hotel's safe, but you never know. I'll worry until you're back inside the room."

Allie missed his touch, his smell, his presence beside her once he left. She threw herself into conversing with everyone she met at the social, even exchanged email addresses with a few women—anything to keep from going back to that sweet agony of temptation.

By the time she made it back, Clay had already closed himself up in his room. Seconds after she came in she saw the sliver of light disappear from under his doorway, proof he'd waited up for her. She smiled, certain that Bruce would have been snoring the minute his butt hit the mattress. But then, Clay was light years ahead of her ex in the areas of consideration and emotional support . . . and if the tub incident was any indication . . . in satisfying a woman's needs.

She shivered at the memory and stood in the middle of the room. Was it so wrong to want more of that delicious feeling? It pulled at her middle, the sweet ache, the need to go to him. She slipped out of her heels and tiptoed to Clay's closed bedroom door. Ready to knock, she raised her fist before remembering that damnable promise.

I said I'd try.

Yeah. Would she accept that excuse from one of her daughters if they went against her wishes? She flattened her hand on the door and rested her forehead against it. She may have to, but she sure as hell wouldn't like it, and the trust factor would be non-existent.

I'll be stronger than that . . . for you and your girls.

Those words . . . that promise . . . they meant something to Clay. She knew if she walked in there he wouldn't refuse her, but he'd regret not being stronger. She couldn't do that to him.

Dammit!

She backed away from the door and returned to her room, one thought running through her mind.

This will-power stuff would take some effort. For sure, now that he'd blown the notion of her sexual need being *inadequate,* clear out of the water.

She went to her bathroom, washed the make-up from her face, and readied herself for bed. She climbed into bed, and reached for her phone to check an incoming text message.

Allie?

She smiled and sent: *I'm here. But I came so close to being there . . . with you.*

Within seconds, her phone rang. She swiped the screen but kept her silence.

"How close?"

"Too damn close."

"Good things come to those who wait, baby. I promise I'll make it up to you."

"I have no doubts."

"Did you meet any interesting people after I left?"

"Nobody new showed up, but I spoke to the couple from Ireland. We exchanged contact information. They want us to visit, as if that's possible."

"It's not out of the question. My passport is current, is yours?"

"I don't have a passport. I've never been out of the country."

"You might want to get one. I was in Ireland for a couple of weeks for some training, but didn't get much sight-seeing in. I'd love to go back."

She bit her lip to keep from saying anything.

"I just wanted to thank you for the game tickets and for accompanying me. This was the best Christmas gift ever."

"I only bought the tickets. You did the rest."

"Yes, but you made it all possible."

"Thank you for making this entire evening so special for me, Clay. This is a memory I'll cherish."

"I plan to fill your life with special memories."

"I don't know what to say to that."

"Say goodnight, Allie."

She grinned, knowing she was about to put a smile on his face. "Goodnight, Allie."

"Sassy pants."

"Smartass."

"Goodnight Allie."

"Goodnight Clay."

Chapter Eleven

New Year's Eve

She stared out over the glasslike surface of Lake Erin, wondering at the mysterious workings of the universe. If anyone had told the Allie of one year ago that she'd be in a brand new relationship with a wonderful man today, she wouldn't have believed it. She let her head fall back against Clay's warmth, rejoicing in the feel of his arms around her. She gasped at the fabulous display of fireworks shot from a boat a half-mile from the shoreline.

Cynthia spoke from beside her. "I'd forgotten how much I enjoyed growing up in a town with events that took place around a lake."

Allie nodded. "I know. I only live eleven miles up the highway, but it's been years since I've been to the Christmas boat parade or the New Year's Eve fireworks show over Lake Erin. It's breathtaking, isn't it?"

"It is, but it doesn't hold a candle to you." Clay's compliment, spoken in a seductive whisper near Allie's ear, sent shivers down her spine.

She closed her eyes and smiled. "Thank you."

"You're welcome." He placed a gentle kiss on her temple. "Would you like a mug of hot cocoa?"

"That would be lovely, but I can get it myself."

"You stay here and visit with your sister. I'll get it for you."

John Michael and Clay headed for the vendor, leaving Allie and Cynthia alone on the boardwalk. Cynthia's laughter worked as a rude interruption to Allie staring after Clay.

"Whatcha looking at little sister?"

"A fine looking man, that's what."

"How was the little getaway to New Orleans?"

"Fabulous! The Saints won, and Le Pavillon Hotel was everything I expected." She spent several minutes describing their accommodations and the people they'd met on the trip.

"Separate rooms?"

"We had one suite with two bedrooms, two baths, and a shared parlor . . . all of it luxurious and gorgeous. I'll never forget it."

"Oh?" Cynthia's brow rose curiously. "Did something *special* happen there?"

Allie pursed her lips and contemplated how to respond to her sister's nosiness. "Let's just say it cleared up some misconceptions I'd had about myself for years." She looked down her nose at her sister. "And that's *all* I'm going to say about that."

"Did the two of you have sex?"

"What did I just tell you?"

"Come on, Al!" Cynthia pleaded. "I'm dying."

"No, we didn't."

"Oh . . ."

Allie faced her sister. "But I wanted to so bad, so at least I know I'm normal."

"Of course you are." Cynthia grabbed Allie's hands and squealed. "I'm so happy for you, Sis."

"You know what? I'm happy for me too, Cyn." She nudged her sister. "So, how goes it in the world of the newlyweds?"

"It's wonderful. I'm crazy in love with my husband in case I haven't told you already."

"Yeah, you have, and even if you hadn't, it's obvious." She looked past her sister to the two men approaching. "They're coming back with our cocoa."

Cynthia glanced at her husband and Clay then back at her sister. "Speaking of obvious, I detect love floating in the air between you two. If no one's said it yet, it's only a matter of time, so I hope you're ready."

Allie beamed at the smile her man sent her way but kept her secret to herself. She figured if anyone deserved to hear it first, it was Clay, and boy was she ready to give him an earful.

Clay parked his truck in Allie's driveway and took off his seatbelt. The second she was free from hers he leaned over the console to capture her soft lips in a single kiss that turned into much more. He finally managed to pull his mouth away and rested his forehead against hers. His truck had been sitting in her driveway for five minutes by then and he hadn't been able to let go of her yet. "Are the girls home?"

She laughed. "Are you kidding? They'd be banging on the truck doors by now if they were." She stroked the side of his face with delicate fingers. "Would you like to come inside and ring in the New Year with me?"

"I thought you'd never ask."

They met in front of his truck and walked arm-in-arm into her house. He used her bathroom break to start two logs burning in the fireplace.

"Perfect," she murmured, with an appreciative glance at the flames licking at the log. "How about a drink? I have something special for our first New Year's Eve."

He nodded. That seemed fitting since he was planning something special for tonight.

She pulled out a bottle of champagne she'd had chilling and two crystal flutes. "How long do we have?"

Clay looked at his watch. "We've got a couple of minutes. You want me to open that for you?"

She handed him the bottle and a dishtowel and then turned her television station to a local channel showing the New Year's Eve countdown. She lowered the volume and turned at the quiet *pop* of cork leaving the bottle. "No foam—excellent job, mister."

He shrugged. "It's all a matter of getting the bottle at that perfect forty-five degree angle; well, that and working the cork off slowly." He filled one glass and handed it to her, then filled a second for himself. They touched their glasses together with a *clink*.

"To us."

She nodded. "To us."

Clay couldn't take his eyes off of her lips as they curved around the rim of the glass. He sipped from his own, the bubbles tickling his nose, and then lowered his head for a kiss. He tasted it on her lips, her breath, the sweet mix of alcohol and Allie, a tempting combination.

She pulled away and caught her breath. "It's not midnight yet."

He smiled and touched his nose to hers. "We'll do it again tomorrow morning."

She returned the smile, her eyes sparkling with laughter. "It shouldn't be long, now." She turned to face the sixty-inch, wall-hung flat screen and laughed. "Here we go."

They watched together as the ball dropped, counting out the last few seconds of the old year. Fireworks lit up the screen and Clay pulled Allie in his arms. "Happy New Year, Allie, and I love you." Her smile melted his heart.

"I love you, Clay, and Happy New Year to you, also."

He lowered his mouth to hers, wanting to savor the moment. "You love me?" he whispered, brushing his lips lightly against hers.

"I do love you." She barely managed to get it all out before he covered her mouth completely. Their tongues melded in a sweet dance, vying for domination, his hands cupped her face while his fingers threaded through her hair.

The buzz and hum of her low, sensual moan had him wanting to lay her down on the couch, or better yet, carry her to the bedroom and make love to her all night long. God help him if she said those words to him tonight—

She pulled her mouth from his. "I want you, Clay."

Her admission shocked him into awareness. "Wh-what?"

She slipped one arm around his neck, cupping the back of his head while the other circled his hips to pull him hard against her. "I want you. I want us to make love tonight."

He took a moment to adjust to this new side of Allie. Unhindered by low self-esteem, untethered by insecurities about her body or her fear of poor sexual performance—*this* lady was ready to explore the new world he'd recently opened to her . . . and there wasn't a damn thing he could do about it. Not if either of them wanted to uphold their ends of the bargain.

He placed his hands on her shoulders and backed off a step. "I can't. God knows I want to, Allie, but I don't want to be the man to disappoint your daughters."

"I'm the one who'd be disappointing them. I only want one chance to see what I've been missing."

His chuckle surrounded them. "Once wouldn't be enough, baby. I can promise you that." He shook his head. "No. I made my own promise and I wouldn't be able to look them in the eye. I'm sorry."

She grabbed her hair in frustration. "You're right, but boy do I want to eat my words."

He pulled her close for a hug. "I know, but all of this is a sign of good things to come."

She stepped away from him. "I hope I don't disappoint you."

"No more of that. I mean it." He linked his fingers through hers and lifted her hand for closer examination.

"I hear you. What's up, buttercup?" She pulled her hand away.

"I'm trying to figure out your ring size. What are you, a five or six?"

She frowned. "Why?"

"So I can surprise you with an engagement ring one day."

She burst into laughter. "That surprise thing is kind of blown already, don't you think?"

"Nah. You'll never see it coming. I just hate the idea of having to take a ring back for resizing. Once I give it to you I won't want it to leave that finger."

"You want to marry me just so we can have sex?"

"I want to marry you because I love you and I know what I want." He shrugged. "But I'll wait, because I know you think it's too soon."

"Thank you for wanting to marry me, and for waiting, and for always finding a way to make me feel special."

"So . . ." He lifted her ring finger.

Allie gave him a luminous smile. "Five-and-a-half."

"Excellent." Clay kissed her finger then moved on to bigger and better things. He lifted her chin, gave her lower lip a gentle nip, determined to get this lady to the altar sooner, rather than later.

Chapter Twelve

Saturday, January 2nd

Clay folded the last towel and placed the stack in his bathroom before answering his phone.

"Daddy, can you talk?"

Clay checked his watch. "Sure, I can't pick Allie up for another half-hour, anyway. What's the problem, Sweet Pea?"

"It's Margie."

He stiffened. His daughter calling her mother Margie instead of Mom wasn't a good sign. "Okay. What's up? Did you get her settled in her place?"

"Yes, but it's every bit as bad as I thought it would be. I can only come in on weekends, and Brian has his hands full with work and Sean. Margie's insurance won't pay for the around-the-clock care she needs, but neither Brian nor I can afford to pay anyone to stay with her. I don't know what to do."

He wanted to tell her that none of this was his problem, but as a father, he couldn't walk away from his kids without offering some kind of assistance. "Is there anything I can do to help?"

"Other than taking care of her when Brian and I can't, I don't know what the heck you can do, Daddy."

"Surely, we can come up with some other solution."

"As soon as you figure something out, I'm all ears."

"What does she have in the way of savings?"

"Not much, from what I gather. She left her retirement alone when she left the U.S., but she can't touch that, of course. She resigned her teaching position in Paris when she came home so she has no salary to draw. God only knows when or even if she'll be able to go back to teaching, considering her frame of mind." She sucked in her breath and released it. "Whatever we do, it will only be for a couple of weeks. She won't be fully recuperated by then, but she'll be able to get around on her own."

"Listen, I'll pay for someone to watch her when you and Brian can't."

"Daddy, that's too much to ask of you, considering . . . considering the way she walked out on you."

"Baby girl, I'd do anything to make things easier on you and Brian."

"You should know she's delusional when it comes to you."

"Yeah, that's the way I see it, too."

"I'm positive she'll take anything you do to help her and blow it completely out of proportion."

"That doesn't matter to me if it's helping you and Brian."

"She *will* twist it around and say you're doing it because you still love her, Daddy. Now, I don't know how serious this thing with you and Allie is—"

"It's serious."

"Well, that's awesome, but aren't you worried Allie may misunderstand your offer to help?"

Clay pictured the woman he loved, and it brought a smile to his face. "Allie is generous and kind enough to understand, but I will talk to her first if it'll make you feel better."

"It would, but I still don't like it. I just don't want Margie doing anything that could come between you and Allie. She's a wonderful lady."

"You don't know how happy I am to hear you say that." Clay picked up the small box from his counter and flipped the lid to stare at the diamond solitaire he'd purchased that morning. Somehow, it didn't surprise him when it happened to be a perfect size five and a half. Just more proof that he and Allie were meant to be together.

"Are you *sure* this is okay with you? It's important you understand why I'm doing this."

Of course, she understood. How could he worry that she wouldn't? Clay was trying to make it easier on Brian and Terri. If he could afford to pay for a caretaker, why wouldn't he?

"Do you still have feelings for your ex-wife?"

His mouth twisted in a sardonic grin. "I have feelings for her, all right. None she'd find flattering, I can assure you. Besides, it's not like I'll even be around her all that much. Terri asked me to help her out today and tomorrow until the sitter comes tomorrow evening, but that's it."

Allie placed one fist on her hip and gave the shears in her other hand a couple of snaps. "Then why would I have a problem with it?"

He smiled and leaned in to place a chaste kiss upon her lips. "Exactly what I thought you'd say." He looked at his watch. "I've got to go meet with the sitters and Terri to coordinate times and salaries."

Allie rolled her lips inward and bit down hard to keep from asking why he had to be involved in that part of it. On the other hand, if she were the one footing the caretaking bill, she would do the same.

"I'll come by later, if it's all right."

She smiled. "I'll be waiting." She stood at the large window of her shop, watching as he walked to his truck.

"That's one fine-looking man you've got yourself, honey."

Allie turned away from the window, faced the client waiting for her in the chair. "Yes ma'am, he sure is, isn't he, Ms. Barb?"

"That's what I just said." The eighty-year-old woman, who came in twice a month for a wash, trim, set, and style on her snow-white locks pursed her lips. "Not that I was listening, Allie, but did I hear him say something about caring for an ex-wife?"

Allie choked back the laugh at her nosy customer's comment. *Not that she was listening?* The woman had leaned so far over in her seat trying to listen she'd nearly fallen out of the chair.

"She was critically injured in a car accident. He wants to help his kids out by paying someone to watch her."

"Oh . . . Well, it's not the footing the bill part that's worrisome. It's the helping his daughter take care of her mother for a while. That means getting her to the bathroom, and in and out of bed. Is he going to bathe her too, for goodness sakes? Aren't you worried?"

Allie kept her mouth shut. She hadn't been worried . . . until now. She pulled the rollers out of Ms. Barb's hair and gave it a quick style to get the woman out of her shop. Let her find someone else's day to ruin.

She drove home, every emotion from fear to loathing running through her mind. She picked up her phone, ready to demand that Clay not have a thing to do with that woman's healthcare, other than pay for it. She ended the call before it rang and threw her phone back into her purse. Either she trusted the man, or she didn't, and so far, he hadn't given her one reason not to trust him. She'd sit on her feelings for now. If she still had doubts, she'd wait and speak face to face with him when he came over later.

A noble intention, only he didn't come over later. He also didn't call until a few minutes past 9:00 p.m.

"Hey babe, I'm so sorry. The sitter who was supposed to start right away had a family emergency and had to pass. We're trying to find someone else, but the other woman can't start until Monday morning. Brian's working twelve hour days right now, but he and Sean will stay there at night to help. Terri will be there until she drives home tomorrow evening. After four years of taking care of Hope, I was able to show Terri how to clean and change the bandage on Margie's incision, and how to get her to the bathroom."

His statement had old insecurities rising to the top of Allie's food chain of inadequacies. She swallowed the lump in her throat. "The bathroom?"

"Well, yeah. She's got a broken leg and five broken ribs, remember? It's impossible for her to get around on her own. She can't use crutches until the ribs heal."

"Dad had one of those potty-chairs by his bed. Wouldn't that be easier?"

"She'd prefer to go to the bathroom. And truthfully? We've all emptied one of those pots more times than we can count for Hope. None of us *want* to do that for Margie." His deep sigh carried to her over the phone. "What's awful is that I can't produce an iota of sympathy for the woman. As a matter of fact, and I may burn in hell for this, but it kind of makes me happy to see her hurting."

"Clay . . ."

"I know, I just said it was awful, I can't help myself. Part of me thinks this is karma. I think of all the pain Hope endured and how her mother barely lifted a finger to help. It's only fitting she should suffer."

Allie bit down on her lip, trying not to agree with him, or let him know how thrilled she was with his take on the situation. Not that she wished her ill.

She remembered the feel of cold, wet gelatin salad being dumped in her lap, the sight of Margie naked in Clay's bathroom, and the nasty text she'd received from the woman, and couldn't stop a low snort from escaping. Who the hell was she kidding? Yes. She did. She wished all kinds of ill on the nasty-tempered, uppity, skinny itch-bay. "So, are you on your way?"

"I'm kind of beat, hon. Is there any chance you could come over to meet me? I could use a quiet evening under the stars. I'll make you s'mores and hot cocoa."

"As tempting as that sounds, I can't. Kayla's got a friend over tonight and I have to be here to make sure Cecily's date brings her home by midnight."

"Oh . . ." His voice sounded heavy with disappointment. "I'll be there in a few minutes, then."

"No, Clay. Stay home and get some rest. We'll have plenty of time to see each other when you get that second sitter hired."

"Okay, babe. Thanks, and I owe you one. I love you, Allie."

"I love you, too, sweetie. Now get some rest." She ended the call, pushed back the uneasiness settling in her chest. He couldn't stand the woman. No worries, right?

Even after Cecily made it home from her date, Allie lay in bed trying to convince herself she had no reason to worry. She fluffed her pillow for the third time that night, telling herself not to be paranoid.

Why couldn't she get rid of this queasy feeling in her stomach?

"Stop being ridiculous, Allie," she scolded herself. "This is only a day or two at the most, just until he finds a second sitter."

She left him alone Sunday. That evening he called, telling her the other sitter had decided to take a long-term job another client had offered. Brian had gone by for a short while but a rambunctious child proved too much for the patient, so Clay had sent them home. She bit back her "beggars can't be choosers" comment, told him she understood he was stuck there for the time being, to take his time, and not worry about her. She didn't call him Monday, surmising he already had more than he could handle. On Tuesday, the 5th, she broke down and called his cell phone.

"Hello?" The dulcet tones of Margie's voice greeted her, about as welcome as an IRS tax audit.

"Margie?"

"Yes, it is. Who's this? Sorry, but it's my husband's phone and all it shows is a number, but no contact name."

Her husband's phone? "I'd like to speak to Clay, please."

"My husband is running an errand for me. Can I take a message?"

She couldn't resist. "You know who this is, Margie, and don't you mean your ex-husband?"

"Old habits," she purred. "Besides, it feels like it did when we were first married. The darling takes such fabulous care of me."

"Tell him I called."

"Of *course* I will."

I'll bet.

"What's your name again . . . Elsie, isn't it?"

"Allie."

"Oh—right. Elsie's that *other* cow."

Allie heard the sound of light laughter until the line went dead. "Bitch!"

Clay walked into the living room. "Was that my phone I heard ringing?"

Margie lifted her head from the couch, shielding her eyes from the light. "I didn't hear any phone ringing. It must have been the television in your room."

"Another migraine?" He picked up his cell to check it. No missed calls or messages from Allie. He was tempted to call her but she was busy at work, no doubt. Damn, he missed her sweet voice.

"A bad one, but that nap helped. They should have ended by now. I hope nothing's wrong."

"The doctor said migraines are a side effect of head trauma for at least two weeks," he reminded her. "You need to give yourself some time to heal."

"Yes, but I feel guilty as hell for keeping you here. You've got the sweetest woman in the world waiting for you."

"She'll be waiting when you're on your feet again. Or we can manage to snag a nurse, whatever comes first."

She tried to sit up on her own, winced as pain cut her breath.

He hurried over to her and helped her to sit. "I keep telling you not to try that by yourself. I'm here to help."

"But I need to do things on my own. I can't have you waiting on me like this. I can't believe it's this difficult to find a sitter for someone like me in a city the size of Lake Coburn."

"I guess it's the short-term job prospect causing the problem. They don't want to pass up a position that will be there for a longer period of time. They're looking at it from a job security point of view."

"If I haven't told you how much I appreciate this, I do, Clay. I just hope it doesn't cause problems between you and Elsi—uh—Allie."

"No problem. She knows how much I love her."

"Y-you're already to that stage in your relationship?"

Maybe it was his imagination but she seemed to pale. "I am. I shouldn't be talking to you about this. It's—callous, in your condition."

"No. Not at all. I'm hoping we can at least be friends, if nothing else. It may make it easier for Brian, Terri, and the grandkids in the future."

"We'll see, Marg." He set his phone on the snack bar and shoved his hands in his pockets. "I bought her a ring already, you know. I'd planned to ask her to marry me this weekend."

Her breath caught and she winced but worked through it. "I ruined your plans. I'm so sorry."

"It'll wait. I just hope she likes the ring."

"Oh, can I see it? I'll tell you if you spent enough on her."

He frowned. "She's not like that. She wouldn't dare ask for a larger diamond."

"That's exactly why I should give it the all clear. Next time you go to your camper, bring it so I can give you a woman's honest opinion."

"It's in my truck."

Her eyes grew round and large. "What if someone breaks into your truck and steals it? You need to get that someplace safe."

He rubbed his hand on the back of his neck. "I guess you're right." It only took him a minute to step into the garage to get the ring from the glove compartment. He walked back inside with it. Just the act of opening the box put a big smile on his face. When she held her hand out for it, he flipped it around so she could see the ring. Clay stayed far enough away so that she couldn't touch it.

"Oh, it's lovely! Could I try it on, please?"

Clay snapped the box closed. "Hell, no. Nobody's touching this ring but Allie." He ignored her pout, wishing he hadn't said a damned thing to her. Allie should have been the first to see that ring, not Margie. He was slipping, dammit—most likely from lack of sleep. It seemed like just when he got to sleep, he had to get up and wait on Marg for one thing or another. He slipped the box in the pocket of his jeans. "What do you want for supper? I know your next words will be you're not hungry, but that's too bad. You need to eat something."

Her brow creased in a concentrated frown. "Is that pizza place on the corner of Edgar and Bryan Street still opened? What was it, Dori and Dave's or something like that?"

"I think it is. You want the vegetarian one, I guess."

"Aw, you remembered," she crooned.

He ignored her again, thinking there wasn't much he didn't remember about her, both good and bad. Clay hoped she realized that no matter how civil they became as friends, hell would friggin' freeze over before he came close to forgetting all the bad.

Friday, January 8th

Allie kept telling herself to be patient with the situation. Inwardly, she was furious enough to spit nails. Not only that, but Clay hadn't returned any of her calls. She knew he was busy; she shouldn't be angry at him. It didn't stop her from being angry at herself. "Take your time . . . don't worry about me," she grumbled. "One of these days I'll learn to keep my big, fat mouth shut!"

Had she known he'd interpret her blessing into "I won't call you again until this situation is resolved," she may have re-thought her words. She'd called him several times during the week, left several messages for him, none of which he'd returned. Finally he called. She'd just finished with her two o'clock appointment, the last of the day.

"Hey, Al. Got a minute to talk?"

"Do I have a minute? Sure, why not? I've got all the time in the world."

Icy silence punctuated the next few seconds of air space. "Did something happen?"

"Why don't you tell me? You must be balls deep in all kinds of busy since you haven't seen fit to answer any of the messages I've left you all week."

"Messages? I didn't get any messages. I misplaced my phone for a couple of days. But when I found it, I checked and didn't see any messages or missed calls."

"I left six or seven voice mail messages. Wait, you *misplaced* your phone?"

"Yep, tore this house apart looking for it. Finally found the damn thing on top of the refrigerator. I don't remember putting it up there but I must have."

Allie sat forward. "Are you kidding me?"

"No, I'm not. I found it on top of the fridge."

"Oh, I understand that part. What I can't believe is that you don't know how it got there. How many people are in that house, Clay?"

"You know it's just been me and Margie since Tuesday."

"Well, then if you didn't put it up there, it must have been Margie."

"I doubt that. She can barely lift her arms to get out of her nightgown. No way in hell could she have gotten it up there."

She stared at the phone. *Get out of her nightgown?* "Did she tell you I called on Tuesday and she answered your cell?"

"No."

"She did. She told me her *husband* was running an errand for her then asked who I was because the only thing that showed up was the number."

"That's bullshit. I have your name programmed in my phone. When you call, your name and picture appear on my screen.

"I told her to tell you to call me. She called me Elsie, like that *other cow,* and yes, she actually said those words to me. You know, on the old milk advertisements."

"Allie, I don't know what to say. I didn't see any messages. I tell you what. Why don't you come over here and we'll straighten some things out. I'm sure it's just a misunderstanding."

"You *cannot* be serious."

"I am serious. I can't leave her alone, but you could come here. The address is 533 Hillcrest Lane. It's at the intersec—"

Allie ended the call, cutting him off midsentence. She fought the urge to throw her phone against the wall, but that was such a guy thing. The girls had already used up her allotment for phone replacements and she'd be stuck buying a new one, so . . . no. Five minutes later, her phone rang again. She answered it with a barely civil "What?"

"Allie, it's me."

Allie closed her eyes at Margie's simpering tone, clamping her jaw tight. If she resorted to name calling, she'd only lower herself to Margie's level.

"I'm sorry, Allie. Truly I am. Why don't you come over and we can talk. The address is 533 Hillcrest if you didn't get it before. We shouldn't leave this to fester. We need to get it all out in the open."

"I'll be there in thirty minutes." She hung up without a goodbye.

Clay held his breath as Margie tried to talk Allie into coming. She held the phone out and looked at it.

She turned her big brown eyes on him, looking like she wanted to cry. "Oh, she hung up on me. I'm sorry."

He released his breath. "What did she say?"

She shook her head. "She won't come. She-she said to tell you to go to . . . well, you know."

Clay rubbed the pain developing at his temple. "That doesn't sound like Allie."

"Clay, go to her. I'll be fine. Go. Spend the evening with her and don't come back until you've straightened this mess. Take my advice. Don't call her. Judging by her attitude, she'd run from you. Just drive straight over there."

He nodded. "Are you sure you'll be all right?"

She raised both hands and dropped them on the arms of her favorite chair. "I can manage until you get back. Just go."

He went to the door and took one last look at her. She made a pitiful patient; too thin, her hair clean, but unkempt, her face pale and make-up free, the bruising under her eyes and on her face still noticeable. "Are you sure you can manage?"

She smiled. "Hurry! Go and make her understand."

He nodded. "Thanks."

Allie found the address, checked the house number when she didn't see Clay's truck in the drive. "533 Hillcrest, this is the right place." She decided he must have parked it inside the garage. She walked to the front of the brick home, a lovely place, even though the flowerbeds and shrubbery showed some neglect.

She rang the doorbell and Margie called for her to enter. She opened the door. "Clay?"

"He's not here, Allie. It's just you and I. The way it should be . . . woman to woman."

She turned to face Margie, seated in an overstuffed chair looking like royalty. She'd styled and fluffed her short brown hair, applied make-up, and painted her lips a pale shade of pink. She wore a gorgeous gown and robe, a peignoir set cut dramatically low in the front. "You look passable for someone who needs twenty-four hour care."

Margie frowned. "Who told you that? I'm capable of getting around by myself. Clay's here because he wants to be here."

"Where is he?"

"He couldn't face you, Allie. He asked if I would be the one to tell you."

"Tell me what?"

"That he doesn't want you anymore."

Allie's gaze narrowed on the woman who sat there looking like she expected her to bow down at her feet. "I don't believe you."

"It's true. He and I are officially back together."

Allie froze as Margie extended her left hand, a beautiful diamond solitaire adorning her ring finger. She swallowed. "I don't believe it. That's not from Clay."

"He bought it yesterday, after he told me he wanted to try again." She lifted a slip of pink paper. "I have the invoice right here if you want to see it."

Allie approached her, took the receipt, and studied it. He'd bought it from a jewelry store in Lake Coburn, and the date showed January 7th, yesterday. "I don't believe you. He said he didn't get any of my messages. You erased them all, didn't you?"

"I did nothing of the sort. He got your messages, every one of them. He listened to them in front of me. I'm telling you, the man is a coward. He doesn't want to face you. He doesn't know how to tell you he's made his choice and that he's chosen me over you."

"I'll believe it when I hear it straight from him." She took a seat on the sofa, placed the receipt for the ring on the end table. "I'll sit right here and wait." She noticed the "tell" in Margie's demeanor, a slight flinch. She was good, judging from her quick recovery. She wanted to give that porcelain exterior coating its first chink, and knew just how to do it. "I know the truth, you know."

"What truth?"

"About Hope."

"What do you know about our daughter?"

"I know that she was your daughter. I know that her blood type was AB, yours is A, and Clay's is O. I know there is no possible way he could have been Hope's biological parent. So I *know* you're a lying, cheating adulteress as well as a manipulative bitch."

Margie's face turned two shades paler. "You don't know anything."

"I do, and Hope knew. That's why she didn't want to turn in that assignment. You know who else knows? Terri knows, and she despises you because of it."

Allie got some satisfaction out of the horrified look that passed over Margie's face. She shook her head. "You thought you were home safe, didn't you? You thought the only other person who knew your secret was dead and buried." Bitterness pulled at the edges of her mouth. "That must be a horrible feeling. Knowing the death of your child didn't accomplish the one thing you hoped it would."

Margie swallowed. "You're going to tell Clay, I suppose, even knowing what that will do to him."

"I would never tell him. That's the difference between you and me, Margie. I won't tell him because it would hurt him. You won't tell him because it would hurt you, and whatever plans you have. I can't see Terri ever telling him, either, but I will sit right here until that man gets back, I can promise you that."

Margie's right eyebrow twitched. "Suit yourself. Whether Clay is Hope's biological father or not is of no consequence. The fact is we did reconcile. I still love my husband, and he's recently discovered he still loves me."

"I still want to hear that from him."

"Fine, but I've thought about it, and I'd prefer if you'd wait in your own car."

Allie stood. "I think that would be preferable to being in here with you." She walked outside, heard the door lock immediately behind her.

Clay drove to Allie's shop first, and found it closed for the day. Then he drove to her house to find nobody home. He waited in his truck until Cecily and Kayla arrived from school. He got out of his truck and approached the girls.

"Do either of you know where your mom is?"

Cecily nodded. "Mom just called me. She said she's waiting for you at your ex-wife's house. She said she would wait there for you until the three of you talked."

He nodded, gave her a quick thank you and left. First thing tomorrow, he'd get Margie another damn cell phone to replace the one she'd lost in the wreck. He'd gotten into the habit of leaving his with her when he left, in case anything happened. The one time he desperately needed it he'd forgotten to grab the damn thing.

He made it to Lake Coburn in record time, found Allie outside Margie's and waiting for him.

"Hey. Why didn't you tell me you were coming?"

"I told Margie I'd be here in thirty minutes. Why didn't you wait for me?"

"She said you told me to go to hell and hung up."

"I did not. I hung up on her, right after I said I'd be here in thirty minutes." Allie's green eyes flashed, narrowing in unconcealed anger.

Clay walked her to the door. It didn't open when he turned the handle.

"Go away, Allie or I'll the police!" Margie cried out, her voice filled with terror.

"What the hell?" Allie faced Clay, wearing a puzzled expression.

"What's going on here?"

"I have no idea. We were talking and she's been trying to convince me that you two are reconciled. I said I'd wait until you got here and she asked me to wait outside. The second I walked out the door she locked it behind me."

Clay pulled his keys from his pocket. "It couldn't have been that quick. The woman can barely walk."

Allie frowned at him and looked as though she wanted to say more, but as soon as the door opened all hell broke loose.

Chapter Thirteen

"Thank God you're here, Clay. Keep that woman away from me. Please!"

"What the hell happened here?"

Allie looked from the bedraggled looking woman sitting in the chair to the mess on the floor. "I have no idea."

"She attacked me, Clay!"

"What?" Allie met Clay's accusing glare. "I most certainly did not. This woman is psycho."

"She may be psycho, but she's recuperating from a car accident. What the hell did you do?"

Allie studied the room. Chairs overturned, books thrown around, picture frames shattered on the floor, the place was a mess.

"Clay, none of this was here when I was in this room. She had to have done it all after I left. You have to believe me." She glared at Margie. "And she sure as hell didn't look like that! She wore a low-cut gown set and she was all made-up."

The woman had scrubbed every bit of make-up from her face, revealing the greenish-purple, but fading bruises around her cheekbones and eyes. Gone was the low-cut peignoir set. In its place was a plain gown, ripped at the front, her styled hair now wild and unbrushed. She looked more like Edward Rochester's crazy, locked-up wife, Bertha, in every version of *Jane Eyre* Allie had ever seen.

She shook her head. "You, woman, are either one foot over the brink of insanity, or you are one desperate, evil bitch. Which is it, Margie?"

"I'm insane? You're the one who attacked me! I can barely move without assistance." She pointed at the side of her face and her neck. "She scratched me, and she slapped me . . . several times." She turned the side of her face forward to show the red splotches.

Allie met the glare Clay leveled on her. "You don't believe this crap, do you?"

"I . . . I don't know what to believe, Al."

Allie stared at him, hurt to the core that he'd even consider believing this conniving, manipulative lunatic's story over hers. She pivoted on her toes and headed for the door, ignoring Clay's plea to wait.

"Let her go, Clay. She scares me."

Margie's pitiful whimper had Allie freezing in the doorway. She may never forgive Clay for believing this lunatic's story over hers, but she could damn sure keep her from getting the one thing she wanted—Clay. She spun around and stared at Margie's hand. "Where's the ring, Margie?"

Clay's head snapped to attention. "What ring?"

"The engagement ring she says you bought her. She said you bought it on the 7th after the two of you reconciled, and she even showed me the receipt."

Clay never took his eyes from Margie. "What did it look like, Al?"

"It's either a white gold, or platinum band, with a round solitaire. You bought it from Clement's Jewelers here in Lake Coburn."

Clay pulled his wallet from his back pocket, opened it, and searched for a minute. "The receipt was in here."

"She's lying, Clay. I didn't show her any ring."

"Margie, stop. The receipt was in my wallet and now it's not. Where is it?"

"She's lying, I tell you!"

He faced Allie. "I didn't buy it on the 7th, Allie. I bought it on the 2nd, for you, but the sales clerk's pen skipped, so she could have made the two look like a number seven. He turned back to Margie. "Where's the ring?"

"She's lying, Clay."

"Where's the friggin' ring, Marg?" He wanted to shake her when her mouth set in a stubborn line. How in hell did she think she could get away with this? He marched to his bedroom, found the box where he'd left it. He opened it, sighed in relief at sight of the ring nestled in the folds of satin. He unfolded the hand-written sale's receipt. Sure as shit, she'd written over the number two to make it look like a seven. The only time his wallet wasn't on him was when he slept. How had she managed that?

On his way to the living room, he paused in Margie's bedroom, noticed a slither of lace sticking out from under her bed. His investigation found the long gown set, nearly see-through and cut low in the front, just as Allie described.

The closed door of her bathroom piqued his curiosity further. He'd brought an armload of folded towels in here this morning and he'd left the door open. He opened it and found nothing out of the ordinary. Various tubes and containers of make-up were all stacked in a case on her vanity, all signs of her OCD propensities. As far as he could tell, she'd used none of it since before the accident.

He stopped mid-spin, nearly missed the out of place bottle of make-up remover, its cap off and lying loose inside the box. Another inspection of the trash bin under the vanity turned up several circular cotton pads, still damp with the remover, and streaked with black eyeliner and/or mascara. His stomach knotted at the thought of how she'd manipulated him from the day he'd set foot in this house.

He headed to the living room, empty except for Margie, still seated, whimpering as she held her face.

"Can it, Margie. I know Allie never touched you." He yanked the door open in time to see and hear Allie's car leave a trail of rubber on the street. She had to be feeling twenty different kinds of betrayal right about now, all courtesy of his stupid self. "Oh, sweet Jesus," he groaned under his breath. "What the hell have I done?"

Margie's low chuckle reached him, turned into a louder cackle, and then into full-blown laughter.

He pivoted, faced the stranger before him. "I'm not sure when it happened Marg, but you've by-passed delusional and transitioned right into full-blown-crazy-bitch mode, haven't you?"

She caught her breath enough to speak. "Call me crazy all you want, but you're just as alone as I am now." Her huge brown eyes looked like something you'd find on a feral animal. "If we're both going to be alone, we may as well be alone together."

He shook his head. "If you were the last woman on earth, I'd still have to pass."

She stood, much easier than he'd thought she could, and limped over to him. "Let me help you to remember how good it used to be with us, Clay, and how good it can be again."

"Since you're a hell of a lot more mobile than you've been pretending to be, you're on your own, Marg."

"You won't leave me."

"You watch my ass." He walked to his room, started shoving his possessions into the duffle he'd ended up bringing over from the camper. Her voice came to him again from the doorway.

"Clay!"

He shoved items into the duffle as fast as he could. Satisfied, he gave Hope's room one last look then shouldered the strap. He turned, paused at the sight of Margie blocking his path. Rather than speak to her, he barreled his way through, not giving one shit if he hurt her, or not.

Despite her one-minute head start, he caught up to Allie on the interstate, an easy enough feat when driving ninety miles per hour to her seventy. He pulled alongside her to check her condition. He'd seen no evidence of tears or erratic driving, only a slight jerk of the wheel when she flicked him the finger. He dropped back behind her again.

He hit the phone icon on his truck's electronic screen and spoke Brian's name. It rang once then went to voice mail, so Clay left him a quick message, explaining the situation. He called Terri, and his daughter answered on the second ring. He told her what Margie had been up to and waited for the explosion.

"Is that all that happened?"

"Isn't that enough?"

"Um, yeah. I guess it is."

Clay couldn't help but feel as though he was being kept out of some loop. "What the hell's going on here, Terri? You're far too unaffected by all this."

"Dad, I'm the one who warned you how delusional she was, remember? Why the hell didn't you listen to me? The woman is evil!"

He slapped at his steering wheel. "I guess you're right."

"I *feel* a monumental sense of relief. From what you're telling me, Margie gets around well enough not to need constant care anymore. I've been wracking my brain trying to mesh my and Ryan's work schedules around trips to Lake Coburn and taking care of Everly. I know she's my mother and I should be glad to do this for her, but I-I can't forget how she treated Hope. Even after the accident. I've tried, but I just can't. And you putting all that aside to help her when you felt the way you did . . . I'm in awe of you, Dad."

"As much as I'd like to take credit for doing the Christian thing, I'm not there yet, hon. I may have ruined my chances with Allie because of that lunatic. If I could go back in time knowing what I know now, I'd never set one foot back in that house."

"Do you want me to call Allie? Maybe I can calm the waters."

"No. It's my mess, I need to figure out a way to fix things." He swallowed the lump in his throat at the thought of how badly he'd hurt her. "If they can be fixed."

She finally interrupted the prolonged pause. "Don't give up, Dad. Brian and I like her. We like her a lot."

"I do too, kiddo." He saw the one-mile exit sign up ahead. "Gotta go. Love you."

"Love you, Daddy. And good luck!"

"Thanks, hon." He hit the end call button. "I'll sure as hell need it." He shot in front of her car so he could get to her place first. He lost her at the first red light of three between her place and the interstate, thankful he'd have a minute or so to get his thoughts together before a face-off with Allie.

After five minutes of no-show, he called her. No answer. After another ten, he called again, left her a message. "I screwed up. I know I did, and I'm so sorry. I saw all the evidence. The gown set shoved under her bed, the dirty make-up remover pads, and I saw her walk a hell of a lot easier than she's lead me to believe she could. Everything you said was true. Please call me."

Ten minutes later, he got out and rang the doorbell.

Cecily came to the door carrying a small white bag she handed to him. "I don't know what you did Mr. Clay, but you did it good. Mom says to give you this and not to let you inside, under any circumstances."

He peered inside the bag and released a groan. "No! These were gifts. I want her to have these."

She held up one hand. "She doesn't want them."

He let his head fall back on his shoulders. "Where is she?"

"I can't tell you that."

"Cecily, please. . ."

"Mr. Clay, I like you, but I love my mom, and I have to live with her. I'm sorry." She reached up on her toes to give him a hug before closing the door on him.

Clay waited until he was back in his truck to examine the contents of the bag, even though he knew what it held. He opened each box, held up the necklace and matching earrings. Wait, she'd been wearing these when he saw her at Margie's house.

His forehead creased in a frown, he started his truck and turned on the street that ran along the side of Allie's place. "Shit!" He stopped his truck and saw fresh tire tracks in the alley running behind her house. Not all subdivisions on this side of town had them, but this one did. She'd seen him and drove in from the back, stopping long enough to drop off the jewelry and leave the message for him.

"Where'd you go, Allie?" He forced himself to think, putting his mind through a sequence of problem solving tactics worthy of MacGyver. He went by her shop, but of course, she wasn't there, and neither was she at her mother's place. That's when he called Johnny's cell phone.

He didn't waste time with small-talk when his cousin answered the phone. "Is she there?"

"What the hell did you do?"

He sucked in his breath. "That bad?"

"Worse. Do not come here. You may walk in here a bull, but if my wife has her way, you'll walk out as a steer."

"I screwed up, Johnny. Bad."

"I gathered."

"How is she?"

"She's pissed. She's hurt, and disappointed in you. My take is she's mostly pissed. What happened?"

Clay gave him the Cliff Notes version of the story. By the time he was finished he was back at his camper. He threw his truck into park and turned off the ignition. "In short, Margie's been manipulating me from the beginning."

"And when Allie tried to tell you what Margie was doing, you didn't believe her."

"Yes, but tell her to listen to the message I left her."

"She did."

"And?"

"Did she call you back?"

He scratched at his chin. "I see your point. Shit. I don't know what to do."

"Let her cool off. Sleep on it. Try again tomorrow."

"I guess you're right."

Johnny's voice lowered. "I've gotta go. I think they're getting suspicious."

"Thanks for the ear, man."

"You're welcome. Goodnight and good luck, Clay."

"G'night."

Clay stepped out of his truck, parked his butt on his favorite chair at the edge of the boat dock. Instead of soothing him, the lap of waves whipped up by icy winds against the shoreline only worked to irritate the hell out of him. The moon, majestic and full, had a bluish hue tonight and he couldn't help but think how much Allie would love it. He surveyed his spot, his little piece of heaven on what Brian had named "Andrew's Pond" nearly seventeen years ago. He loved it here. Allie said she loved it here, too, had told him on countless occasions how she couldn't wait to fish once the weather turned warmer.

He dropped his head on the back of his chair, aching to see her, hold her in his arms, and hear her voice. What could he do? How could he tell her what a fool he'd been if she wouldn't speak to him, see him?

Show her.

The words came to him, soft and clear, as though they'd been whispered directly into his ear. The familiar chill at the back of his neck, one not caused from icy winds . . . Hope. Her image, frail and thin, her skin pale nearly to the point of transparency, materialized in his mind. Jesus, he missed his daughter. He tried to picture her well and healthy, but all he could manage was how she looked the last few months of her life, when the thought of not having her had been too unbearable to face. He remembered the feeling, the ache of knowing he'd never see her again. Here he was, facing the same ache at the impending loss of Allie.

Over two years, and he had yet to visit that cemetery since the graveside ceremony. He'd walked away before the crew had lowered the coffin into the ground, promising himself he'd never go back. His mom, who visited regularly, reported that the headstone was lovely, but he didn't care. If she got comfort from sitting there beside a cement slab, more power to her. No headstone could replace his daughter, and the thought of her body being in that cold, dark place made his stomach roll.

Make her see.

He groaned at the second sudden chill down his spine. "Okay Hope. I know. I know what I have to do. I just don't know how to get it done." He leaned forward, rested his arms on his thighs. "You'd like Allie, I know you would." He sat outside until the skies darkened from an approaching storm. The wind picked up, bringing a splattering of icy raindrops with it. He entered his camper, going through his nightly routine in a zombie-like manner, locking the door and turning up the heat.

He took a hot shower, knowing the place would be toasty warm by the time he finished. Afterward he sat in his recliner, staring at the 3D flames of the electric fireplace, wishing Allie were with him. He called her again and this time she answered.

"You have to stop this, Clay. I don't want to play these games, and I don't want to cringe every time my phone rings."

"Allie, I'm so sorry. You have to understand that I was exhausted, and sleep deprived, and I was only there to make it easier on my kids."

"And I accepted that. I didn't like you being there, but I accepted it. That's not what breaks my heart."

"The Margie she showed me and the person you saw and spoke to were two completely different people. I had no idea."

"And based on your history with her, you couldn't fathom that she may have been deranged and lying to your face?"

"Until recently, I'd never known her to be a liar; selfish and uncaring, yes, but not a liar."

"Need I mention the crazy phone messages, the gelatin salad, and the bathroom incident in your camper?"

He sighed. "I said until recently."

"And with all those instances still fresh in your mind, and faced with two versions of stories, you were still ready to believe that mine would be the lie."

"I-I don't know what I thought. But I believe you." He held his breath, hoping . . . praying she'd forgive him.

"You left out one word, Clay, one simple word that makes all the difference in the world to me. Now . . . you believe me *now*, after seeing the evidence. You couldn't . . ." Her voice cracked but she made an instant recovery. "You didn't have enough faith to believe the person you claimed to love, over the deranged, delusional woman who walked away from you and her dying child."

He'd done that to her. The depth of his betrayal slammed him like a wrecking ball. How could she ever forgive him?

"You're right."

"I know I'm right. Now—remember that I received a naked photo of you in the shower and a nasty text message from that woman as evidence, and I still believed you, over her."

His heart sank at her words, fearing the worst. "I know. I'm so sorry."

"It's too little, too late, Clay. Besides, I'm not even angry any more. I knew all along not to let my dreams get too far ahead of reality. I let you get too close and learned a valuable lesson."

"Aw, baby, please don't say that. Please don't close yourself off because of my stupidity."

She released an exhausted sigh. "Listen, I can't turn my phone off in case the girls need to call. Please don't call me again."

Before he opened his mouth to speak, the line went dead again. "Shit."

He skipped any effort to eat, tried to watch some television, but even the boxing match on a premium channel didn't hold his interest. Tired of trying not to think about the terrible, awful day, he shut everything down and went to bed.

Build it and she will come, Dad.

His eyes flew open. The message from his dream spun around in his mind like his laptop's 3D screensaver display. No whispered words of Shoeless Joe Jackson from Hope's favorite movie, Field of Dreams, no sound at all, just an image of the words . . . along with the first hint of an elaborate plan to get Allie back.

The next day he returned to work in south Texas. He spent a couple of hours his first day working on a sketch. Over the next week and a half, he sent and received design files back and forth to a friend of his. By the time he made it home on the 21st, Clay was prepared to put his plan into action.

Then the unthinkable happened.

Chapter Fourteen

Friday, January 22nd, 10:00 a.m.

Clay sat across from the desk in his contractor's office, a set of plans spread between them. "So, when do you think you can get this thing started?"

"I believe my guys finished the dozer and box blade work today. Tomorrow my crew should be able to start the prep work for the slab. If the weather holds off, we should be pouring in a couple of days."

"Sounds good, Bob. I'll see you tomorrow, then." He stood and shook hands with the man.

"It's going to be an exceptional set-up, for sure."

"I think so." Clay's phone buzzed with an incoming call. He glanced at the name flashing on his screen and tapped to answer it on the way out the door. "Hey Son, what's up?"

"Pop . . ."

Brian's tone, the crack in his voice, had Clay clenching his fist against his forehead and praying his grandson hadn't been hurt. "What's wrong?"

"It's Mom. Sean and I came to check on her this morning and she was unresponsive. I called the ambulance, but they couldn't bring her back. She's gone, Pop."

"Aw hell, Brian. I'm so sorry." He stepped into his truck. It roared to life when his key turned in the ignition. "What happened?"

"She overdosed on pain medication. She killed herself."

"Son, maybe she just lost track of how many she'd taken."

"No. She hadn't been taking anything but OTC pain relievers. The last refill of her prescribed meds was full when I went a couple of days ago. Today—empty."

Clay ranted inwardly at Margie for leaving their two oldest kids to deal with her legacy of suicide. An immediate wave of guilt washed over him for thinking such an awful thought. "I'm in Lake Coburn already. Where are you?"

"I'm at Mom's house, but I need to go to the hospital and I don't want to bring Sean."

"I'm just around the corner from you. I'll be there in two minutes."

He entered the house, found signs everywhere of the team of EMT's that had worked on Margie, apparently without success. He wrapped his son in a hug. "I'm sorry, Son."

Brian stepped back and wiped his eyes. "Thanks, Pop."

Clay lifted Sean in his arms and hugged him. He faced Brian. "How much of this did he see?"

Brian shook his head. "I sent him to the room to watch TV immediately. By the time he came out they'd already left with her." He passed a hand through his son's curls. "Hey, little man, you're going to stay here with Pop, so I can do something for Gramma Margie, okay? You be a good boy."

Sean nodded. "I will."

Brian stopped at the door and turned back. "I already spoke to Terri, and I just left a message on Jacques Bessette's voice mail. I left my cell number and yours too, in case I'm not in a position to answer. I'm not sure which he'll call first, so you may have to speak to him, Pop."

"Not a problem."

"He doesn't know. I didn't tell him, just asked him to call."

Clay gave his shoulder a pat. "You can count on me to be sensitive to the situation, Son. The man was her fiancé not long ago."

Clay ended a call with Terri a few minutes later, confused by her guarded reaction to Margie's death. Still pondering the somewhat mysterious conversation with his daughter, he answered a call from a strange number. "Hello."

"*Bon jour* . . . uh . . . hello. My name ees Jacques Bessette, and I had a message from *Monsieur* Brian Andrews to call one of two numbers. Is thees Brian?"

The man spoke perfect English, although in a heavy French accent. Regardless, Clay had no problem understanding him. "No, Mr. Bessette. I'm Clay Andrews, Brian's father and he had to go to the hospital. I'm afraid I have some bad news for you regarding Brian's mother, Margie. I'm so sorry to have to tell you this, but she passed away earlier this morning."

"*Oh, mais non.* I am sorry for your loss, *Monsieur* Andrews."

"Well, It's more my children's loss than mine. I had no kind of relationship with my ex-wife. I'd thought for a few days we could at least be friends, but her actions made that impossible. I'm afraid my last words to her were far from kind."

"I see. I am sorry. I am at a loss as to how to respond. The last time we spoke, she mentioned a *réconcilier, non?*"

"Never. I'm afraid Margie had grown quite delusional, and more than a little manipulative."

"*Mais oui,* I believe you are correct. *Comment at-elle morte?* Oh, *excuse-moi,* but how did she die?"

"We . . . we believe she overdosed on pain medication."

"Suicide?"

"We think so, but nothing's been verified." Silence, thick and heavy, greeted him. "*Monsieur Bessette?*"

"*Oui.* I am here. I am sorry to hear this . . . but . . . I cannot say that I am surprised."

"I admit I am. I thought Margie was too self-centered to take her own life. Excuse me, but you don't sound all that upset at the news."

"*C'est compliqué*, Monsieur Andrews. I'm afraid we parted ways badly. My last words to her were unkind as well." His sigh carried over the airwaves to Clay. "I weel take the earliest flight I can to America. I have many questions about a certain matter."

"Questions?"

"*Oui.* But it is a delicate situation. I'm afraid we have things to discuss that require a man to man introduction."

Clay gave the man's statement careful consideration. "This is my cell phone number, Mr. Bessette. Try to get a connecting flight to the Lake Coburn, Louisiana airport if it's at all possible. If you let me know your flight schedule, I will be there to pick you up from the airport."

Brian made it back just past noon and took Sean home. Clay stopped at the Post Office on the way home to check his mail. Once home, he separated the junk mail and discarded it in the trash before turning his attention to the more important stuff. A business size envelope addressed to him with Margie's name and address in the upper left hand corner caught his attention. He tore the edge to open it, pulling out a single sheet of paper filled with her neat script.

He leaned one hip against the island and closed his eyes. "Dammit, Margie . . . haven't you done enough damage for one lifetime?" He folded the letter, instinctively knowing it wouldn't be good news. He pulled out his phone and sent Allie a text.

Not sure if you heard, but Margie committed suicide earlier today.

Her reply was brief and instant. *I'm sorry.*

His shaking hands fumbled with the keypad and it took him several tries to get the next text sent. *She sent me a letter. Haven't read it yet, but have a feeling in my gut this is going to be catastrophic.*

Her response was unexpected but welcomed. *I'm on my way. Don't read it until I get there.*

Clay tried to wait for her. He paced the floor for five minutes, staring at the tri-folded sheet of paper. Did he want to appear that vulnerable in front of Allie? No. He grabbed the letter, thinking it'd be best to know what he was dealing with beforehand. He unfolded the paper and took a deep breath before he began to read.

Clay,

I know I've made a mess of things from the beginning to the end. I've never been good at showing my emotions, especially with the children. You were always better at that than I was, but I have done something unforgiveable. I know that. I've always been too much of a coward to face it. I was a coward years ago when Hope was conceived, when she got sick, when she was dying, and I still am.

I had an affair with Jacques Bessette seventeen years ago. I'm not proud of it but it's all bound to come out now. I met Jacques at a five-day seminar in Atlanta. He was a complete stranger in a place he'd never been before, and I took advantage of the situation. I told him I was separated from my husband and getting a divorce. Please don't blame him for this. Once he went back to Paris, he tried to contact me. I told him we'd reconciled and he left it alone.

Then I found myself in the worst predicament of my life. Pregnant with a third child, which I said I'd never have, and suspecting you may not be the father. You were adamant about me keeping it, and finally convinced me. I went along with it, hoping the child I carried was yours.

From the moment Hope was born, I knew who her biological father was. The older she got, the more prominent Jacque's features became on our daughter's face, and the more threatened I felt. She was a daily reminder of the ticking time bomb eating away at my marriage, at my life. I tried not to resent my daughter, but I'm afraid I failed, just as I've failed at so many other things in my life.

Clay collapsed on the couch, his stomach rolling with nausea, his heart pounding in his chest. Hope not *his* child? This couldn't be happening. He wanted to quit reading, but he couldn't. As sick at heart as his recent discovery had made him, the next sentence had him wanting to scream.

I never dreamed Hope would be the one to face-off with me first about her parentage.

"Oh . . . dear . . . God." Clay clutched his head with one hand. "Hope . . . knew?" He raised the letter with his other.

She came to me with a page of blood types she'd printed out for her extra credit Biology project. She'd just discovered our types, and told me she knew you weren't her biological father. I told her a little about Jacques, without giving her his name. Hope knew he was French and lived in Paris, and that he'd been under the impression I was divorcing during the affair. It tore her up, the wanting to know him and not wanting to see you hurt. She left it up to me to tell everyone the truth. She asked me not to tell her the man's name unless I was willing to tell both you and "The Frenchman" the truth.

I contacted Jacques, with every intention of telling him. He told me he'd never married and couldn't have children and had never forgotten the week we spent together. I told Hope what I'd learned about him. She knew I was going to him, but I told her it was to tell him face to face and then come back and tell you. Only, I never returned. I think she knew all along that I wouldn't. Hope knew I was a coward. She told me she didn't have long and wouldn't be the one to break your heart, so I knew I was safe. Before I left, she gave me two letters. One addressed to you and the other to her biological father. She asked me to make sure you got them both after she was gone. Then she thanked me, Clay. She thanked me for allowing you to raise her as your own.

Both letters are in a safe deposit box at The First National Bank in Lake Coburn. I told them I was leaving the country and they've been instructed to let you open the box. I'm enclosing the key. All I can do is ask you to get the other letter to Jacques. If you choose not to, I can't blame you.

I'm sorry, Clay. Please believe that I never meant for any of this to happen. Once it did, I was too much of a coward to face up to it. I've hurt you, I know that. But you must realize one thing; as badly as you're hurting now, it can't come close to the devastation Jacques felt when he discovered he'd had a daughter he never got to meet.

May God forgive me even if you or Jacques never will . . .

Margie

Clay sat there, stunned, sad, sick at heart, until the slam of a car door shook him from his thoughts. He called out to come in at the urgent knocking.

Allie jerked the door opened and walked inside, her eyes wide and questioning. Her gaze landed on the letter clenched in his hand. She took a deep breath and walked to the couch, stopping in front of him.

"Hope . . ." A huge lump in his throat stopped the rest of the words from forming.

She dropped to her knees before him, took his hands in her own, her eyes brimming with tears. "I know."

"How?"

She sniffed, using her pinkie to wipe her eyes. "Kayla did that same extra-credit project this year. I helped her to study for the quiz and she memorized the chart. When you said you were O type, I knew."

"But you didn't say anything. Even after Marg . . . after I . . ." He choked back the sob building in his throat.

She squeezed his hands. "I couldn't be the one to hurt you like that."

"Part of me feels as though I've lost Hope all over again."

"You shouldn't, Clay. Does DNA matter when it comes to the love between a parent and a child?"

He clamped his jaws shut and shook his head, tears flooding his eyes. He pulled her close, wrapped his arms around her, and held on until both of them got their emotions under control.

"There are two letters in a safe deposit box at her bank. They're from Hope. I've got to get them today." He stood and helped Allie get to her feet. "I know I have no right to ask, but I'd appreciate you coming with me."

She nodded, too emotional to speak.

Neither of them spoke until his truck was already on I-10 westbound and headed back to Lake Coburn.

Allie pulled a tissue from her purse and wiped her eyes. "How are Brian and Terri?"

"Brian found his mother, so he was torn up about it. Terri is somber, but not all that upset or surprised."

"She knows already, Clay. Hope told her after Margie left town."

Clay thought about Terri's low opinion of her mother the past couple of years, realized it explained a lot. "I'm glad Hope was able to confide in her big sister. I'll speak to both Brian and Terri when she comes in from Natchitoches."

"In the letter . . . did she say who he was?"

"It's the guy she was with in Paris. Jacques Bessette is his name. I spoke to him earlier today, and according to her letter, he knows. I think that's why she left Paris. He's flying in for the funeral, so you'll get a chance to meet him." He looked at the spot where their fingers linked over his truck's center console. "That is, unless this is temporary." He checked the roadway then reached up to place his hand on her face. "Please tell me it's not, because I am so in love with you it's ridiculous."

She cupped her hand around his face. "I just spent two miserable weeks without you, Clay." She lowered his hand and linked her fingers through his. "I've learned how much stronger I am. I've discovered I don't *need* a man around me to make me feel worthwhile."

His heart sank at her words. "Allie, please—"

"I do *want* you in my life, but only if you promise never to doubt me again."

He leaned over to kiss her fingers clasped in his hand. "Never again, hon. I promise. I love you."

"I love you, too."

"How are the girls?"

"They've been annoyingly attentive and well-behaved since our split. I think they were afraid at first that I'd cut my wrist or something, but they finally relaxed. They miss you, though."

"I've missed them, too."

They were quiet the rest of the way to Lake Coburn. It took less than fifteen minutes to get the contents of the safe deposit box and get back to his truck.

Allie placed her hand on his arm. "Would you like me to drive so you can read your letter now?"

"I think I'd better wait until I get back home."

Neither of them saw any point in trying to make small talk on the way home. The presence of the two letters sitting on the dashboard hung between them. The atmosphere inside the truck was as dark and heavy as the skies just before a hurricane makes landfall.

Finally home, he helped Allie down from his truck and grabbed onto her hand like a drowning man reaching for a life preserver.

"Clay, do you want to be alone for th—"

"No!" He pushed her toward the camper. "I want you with me, Allie." He paused, thinking of her other obligations. "Can you stay? Do you need to get back to the girls?"

She reached up, placed a calming hand on his face. "No. The girls will go to Bruce's straight from school and stay until Sunday evening. I'll stay."

He nodded and took a shaky breath as he followed her into the camper. They stood looking at each other. He grabbed her hand and pulled her along with him to his bedroom. "I want to read it in here, with you in my arms. Do you mind?"

She gave him a sweet smile. "Of course I don't mind." She took off her shoes and climbed into the center of his bed. He pulled off his sneakers and propped four pillows against the headboard. Once situated, he pulled her close to his side and kept his arm around her. He took one deep, shaky breath. "Will you do me one more favor and read it out loud to me? I doubt if I'll be able to get through it if I do it and I want us to hear it together."

"Sure, if that's what you want."

He handed her the envelope with "Daddy" written in Hope's handwriting.

Allie took the envelope, held it close for a moment, while saying a silent prayer for help in reading it to Clay. She slid her nail under the flap the length of the envelope and pulled out four sheets of paper. She sucked in her breath at the neat script in blue ink, cleared her throat, and began to read:

Hey Daddy,

I suppose you know what's what by now. I've asked Mom to give you this letter if she ever gets the courage to tell you. I want you to know that in my eyes, it doesn't change a thing. I couldn't have chosen a better Dad for myself if I'd had the chance.

I figure God had a hand in making Mom do what she did nearly fifteen years ago. If she hadn't, I wouldn't be me. If she'd done the "right thing" and told you and my biological father about me, I may never have gotten to experience having you as a dad. I mean, heck, she could have packed me up and raised me in Paris, France with that other guy. Yes, I got her to tell me that much. I didn't want to know his name, because, well, that would have been too weird. Besides, you know how crazy genius I am with my web researching skills, especially after treatments when I'm bored and too sick to get out of bed for two days. I would have looked him up on the Internet, and gotten obsessive about it. Next thing you know, Interpol would have been knocking on our door. As awesome as that would have been, it would have been impossible to explain to old Mrs. Boudreaux (aka Mrs. Buttinski) next door, don't you think?

I thank God I didn't grow up in Paris. They walk around with loaves of bread under their arms, and that's just about the nastiest thing I've ever heard! You know I pride myself on being the "Carb Queen" of this family. I earned the title fair and square by going through a loaf of bread every three days. I do enjoy my sammiches, but I refuse to put anything in my mouth that has been anywhere near someone else's pits. Nope—armpits are only good for making fart noises, and I should know—I have a trophy to prove it!

Not only that, but they drink wine with everything. I don't like wine, and believe me when I say I've snuck enough of mom's wine to know I could never develop a taste for it. No, I'd be a beer girl, for sure. If I had the chance to grow older, I'd strive to be like my big brother, Brian, and learn to guzzle an entire beer, and then get through the alphabet in a single, alcohol-smelling burp. There's your silver lining, Daddy. You'll never have to bail my juvenile delinquent butt out of jail for public intoxication.

Question: Can cops arrest people for public obnoxiousness? Terri insists no one does obnoxious better than me when I put my mind to it.

I adore my siblings. I love Brian for choosing to raise a child on his own. He told me he learned everything he knows about being a good dad from you. There's another silver lining, Dad. If Mom hadn't turned the reins of raising me completely over to you (let's not kid ourselves—everyone knows that's exactly what she did) then Brian may not have fought as hard to keep Sean's mom from aborting him. He may not have thought it was possible to raise Sean as a single parent. You're the one who showed him it was normal for fathers to change poopy diapers and get up for midnight feedings. I can't even stand to think of a world without our adorable little Sean in it. I love my nephew so much it hurts. I'm glad he won't be old enough to miss me when I'm gone. It's bad enough the rest of you will.

I guess you also know that I unloaded on Terri about the whole blood type thing. You can't be ~~pissed~~ mad at Terri. (Sorry, I know you don't like me to say "pissed") I made her promise not to tell you she knew. She got it out of me one day—took advantage of me in a moment of weakness, and wouldn't quit nagging me until I blew up and told her. Poor thing is so ~~pissed~~, I mean mad at Mom and has decided never to speak to her again. From what I can see, it hasn't been much of a change. Terri told me she's always resented Mom for resenting me being born. I know, right? Like I had any control over the situation. I think I've always known Mom never wanted a third kid. Heck, I've known for so long, I can't remember how I found out, but it doesn't matter.

I know Terri and Ryan have been working hard to have a baby (although the way the two of them talk, it sounds more like fun than work to me) so that I could have another niece or nephew to love. If she and Mom had been closer then Mom leaving us would have been a heck of a lot harder on Terri, don't you think? Anyway, I'll regret not getting to see any of Terri and Ryan's kids. I told her I have a feeling her first one will be a girl. I even hinted that I've always liked the name Everly for a girl. I read it in a book once and fell in love with it. She told me she likes Hope Everly, but I think I've convinced her that Everly Hope sounds better. The poor kid should have her own identity. I don't want people in Lake Erin to meet her and immediately think of her dead aunt. I know she'll be beautiful, because Terri is Homecoming/Prom Queen material, and secretly, I've always thought Ryan was a hottie. I know people divorce a lot these days, but I hope they make it. They're good together.

You, Brian, Terri, Ryan, Sean, and me . . . Together, we made a great family, didn't we, Dad? I've loved every minute of it, except the ones I spent hurling after treatments. (Dry heaves suck—big time!) But, even the trips to Houston for treatments were like mini-vacations for me, because I got to be with my dad.

I guess I'm trying to tell you not to be sad for me, and not to be too angry at Mom, or even at "the Frenchman". If Mom is telling the truth, he thought she was divorced and when he found out differently, he left her alone. None of that matters. I've had the best life of any thirteen-year-five-month-twenty-eight-day-old kid (so far) I know. I grew up feeling loved by so many wonderful people, and I was happy. There are millions of kids out there who don't get a year, or a week, or even a day out of their entire lives to experience the kind of happy that I've been. I know I'm blessed.

In group therapy the other day, one of the girls said she was sad she'd die before she got the chance to have a real boyfriend and a fabulous first kiss, and dates, and sex, and stuff like that. I regret not being able to provide more cousins for Sean and Everly Hope, or whoever, to cut up with during the holiday get-togethers. I know it's kind of putting the cart before the horse, as Maw Maw Jane says—I mean there can be no baby without all the other stuff first, right? I guess I'm sad I won't give you a grandchild *to love, because I can already see that you're every bit as great of a grandfather as Pops was to me. I know you're going to go fishing with them, and take them to movies even if you don't like what's playing, and take them for ice cream, and sit through T-ball, baseball, softball, soccer games, and whatever other sports they play. I'm betting you'll sit through dance recitals if Terri has that little girl.*

Here's the important part, Dad. I don't want you to be alone when you do all these things. I doubt you and Mom could ever make it work after this, but that's okay. Find someone else. It shouldn't be difficult for you, because my entire soccer team used to drool when you showed up early to pick me up from a practice. And everybody knows you're a great guy. Find someone who likes to laugh, but not at other people, cuz that's just mean. Find someone you can't wait to go home to at the end of the day, someone who'll love you enough not to ever look at another guy. You deserve that because you'd never look at another girl. Try to find someone who likes to fish because that's something you can do together when you're old. Build that cabin on Andrews Pond that you always talked about building.

Most of all, be happy, Daddy. Because if I can find a way to bug you until you are, I will do exactly that.

I have a few requests for you. When you hear wind chimes tinkling in the breeze, think of me and how much I loved the sound. When you see a puppy or a kitten, stop and play with it, and take the time to pet older dogs because they need love too. When you hear a baby or a toddler belly laugh, remember how I would tickle Sean until he peed his pants. Go to the occasional girls' soccer or softball game for me if you have time because seeing you there will make my teammates happy. Dye eggs for Easter. Pop fireworks for the 4th of July. Carve a pumpkin for Halloween. Keep putting out that hideous turkey I made in 2nd grade out of a milk jug for Thanksgiving. Decorate a real tree for Christmas so you can smell it when you walk into the room. Watch the ball drop on New Year's Eve with someone you love just like we always did. Last (but this is a biggie because I know how you tend not to see anything but the roadway when you drive) when you see a field of sunflowers, stop your truck, get out, and enjoy the view. Even better, take a walk among the flowers, Dad—close your eyes and think of me when you do, and I will be there with you."

Thank you for being the best daddy in the world to me. Thank you for caring for me when I was too little to care for myself, for bandaging all my boo-boos, taking me to my first days of school, taking me to T-ball, and softball, and soccer practices and sitting through the games, and for taking care of me when I was too sick and weak to lift my own hand. Thank you for loving me so much I never felt unloved for a single second.

Just saying "I love you" doesn't cover it nearly enough, but I do. I love you forever, and even though I've got another "father" out there, YOU have always, and always will be my Daddy.

Always,
Hope

P.S. I don't know if you're interested in seeing a video version of this or not. In case you are, I made two versions, one for you, and one for "the Frenchman". They're on jump drives and Terri has them. I didn't want to trust Mom with both versions in case she chickened out and destroyed them.

Allie's quiet sniffles punctuated the otherwise silent bedroom. Clay lay there, his eyes closed, his arm around the woman he loved, letting his daughter's message infiltrate his mind, his entire being. "Thank you for reading that. I know it couldn't have been easy for you."

"You're welcome. Thank you, for allowing me to be a part of that."

"I love you, Allie."

"I love you, Clay."

"Will you marry me one day?"

"We'll see."

"Is that the best you can do?"

"Good chance."

He lifted his head to gaze at her, a single eyebrow lifted in dramatic fashion. "Seriously?"

"What? You haven't asked me properly, yet. And the only ring I've seen was on another woman's hand."

"That's going back to the jewelers tomorrow."

She nodded. "Good. Can you get your money back for it?"

"I don't want my money back. I want another ring."

"Get something with a smaller diamond."

"Do I have to get a smaller diamond?"

"No. I was only trying to be polite. I loved the diamond."

He chuckled. "Good to know. Any particular shape or cut you prefer?"

"Round is perfect."

"How about the finish—yellow, white, or platinum?"

"I prefer yellow gold."

"Now we're getting somewhere."

A minute of silence passed between them. "Clay?"

"Yes?"

"Are you all right?"

He paused and mentally checked items off a list. "I believe I am, Allie." He turned onto his left side to face her. She rolled toward his body, hooked her left foot around his right calf, and settled her face into the crook of his neck. They lay there, the sound of the wind chimes ringing in the winter wind, lulling them into a state of contented drowsiness. *Hope.* How could he not think of her when he heard them? The chimes had been included in the box of treasures he'd taken from the house before her funeral.

"I love the sound of those chimes." Allie's sleepy admission made him smile.

"They're my last Father's Day gift from Hope."

"That explains why they're so soothing."

Her lengthy pause had him believing she'd finally fallen asleep, but she hadn't.

"I didn't know Hope liked sunflowers too."

"Uh huh, her room was filled with them." He smiled, imagining his daughter's room. "Pictures, posters, stickers on the windows, silk arrangements, dried arrangements, figurines, sun catchers, and wind chimes . . . even her bedsheets. The kid was obsessed with them."

Allie smiled, her eyes heavy with sleepiness. "I think Hope and I would have gotten along beautifully." She yawned and settled again.

"I know you would have, Al," he whispered. He draped his arm over her waist to pull her closer, sighing with absolute content. This woman could not have been a better fit for him if he'd built her from scratch. His last conscious thought before joining Allie in sleep was the certainty that Hope had somehow led him to her.

You did good, baby girl.

Saturday, January 23rd

Clay answered the door, dressed in dark blue jeans that hugged his hips, with a long-sleeved, pressed, dress shirt. He held out one hand to help her up the steps of his camper. She stepped inside and his left hand came forward with the huge arrangement of flowers he'd been hiding behind his back.

"Oh, how beautiful! Thank you, Clay." Allie closed her eyes and inhaled the sweet mixture of fragrances from the rose, carnation, and calla lilly bouquet. "These smell delicious." She glanced at the pot on his stove top. "And so does whatever you've got simmering in there."

"Beef stew. Are you hungry?"

"Starved, there must have been three Mardi Gras balls tonight, and I think half the women attending them had appointments with me. I've never done so many up-do's in one day. I worked right through lunch until five o'clock."

"Sit, rest your feet. How about a glass of wine first?"

She soaked in her surroundings. He'd made the effort to light several candles, and there was a country ballad playing softly in the background—all of it upping the romantic mood. "That sounds lovely."

"Or maybe you'd prefer champagne?"

"Champagne? Is this a celebration of some sort?"

He shrugged. "Could be." He turned his attention to the flowers. "The roses are fragrant, aren't they?"

She raised the boquet to her nose, breathing them in. "They are."

He pointed to the largest flower in the center. "That one smells the best."

Allie turned her attention back to the flowers. She paused, catching the sparkle of . . . something. She leaned in to give it a closer examination. Her hand froze on the petal as she released a small gasp.

There, nestled between the petals of a bright red rose, was a beautiful ring, a solitaire round diamond seated atop a band of yellow gold. "You even warned me you would do this, and I'm still surprised."

"So, what do you think?" He removed the ring and held it in front of her. "Better?"

"Much better."

With Little Big Town's "Bring it On Home to Me" flowing through the room in soft vocals, Clay got down on one knee. He took her left hand in his and cleared his throat. "Allie Elizabeth Sarver . . . you're the fric to my frac, the tick to my tock, the marshmallows on my cup of hot cocoa. I love you and I want to be there for you and your daughters until God takes me from this earth. Would you do me the tremendous honor of becoming my wife?"

She blinked several times to clear her eyes and nodded. "I love you, Clay, and I will . . . er, yes!" Allie held her breath as he slipped the ring onto her finger, a perfect size five and a half. She set the flowers on the couch after he got to his feet, and stepped into his embrace. His mouth covered hers, his tongue probing, heating her, anniahlating her resistance. She pulled back, light-headed, and laid her head on his chest; staring at her hand resting in his, at the ring on her finger, loving the look of it. "I love this ring."

"How about that champagne now?"

She lifted on her toes to give him a final kiss before he stepped away. "One glass, but then I need to eat something or I'll faint from starvation."

He uncorked the bottle and poured her a small amount in a champagne flute. "I bought these today, you know. Most days I drink my alcohol from the bottle, unless it's a high-ball glass or a red solo cup."

She giggled as the bubbles tickled her nose. "I'm honored."

"If you can spare a few minutes more, I have another surprise for you." He pulled out a large roll of white paper and handed it to her. "These are for you."

"What's this?" She placed her glass on the kitchen counter and unrolled the plans onto the immaculate surface of the granite island.

"It's our cabin on Andrew's Pond."

She gazed at him. "You're taking Hope's advice?"

"Look at the date on those." He pointed to the bottom corner of the plans. "I started working on this right after I acted like a dumbass. I dreamed about Hope and she told me to build this and you'd come."

She crossed her arms. "Was it a whisper like in "Field of Dreams"?"

He shook his head. "No, I didn't hear anything. You know that 3D screensaver on my laptop?"

"The one that says 'Carpe Diem'?"

"Yes. That's what I saw, a message that said 'Build it and she will come, Dad'. That was Hope's favorite movie, so of course she'd find a way to use it get my attention."

Allie couldn't stop the light-hearted burst of laughter. "She said she'd bug you until you did what you could to be happy." She looked down at the plans. "So, walk me through this."

He described the spot he'd chosen to build, which was just behind the camper, and why she hadn't noticed the on-going, slab-pouring process.

"As of now, it's right at two thousand square feet, but if you want to add anything more to it at this stage, we can. That's why I'm showing you the plans now. The girls will each have their own room for as long as they want to call this place home."

"So, this will be a permanent home and not just a cabin retreat?"

"That's the idea, unless you don't want to live out here all year."

She squealed and threw her arms around him. "I would adore living out here, Clay. Do you think you could build a walkway from our bedroom door that leads to the pond?"

"Baby, I'll build one so that you can walk outside in your pj's and cast a line, if that would make you happy."

She nodded. "I believe it would, now feed me before I pass out from hunger."

Once her belly was sated, they propped themselves up on his bed to give the plans a thorough examination. Allie gave him her perspective on a few things. She'd prefer a larger window over the sink area, and told him she'd always wanted double wall ovens, one of them small so it wouldn't heat up the whole kitchen during the summer months. She didn't care for the arrangement of the laundry room, and sketched out her own idea. Rather than be upset about any of the changes, her input thrilled Clay.

"This is your home, too. Do you want to get the girls involved? Maybe they would like some say-so over the closet sizes and such?"

She waved off that idea immediately. "The closets you have here are already twice what they have now. No, if we get them involved, there'll be no end to it. They'll both be off to college soon, and after that, they'll be in places of their own. Let's concentrate on what you and I want this place to be for us."

Clay rolled up the plans and dropped them on the floor beside the bed. He pulled her in his arms, their legs entwined. "How is it you know exactly what to say to put a smile on my face?"

"Well, sweet man, it's not all that difficult when we both want the same things."

He scooted them both lower onto the bed then rolled on his side to face her. "If that's the case, then you should know what I'm wanting right about now." He waited, the mellow sounds of Keith Whitley's "When You Say Nothing at All" reaching them from the living room.

She nuzzled his neck. "I believe I do, Clay. Does that mean you've reached the end of your resistance?"

"All I needed was a commitment from you. The way I figure it, if we can set a wedding date in the next few minutes, I'll be good to go." If he had his way he'd marry her within the week. Time to see if they were on the same page.

She pulled away from him long enough to grab her phone from the nightstand. "When will the cabin be move-in ready?"

"I added a bonus clause if the contractor had it ready by April 15th. Taking his reputation into account, I'm fairly certain he'll do it unless we throw any major plan changes his way."

Allie's lips pursed as she swiped at her screen. "April 24th is a Saturday."

"He frowned. That sounds so far away. Do we have to wait that long?"

"I want to start our marriage in our cabin on Andrew's Pond. Cecily will graduate from high school the middle of May, so I'd like to be married before all that chaos."

He pulled her close, brushing her hair back to kiss the side of her neck. "Sounds wonderful, Al. If he doesn't make the deadline, how about we give him extra time by going on a long honeymoon?" His wheels started turning. *Ireland maybe?* Note to self: start working on that passport for Allie immediately.

"I don't need to go any place fancy. If I could have a week in this place with you all to myself, I'd be satisfied."

He captured her lips in a kiss that lingered. Satisfied . . . just the sound of those syllables rolling off her tongue had him ready to please her. When the next song began from his playlist, he recognized it immediately. It had been their ultimate downfall at the hotel in New Orleans, the song that had them running to the roof for the equivalent of cold showers.

"That song again," she groaned.

He smiled, thinking Ed Sheeran's words and melody couldn't do anything but further his cause tonight. If things went his way, he was minutes away from breaking in this king-size mattress for something other than sleeping. "April 24th it is. I can guarantee one thing. No matter where we go, I'll make sure you're good and satisfied."

"Mm . . . I like the sound of that."

"You should start thinking of excuses for your girls, babe. I'm about to put a smile on your face that'll call for some kind of explanation when you get home." He slid his hand under her shirt, placed a series of tender kisses on her belly.

"The girls are at their dad's for the weekend, remember?" she murmured. "Besides, I heard them say something about you putting a ring on it, so . . ."

He clasped her left hand, stealing a quick glance at the glittering diamond on her ring finger, smiled as she spoke the words that would give them both what they craved.

"You may proceed."

Chapter Fifteen

Sunday, January 24th

A tall man with a single duffle bag rounded the corner of the walkway. From a distance, he looked like Robert Downey, Jr.—the same dark hair and coloring but on a beefier, six-foot-tall frame. Something about the way he carried himself told Clay he was Jacques. As he approached, there was no doubt in his mind. He walked toward the man and stopped before him, stared into eyes the exact shade and shape of Hope's. He would be lying if he said it didn't rattle him. He had to take a big breath to steady his nerves before speaking. "Jacques Bessette?"

"Yes."

Clay extended his hand. "I'm the man who had the great privilege of being your daughter's dad."

Jacques stared at him for several seconds before taking his hand. His eyes misted over and he and Clay joined for a manly hug and slap on the back. "*Merci beaucoup, Monsieur* Andrews."

Clay stepped back and stared at the man. "Call me Clay, please. My God. I always thought Hope looked like her mother, but she didn't. She looked exactly like you. No wonder it drove Margie crazy."

Jacques wiped his eyes with the cuff of his jacket. "When did you discover thees?"

"Not long after I spoke to you on Friday. I picked up my mail and found a letter from Margie. She told me everything. The fact that you wanted to speak man to man is testament to your fine character."

"It is no less than what you deserved."

Clay glanced at the duffle. "Do you have any more luggage to claim?"

"Non. I try to travel light when I fly. They've lost my luggage too many times to count."

"I understand." He waved him forward. "This way. *Par ici.*"

Jacques' eyes widened at Clay's modest attempt at the French language. "*Tu parle français?*"

Clay held out his thumb and index finger, indicating a small amount. "*Un peu. Vous êtes en Louisiane, mon ami.* You're in Louisiana, my friend." He grinned. "That's about it, though. If you ask for more than that, I'd have to start digging through the Cajun French cuss words I learned when I was twelve. *C'est tout.*"

He waited until they were in his truck before reaching onto the dashboard for the long, white envelope. "This is for you, Jacques. It's from Hope. She gave it to Margie to give to you. Margie's letter to me told me where to find it. My fiancée and I read mine in the privacy of my home. It's your choice." He reached inside his coat pocket and drew out a memory stick. "There's a video version of it on this jump drive. Our daughter liked to cover all the bases. My older daughter, Terri, also added more videos of Hope for you, along with a slideshow. She said she filled it up for you."

Jacques took the stick from him, held it and the letter to his broad chest. "Thank you, my friend. And I weel thank Terri when I see her. I am astounded by your family's generosity." He wiped his eyes and stared straight ahead. "Can you tell me where we are we going?"

"I thought I'd take you to the cemetery first, to see Hope's grave."

Jacques nodded. "Bon. I will wait and read the letter there. It weel be fitting."

"As you wish." Clay cleared his throat. "This will be the first time I've been to the gravesite since her funeral. I-I couldn't make myself go back there."

"Eet is understandable." Jacques shrugged his broad shoulders. "*Elle n'y est pas de toute façon.* She, her soul, ees not there, non?"

"That's my take on it, but, I thought it may give you some comfort." He readjusted his hand placement on the steering wheel. "What's the story with you and Margie? Brian had been under the impression the two of you were in good shape before Margie came running back to the states. Weren't you engaged?"

"Our relationship—*c'est compliqué*. Three weeks before Christmas, we went out with friends. She had too much wine with our dinner so I had to bring her home. After we got home she drank more wine and confessed that we had a child together."

He put a hand over his heart. "*Bon Dieu!* You have no idea what that did to me. I was so happy. I have always wanted children. I had testicular cancer several years ago and the treatments left me sterile."

His tone turned somber. "When she told me about our daughter's death two years earlier . . ." He turned in his seat to face Clay. "Two years, Clay, but she found me two and a half years ago. Then I remember her going back to the states for an early Christmas with her children.

I confronted her with it, and she admitted that was when she went home for Hope's funeral. She admitted she'd left you and our sick daughter six months before Hope passed." He shook his head. "I couldn't believe it. I felt so betrayed, as betrayed as you must have felt when she walked away from you and Hope.

I ask her thees. I ask her how a mother can leave a sick child behind, and a husband to take care of that child alone.

I ask her how she could rob me of a chance to meet my daughter. If she had told me then I would have come immediately. I would have thrown myself at your feet, Clay, and begged you to allow me to help you care for Hope."

He choked on an anguished sob. "My heart . . ." He slapped his hand over his chest. "Eet was shattered. I told her to get out, to go back home to the states and make amends with the family she betrayed if you all would allow. I told her to do it while she still had the chance. I accused her of being a heartless woman."

Jacques stopped speaking to wipe his red-rimmed, exhausted eyes with the sleeve of his jacket.

Clay swallowed the lump in his throat. "I'd had the privilege to have Hope all to myself for thirteen and a half years at that point. I would have allowed you the chance to get to know her." He met the other man's dejected gaze. "I'd have let you care for her, if you'd so chosen."

"You are an honorable man. I have no reason to doubt what you say."

Clay steered his truck into the gates of the cemetery and drove around to the far side of the huge lot. Despite the two years since his return, he found the spot in under a minute. He parked the truck and the two of them got out and walked the few feet to the granite slab littered with small bundles of flowers with notes attached.

"Brian mentioned that her soccer and softball teammates still come regularly to bring flowers and mementos."

Jacques leaned over to get a good look at the picture of Hope set in the granite headstone. "*Bon dieu!* She looks like *ma mère* as a girl." His emotions got the better of him and soon his shoulders shook with deep, wracking sobs.

Clay placed a hand on shoulder, if only to let him know he wasn't alone.

Reining in his emotions, Jacques wiped his face on his jacket sleeve again. He studied the wealth of items arranged on the slab, everything from team snapshots *decoupaged* onto pieces of wood, stuffed animals, and crosses, to macramé rosaries. "She . . ." Jacques had to give his throat a brusque clearing to continue. "She must have been a good friend to have them all remember her in such a way."

Clay nodded. "She had good friends and she was a good friend. The entire junior varsity teams, both softball and soccer, came to the funeral in their uniforms. Hope would have loved it. She would have been so honored."

"Soccer . . . she played football?"

Clay recalled that the U.S. was the only country in the world that soccer wasn't called football. "Oh yeah. She was a goalie."

"*Ne me dites pas!* Don't tell me! That has always been my position. I love the game."

"She did too, and she was good at it. She allowed few goals."

"And baseball?"

"Softball for girls; she was the catcher, which is an extension of a goalie, in my opinion. She had a heck of a throwing arm. She was fast, accurate, and could hit anything they threw at her. Our little girl has always been an excellent athlete, Jacques. Like her father, I'm guessing," he added, hoping to lighten the man's heartache.

"*Ah, bien.* I wish I could have seen her in action."

"I have hours of video for you. My fiancée, Allie, and her daughters have been compiling it all onto CD's for you to take home with you."

"You have a fiancée? You didn't mention that when we spoke on the phone, *non?*"

"As of last night." Clay couldn't keep the smile from his face at the memory of last night, and this morning, and again before he left for the airport. All three experiences had been truly satisfying for both of them. "The wedding is set for April 24th."

"She makes you happy, *oui?*"

"We make each other happy, Jacques."

"*Ah, bien.* That ees what it ees all about, yes?" He squinted, as though mentally calculating something. "My second child is due on April 30th."

Clay frowned. "Second child? I don't understand."

Jacques mouth spread wide with a genuine smile. "*Oui,* I am having another daughter. You see, before I had the treatments for the cancer, I had my *sperme* frozen. Last May, two good friends of mine agreed to assist me to have a child of my own. The woman, Chelle, had a procedure . . . ICSI . . . a *sperme injection*. She is married to my oldest friend, Phillipe, and they have two other children. She ees not interested in raising another child, and has agreed to give me sole custody of our daughter."

"Did Margie know about this?"

He nodded. "*Oui.* I asked her first about the other process, *la fécondation in vitro . . .*"

Clay had to guess at that one. "In vitro fertilization?"

"*Oui.* She wanted nothing to do with carrying a child. We got in a huge argument when I brought up Chelle being a surrogate mother for our child. She wanted no part of that either. It turns out, she wanted no part of a child, period. When Chelle offered both her egg and her womb, I paid for the procedure and kept my silence until a few months ago. I decided eef Margie didn't want my child, she didn't want me either, and she could leave. She didn't like eet, but she stayed, until the drunken confession. At that point, I took any choice out of the equation."

"Well, it looks like you must have been a good friend to Phillipe and Chelle if they're agreeing to this."

Jacques nodded. "I have two younger sisters, but Phillipe was like the brother I never had. I would do anything for those two."

"One more way our daughter was like you."

Jacques smiled again. "I think she may have taken some instruction from you, also, Clay. You are a generous man, sharing her with me this way."

"None of us asked for this to happen, but it did. It's the right thing to do." He pointed at the letter in the other man's hands. "You want me to leave you alone to read that?"

He shook his head and lifted the letter to open it. After staring at the page, he made an apologetic plea. "I'm better at speaking English than reading it. I could use some assistance if it's not too much trouble?"

Clay reached for the letter and took a deep breath, honored that Jacques thought enough of him to ask. He unfolded it, read the first line, and wondered if he could get through it without falling apart.

Mon père,

I'm sorry, but I don't know your name, only that you're from Paris, France. Father sounds too stiff and formal, so I'm relying on an Internet translator for help.

If you're reading this, you've heard that you have a daughter. Mom told me you don't have any other children and that makes me sad. No children, no grandchildren, no great grandchildren . . . It's a sad cycle, and I'm praying that changes for you one day. At least after I'm gone my dad will have Brian, Terri, my nephew Sean, and any future munchkins they bring into the family.

For future reference, I'll call you my father or mon père, but I'll call the man who raised me, my dad or Daddy.

I don't want you to feel sad about anything you think I may have missed out on because I grew up in the U.S. I've had a great life. I was happy. Mom wasn't exactly affectionate or loving but Dad, my siblings, and my grandparents made up for it. I had the best father I could have ever hoped for.

I want you to know that, when it came to my parentage, I always felt off, somehow. Some days, I'd look at Dad and Mom, then at myself in the mirror, and wonder where the heck I came from. I'd asked Mom what you looked like and she showed me an old snapshot she'd taken of you, I guess during your week together. So, it was you fourteen years ago. I can't describe the feeling of finally seeing someone who looked like me. If I could talk to you I'd ask where this hair came from. Everyone keeps telling me I get it from Mom but I can't see it. So I'm thinking that comes from your DNA.

I don't hate Mom for what she did. Like I told Daddy in his letter, I guess God did what he had to do to get me here.

And I sure don't hate you. If Mom is telling me the truth, you believed they were getting a divorce, which wasn't true. In other words, I know you aren't to blame. I'm sad for you. I know how hurt and angry you'll be when you find out about me and I can't blame you for that. Mom isn't brave enough to tell Dad about you, or to tell you about me. The way I see it, they both have to happen at the same time or it won't work. And I don't have that much longer, so I'm thinking we'll never get to meet.

I wonder about you, though. Like, do you like sports? Mom wasn't athletic at all, but Dad played American football, basketball, and baseball, so he thinks I get it from him. I'm betting you at least play soccer, or football, as it's called in France. I play girls softball and I like it, but I love soccer even more, especially being a goalie.

I'd also ask if you enjoy Science as much as I do. I freaking love it. As a matter of fact, it was my love for extra credit Science projects that brought about this entire blood type fiasco. I always brought projects to work on during chemo treatments. I knew my dad's blood type was O and I was AB. Imagine my surprise when I discovered that was literally impossible. I ditched the project ASAP and talked to Mom about it. Funny, I'd always heard that saying "Mama's baby, daddy's maybe" before, and I always thought it was funny. Well, guess what? It's not so funny when it applies to you.

Anyway, I'm over it.

Even if it's sucky for you, it's better for me that there aren't any half-siblings from you that I'd leave behind without ever meeting. The idea of that would break my heart. Every day, I hope that Mom finds the courage to tell both you and Dad what she did before it's too late.

Sometimes I think having someone else to share in the heartbreak would be better for Dad. He's holding on to me so tight that I worry for him. Some days I want to tell him not to love me so much, that I know I don't deserve it, because I'm not of his blood. But I know if it was him in this bed instead of me, I'd do the same thing.

I hope my father and my dad have the opportunity to meet one day, and if you do, that you look past all the betrayal and become friends. After all, neither of you betrayed each other. That's Mom's fault, not yours or Dad's.

I have two wishes for you and Dad. First, that you both fall in love with people you can be happy with until you're old and gray. Second, that neither of you get weighed down by anger or sadness when you think of me. As a matter of fact, there are only three things you need to remember when you think about me.

Remember that I was happy . . . Remember that I was loved . . . and remember that I was HERE!

I have nothing but love and gratitude to you for giving me life.

Ta fille (your daughter),
Hope

The two grown men stood there, both sobbing over the daughter they'd both lost. They hugged then sat on the slab of Hope's grave, both too exhausted and emotional to stand any longer. After a while, they calmed. Masculine sniffs cut through the sound of icy, dry wind and leaves skipping and dancing over the ground.

"Was your letter that emotional?"

Clay nodded. "*Oui.* Although she did make us laugh." He told Jacques the part about people carrying loaves of French bread under their arms.

"Ah, *baguette.* It ees true! *Américains. Vous êtes tous si germophobic!* You Americans, you are all germophobics!"

Jacques burst into laughter at Hope's desire to burp her way through the alphabet like her brother.

"*Oui, une bonne bière*—A good bottle of French beer can create the same alphabet-burping abilities. I could have taught her that one myself." He chuckled. "Hope . . . she had a good sense of humor, *oui?*"

"She did, Jacques. That kid could make me laugh. I miss her corny jokes. I miss her laughter. I miss the way she loved puppies and dogs of all ages, and adored kittens but barely tolerated cats."

"*Ah, chats!*" Jacques spit twice on the ground. "*Je déteste les chats!* I hate cats, irritating creatures who barely tolerate humans."

Clay reached out and brushed his fingertips over the sunflowers etched into the granite headstone. "I miss the way she loved sunflowers."

"Sunflowers . . . ah, *tournesols. Ma mère* was from the south of France where they were plentiful. They were her favorites, too."

"I hate that she never got to meet my fiancée, Allie. She could have been the kind of mother to Hope that Margie never could be."

This time it was Jacques that put his large hand on Clay's shoulder to comfort him. "*Vous l'aimiez assez pour à la fois une mère et son père.* It sounds like you loved her enough for both mother and father. Hope missed nothing."

Clay smiled. Jacques was so right. Hope missed nothing, but oh, how he missed Hope.

Chapter Sixteen

April 24th

Clay led his new bride to the middle of the floor for their first dance as a married couple. When asked by Allie if he had a song preference, the choice had been easy. "Thinking Out Loud" would forever be the song he would remember as a celebration of firsts with her: from their first night in the same hotel suite and the bittersweet agony of having to resist her, to the night of ecstasy when they first consummated their love. They had dissolved into laughter when she showed him her list of possibilities, with the same song gracing the number one position. More evidence they belonged together.

They stood in the center of the darkened room, under a canopy of twinkling lights. "You ready to show everyone how young we still are, Mrs. Andrews?"

Her eyes sparkled with laughter as she nodded. "I can handle it, Mr. Andrews."

He grinned. "Let's blow 'em away, baby."

The first mellow chords began, and there, amid a quiet crowd, they began the dance routine choreographed for them by a friend of Allie's, a local dance instructor. The two of them twirled and turned their way through the soft-rock-with-a-pinch-of-blue-eyed-soul song, working the crowd into an excited frenzy. The routine drew to a climactic close in the center of the floor—with Allie bent backwards over Clay's arm. He punctuated the performance with a tender kiss to his new wife's smiling lips, as the room erupted in a clamor of applause and whistles.

He'd no sooner returned her to a standing position when her daughters—no, *their* daughters, because they were his now, also—swarmed them.

Cecily, usually so reserved in crowds, was the first to throw her arms around her mother. "Mom! Oh my God, that was so awesome!"

"I had no idea you could dance like that!" Kayla joined in, hugging her mother. "It was beautiful and impressive, and I'm so proud of you, Mom."

Allie beamed at her daughters. "Clay got the idea from that video you showed him. He paid for a private choreographed dance session and our instructor designed this routine just for us. It was simple compared to the dancing they did in that video, but I think it fit us."

Clay couldn't stop grinning at his wife, her face radiant with beauty and happiness. It gave him a tremendous amount of pleasure to see these two girls treating their mother with the love and respect she deserved.

Cecily turned to give Clay a hug. "I'm so happy for you guys."

"Thank you, Cecily. That means a lot to me." He nudged her with his elbow. "I think she's keeping me."

Cecily laughed. "She'd better, Pop. Kayla and I like having you around."

"Even if it means we're moving you out of town and to 'the boonies'?" There had been mutinous talk of her moving in with her dad when Allie had first approached the girls with the news of moving to the country.

"Nah, I'm used to the idea. Besides, the cabin is beautiful, my room and closet are huge, and I've recently discovered that I love, love, *love* to fish."

Kayla entered the conversation, clapping her hands in excitement. "And I can't wait to get the dog you promised me." She pointed her finger at him. "Don't think I'll let you forget, either."

Clay laughed and pulled her in for a hug. "No chance of that. I promise, as soon as we get back from the honeymoon, we'll put the word out that we're looking."

"Do you think we could try the pound first, Pop? I'm thinking the perfect dog is there, waiting to be adopted by a family like ours."

He had to swallow the sudden lump in his throat at her comment. Hope had asked to adopt a dog from the pound, also. She had walked in, seen Evie, one of several rescued puppies, in one of the cages, and it was love at first sight for both of them. He could only hope Kayla had the same kind of experience. "I think that's a great idea, Kayla."

He met his wife's adoring gaze and had to blink several times to clear his eyes when she mouthed the words "Thank you." Clay shook his head and placed his hand on the back of her neck. He pulled her close to rest his forehead on hers, had to clear his throat in order to speak. "Thank *you*, Allie. For giving me back part of what I'd lost—and for keeping me."

She cupped his face in her hands. "Always, Clay. Always."

Epilogue

July 26th

Clay scanned the people scurrying around the passenger pick-up area of the airport in Marseille. "I see him!" He grabbed Allie's hand and pulled their luggage cart in the direction of the big man. He called his name and Jacque's head whipped around to face them, his face wreathed in a huge smile.

"*Mes chers amis!* Welcome! Welcome to France!" He pulled Allie to him first for a hug and a kiss on each cheek before enveloping Clay in a one-armed bear hug. "How was your flight?"

"Relatively uneventful, thank goodness. Thirty minutes from Lake Coburn to Houston, and we slept through most of the red eye from Houston to Frankfurt," Clay admitted. "Our layover in Frankfurt was just long enough to take a mini tour of the airport before boarding for Marseille."

"And our luggage followed us all the way here." Allie placed her hand on the navy blue nylon sling resting around Jacques' torso. "May I hold her, Jacques?"

"*Absolument.*" Jacques freed his three-month-old daughter from her sling. "Wake up beautiful girl. It's time to meet your *marraine et parrain Américain.*" He pressed a soft kiss on the child's forehead before turning her to meet her American godparents.

Allie's gasp of delight eclipsed Clay's complete loss of breath.

"She's beautiful! Oh come here, *petite fille!* Oh Jacques, she's gorgeous." She cuddled the child, pressing soft kisses to her forehead. Allie turned to look at Clay, the smile on her face fading when she did. "Honey?"

Clay stood there, too emotional to speak as he gazed at his and Allie's godchild. Their trip to Paris had a dual purpose: to spend part of their delayed honeymoon in the company of a dear, new friend and to participate in the holy baptism of said new friend's baby girl. "My God, Jacques . . ."

He couldn't finish, had to cover his mouth with one hand to keep his emotions in check.

"I know, *mon ami*. Judging by the pictures you gave me, she ees the identical image of her sister at that age, is she not?"

Clay nodded. "She is." He reached out to pass his fingers through the soft as silk curls the same color as his baby girl's hair. "Allie?"

Without another word, his beautiful wife placed the child in his arms. The infant raised her big, brown eyes to gaze up at him. As though she knew she was something special to him, she gave him the sweetest, most angelic smile. The infant raised her little fingers, touched his trembling lips, and gave him a coo filled with adorable sweetness.

And he disintegrated like a cheap, wet, paper towel. He sobbed once, fought to control his emotions when she looked like she would cry along with him. "I'm sorry, sweet girl. It's just that you look so much like another baby girl, it's uncanny." He lowered his head to her face and she grabbed his lips with both hands, just like his Hope used to do.

"Hope Elena Bessette," he whispered. "You are every bit as beautiful as your big sister. Yes, you are, and I pray, for your daddy's sake, that you are just as smart, and funny, and kind, and loving, and athletic, and talented as she was. I was privileged to be your sister's daddy, and you can't possibly know how happy your daddy made me when he asked me to be your *parrain.*"

He kissed her forehead and held the infant close before peering at his host. "Thank you for this."

Jacques nodded. "After all you have done for me, it feels right." He took a deep breath and released it slowly. "I know you must be exhausted, but we still have a short drive to my home in Avignon. Eef you two are hungry there ees a quiet place not far from here, my favorite place to eat in Marsielle."

Allie sniffed and wiped her eyes. "We're famished."

Jacques gave them a brief nod. "Let's get you fed. Thees place I take you is owned by friends of mine—out of the way and quaint, but the food is excellent."

After loading their luggage into Jacques SUV, it was a quick drive to a small café with a gorgeous view of the Mediterranean Sea. The three adults seated themselves at a table outside along the quiet street.

Clay sat back, enjoying the street view. "It's nice out here—back home they're in triple digits right now."

"And the humidity is unbearable." Allie turned the baby's car seat so it faced her. "It's nice out here, isn't it, *ma petite fille?*" Hope grinned at her and kicked her feet.

Clay watched, in quiet satisfaction as his wife elicited smiling and excited coos from their godchild. His gaze shifted to Jacques, and he recognized the look of adoration on the man's face. "Nothing compares, am I right?"

Jacques shook his head. "Every day I look at her, thees tiny miracle of mine, and I am amazed. She grows too fast before my eyes."

Clay smiled, remembering how he'd felt the same way about his own children. How he'd come in from extended stays at work and be shocked how quickly his children had grown, how much they'd changed while he'd been away. "Do you miss the bustle of Paris, compared to the Avignon countryside?"

"Not at all. Before I had Hope, I had to fill my life with other things to do. Now thees little one fills it for me. My parents would be glad to know I moved into the family home permanently. I love my teaching job at a smaller private school in the area."

Clay picked up the menu to try to decipher the dishes, all listed in French, of course. "Is that where you plan to send Hope one day?"

"Yes, I want to work where my daughter will be attending, so I can keep an eye on her, as well as her teachers."

Clay laughed. "Papa Bear will be on guard at all times, right?"

"Absolument!"

"Do they have sports in private schools here?"

"Thees one doesn't, but I will make sure she learns the game of football, you can be assured of that." He winked at Clay. "Maybe teach her how to protect the goal, eh?"

"Something tells me she'll be a natural at it."

A gentle breeze circulated around the four of them, setting into motion a set of wind chimes hanging not far from them. The tinkle of glass on glass had the three adult heads turning in unison toward the sound.

Clay's face stretched wide in a smile as he exchanged glances with Allie and Jacques. "Hope . . ."

His appetite sated with wonderful seafood fresh from the Mediterranean Sea, Clay stared out at the gently rolling landscape of the passing scenery. Allie's excited squeal drew his attention.

"Oh, Clay . . . look!"

Clay turned to look out of the opposite window of Jacques' late model Renault Talisman. He caught his breath at the spattering of sunflowers growing wild along the roadway. "Oh, man. Hope would go crazy if she saw this."

Jacques low chuckle filled the inside of the vehicle. "If you two think that is something, prepare to be blown away, *mes amis* . . ." He steered the car around one last turn in the roadway, laughed out loud at Allie's cry of delight. He pulled the car over to the side of the road and shut off the engine. "It is something, non?"

Clay and Allie's doors opened simultaneously. They exited the car and met in front of it, Allie's hands seeking his. He laced his fingers through hers and together they walked to the opposite edge of the roadway.

There before them, were dozens of acres of sunflowers in full bloom. Hand in hand, they approached the field's edge. With one last glance at Allie, Clay stepped inside the sea of brown faces ringed with golden coronas, pulling his wife with him. He closed his eyes, inhaling the earthy sweetness, and felt *her* presence, as surely as if she were standing beside him. Seconds later, Jacques joined them, carrying his child.

"May I?" Clay reached for his daughter's namesake. He stood there, with baby Hope in one arm and his teary-eyed wife in the other, overcome by an immense sense of balance. He could almost feel *his* Hope settling . . . almost hear her release a satisfied sigh. Things were as they should be. He closed his eyes, remembering the words she'd left for him.

". . . take a walk among the flowers, Dad—close your eyes and think of me when you do, and I will be there with you . . ."

What a blessing his daughter had been to him . . . and now, he'd been blessed even more. Allie was the new center of his universe for as long as God saw fit to keep them together. Clay had no way of knowing what the future held, but . . . there was always hope. Hope for a long, wonderful lifetime of happiness with the woman he adored.

He was determined to hang on to that hope through good times and bad.

Bon jour! I hope you enjoyed Allie and Clay's story about finding love during the Prime of Life. It's not required, but I'd adore hearing your opinions. So, if you enjoyed the story, and even if you didn't, please consider leaving a review with Goodreads and/or your favorite retailer. ALL reviews, good or bad, are a learning opportunity!

~ Merci Beaucoup (Thank you so much) ~
Lori Leger

Acknowledgments

Shout outs to KSB and the book clubbers . . . you know who you are, for the assistance in catching those annoying little typos and gaps. If I could find them all myself, I wouldn't need you ladies. Thank you!

Thanks to my son-in-law, Ryan LeJeune, for the interview and for helping me to understand both his and Clay's profession.

Thanks Vanessa W. for strongly suggesting "Thinking Out Loud" as a song choice. You know your blue-eyed soul music!

As always, I need to acknowledge and thank the love of my life, Michael, for letting the housework slide when I'm eyeball deep in writing, editing, formatting, reading/reviewing, proofreading, contest judging, or cover designing deadlines. You're the best, baby . . .

La Fleur de Love Series: Romantic Suspense
with a Cajun flair!

Halos & Horns Series: Where residents of Louisiana and
Texas cross state lines to find romance.

Read Cathryn & Zachary's four-part love story first . . .

FULL CIRCLE LOVE

LORI LEGER

Then meet Zach's dad, John Michael. Sexy is as much a part of his DNA as those Ferguson-blue eyes.

RUNNING Out Of Rain

Eventually, all storms break for a little sunshine . . .

PRIME OF LOVE: Book One
LORI LEGER

In Book Two of the Prime of Love series, HANGING ON TO HOPE, I've created a family affair by introducing John Michael's sister-in-law, Allie Sarver, to his cousin, Clay Andrews. Both are hurting from personal loss...but sometimes you need to lose all hope in order to find true strength...

HANGING On To Hope

PRIME OF LOVE: Book Two
LORI LEGER

LA FLEUR DE LOVE SERIES
Some Day Somebody (Book 1), Last First Kiss (Book 2), Hart's Desire (Book 2.5 – A Novella), Brown Eyed Girl (Book 3), Heaven in Your Eyes (Book 4)

HALOS & HORNS SERIES
Green Eyed Temptation (Book 1), Sarah Smile (Book 2), Meagan's Marine (Book 3), One Year to Forever (Book 4), Tinseled Up in Texas (Book 5 Novella)

PRIME OF LOVE SERIES
Running Out Of Rain (Book 1), Hanging On To Hope (Book 2), Settling For More (Book 3)

Full Circle Love
(Four short stories about one couple, Cat and Zach, taken from the Seasons of Love Anthology series)

Christmas 911 – Stand-alone Christmas suspense with **The Wild Rose Press**

Non-Fiction Article in Writing After Retirement, Publishers: Rowman & Littlefield

SOCIAL MEDIA LINKS:
http://www.lorileger.com (also for newsletter signup)
http://www/facebook/llegerauthor
http://www.facebook/lorilegerauthor
https://twitter.com/LoriLegerAuthor (@LoriLegerAuthor)
Instagram: lorilegerauthor
http://cajunflair.wordpress.com
https://www.goodreads.com/author/show/5171074.Lori_Leger

About the Author

Award winning author, Lori Leger, adores writing stories set in southwest Louisiana, where good Cajun cooking, helping your neighbors, and saying 'y'all' is as normal as hurricanes, heat, and humidity. She has twelve full-length novels, two novellas, and five short stories published in four series: La Fleur de Love, its spin-off, Halos & Horns, Seasons of Love, Prime of Love series, one stand-alone Christmas suspense published with The Wild Rose Press.

She's contributed to the Sweet & Savory Cookbook of Amazon Authors, published by Top Ten Press. Lori also has an article published in the non-fiction book Writing After Retirement: Tips From Retired Writers, published by Rowman and Littlefield Publishers, and edited and compiled by Carol Smallwood and Christine Redman-Waldeyer.

Her fourth novel in the Halos & Horns series, "One Year to Forever" won 2015 Romance Novel of Excellence award from InD'tale Review magazine.

www.ingramcontent.com/pod-product-compliance
Lightning Source LLC
Chambersburg PA
CBHW051955220626
47052CB00004B/955